operation mom

My plan to get my mom a life and a man

Reenita Malhotra Hora

ZENITH PUBLISHING

Copyright © 2022 by Reenita Malhotra Hora

Cover Designer: Fiona Suherman

Supervising Editor: Shannon Marks

Editing Assistants: Courtney Smith, Jessica Duvall, Madison Newman

Publishing Assistant: Lisa Wood

ISBN 978-1-958503-08-9 (paperback)

ISBN 978-1-958503-09-6 (hardback)

chapter
one

IT ALL BEGAN with Deepali wanting to experiment with her sexuality.

"It's about discovering the feminine mystique," Deepali said. She peered out of the corner of her eye towards the far end of the school canteen, twirling a thick lock of hair that hung down over her left ear.

"That's a book by Gloria Steinem...No, Betty Friedan," I replied.

"Yaar, don't be so literal. Just think about it. If you kiss a girl, maybe you'll understand how a boy feels when he kisses you. It's an experiment." Interesting...the only thing *I* had experimented with was sulphuric acid in a lab.

"There must be *something* you want to experiment with this summer," Deepali continued, scrutinizing her perfectly manicured nails. "Something that you are obsessed with, that you love. And that Aunty Veena probably despises you for."

It was just like Deepali to have a dig at Aunty Veena, my mom. She did it only to test boundaries; riling me up was a matter of entertainment for Deepali. It had been ever since we were five. Every play date, every sleepover. Deepali was convinced that I was too over my head in trying to please my mother, so she did everything possible to encourage me to rebel. Although this trait had annoyed me throughout our twelve or so years of friendship, it was definitely a truism that helped me confront my inadequacies. Isn't that what BFFs are for?

But back to being obsessed. Yes, I knew all about that. In no particular order, I was besotted with:

1. Ice-cream
2. Puppy dogs
3. Ali Zafar
4. Roller-coaster rides
5. Sleeping in on weekends.
6. Dev

Okay, okay, I admit that's not entirely true. So let me rephrase.
In *this* particular order, I was crazy about:

1. Ali Zafar
2. Ali Zafar's voice
3. Ali Zafar's eyes
4. Dreaming about Ali Zafar
5. Ice-cream, puppy dogs, roller-coaster rides, sleeping in on
   weekends, Dev.

No, not Dev! Perish the thought! He was far from being anywhere
near my league. In recent days, I had more exposure to this particular so-
called love interest of Deepali's. Yes, I choose my words carefully, but as
long as the 'so-called' part was still valid, I needed to put him out of my
head and focus on Ali Zafar, Pakistan's hunkiest singer-songwriter who,
until my very recent experience with Dev, had been the object of my
attention since I was fifteen.

Mom could never stomach my obsession with Ali Zafar. As far as
she was concerned, two years was way too long to have a teen pop idol
crush. "For god's sake, Ila, get a grip," she would grumble, perhaps on a
weekly, if not daily, basis. I couldn't understand why it so riled her, but I
did try to reason. "I'm in love, Mom. You were seventeen once. You
should know the deal."

"Yes, I do know the deal." She was, as always when it came to Ali
Zafar, dismissive. "The deal being that, at seventeen, you can't tell love
from the backside of a bus."

Mom's metaphors are so confusing. "Ali Zafar is a beautiful man. He can hardly be compared to the backside of anything."

"Still, you should set a more achievable target."

Should. Conversations with Mom are always peppered with the word. Ila, you *should* this; Ila, you *should* that. Perhaps I *should*, but in my eyes, just one target counted—Ali Zafar. He was definitely more achievable than Dev.

I've never been much of a groupie, but I figured I could spend most of the summer following Ali around the country from concert to concert. Some people travel, some do internships. I could make an art out of stalking my celebrity. If not an art, a science. That's what I wanted to experiment with.

Recently, while shopping at Phoenix Mills, I couldn't help but notice a horde of people and cars in front of the mall. I finagled my way into the crowd, anxious to find out what the fuss was about. A big black sedan drove up to the front. *A sedan in Mumbai? Must be some big shot.* The car door opened and out stepped a black tank-topped, skin-tight-jeaned Ali Zafar, bodyguard and all! A lady-killing machine. You should have seen the jaw-dropping entourage cluster around him as he sauntered over to the popcorn vendor.

My heart pounded harder and harder with every step he took farther into the mall. He took off his dark glasses and smiled at the crowd. At one point, his eyes actually met mine—the ultimate moment of romantic connection.

"Hey, babe," he said with a twinkle in his eye.

Of course, I couldn't say anything. What can one possibly say in response to a 'hey, babe' from the world's hottest teen pop idol? I just stood there, frozen to the bone, trying to conceal the embarrassment that spread through my being. What I was actually nervous about, I have no idea—the sheer thrill of being acknowledged by my heartthrob had rendered me utterly useless.

Within seconds, he had left me for someone else at the other end of the crowd. He posed coyly for photos with some girl and then with another girl, both of whom had been frantically pushing and shoving to get framed with him. And then his bodyguards skillfully maneuvered him into the lift.

What a colossal idiot I was. Instead of standing there like a victim of Medusa, I should have gone right up front and demanded a photo with him. I hate it when my nerves take over my powers of judgement.

That was two months ago but, of course, I haven't stopped thinking about it. Every day since, I have become increasingly obsessed with the idea of tracking him down.

——

"And why shouldn't you track him down?" Deepali said, staring at her nails. We were perched at the end of the very last table at the entrance of the school canteen. It was Deepali's prime 'eye candy' spot... the in other words, the spot that allowed her to be eye candy to every passing male. Deepali insisted it was something about how the sunlight floodlight that part of the canteen during the morning tea break— apparently, it somehow encircled her like a halo from the heavens. Whatever! It was the last day of school and I wasn't about to argue.

"In fact, if you can get Aunty Veena to successfully back off then that, my friend, is one example of the perfect summer project."

She was absolutely right! As always, Deepali knew how to read my needs and endorse my desire for a life of independence, so I braced myself to talk with Mom.

"I rightfully deserve that photo," I said to Mom at dinner one day. "And more."

"More?" She looked at me, vexed. Then she crossed her arms, pursed her lips, and raised her left eyebrow. A tell-tale sign that she was about to psychoanalyze me.

"You know, if I'd spent my teenage years lusting after a boy in a poster, I'd never have got into college," she sneered.

Sometimes I wish Mom was a little more 'motherly' in the way she talks to me.

"It's not lust!" I replied indignantly.

"Right, I forgot. It's *love*. The kind that you get in fairy tales," she said. Her raised eyebrow had now begun to twitch.

"What's wrong with fairy tales? You brought me up on them."

Mom took a breath in perfect sync with her eyebrow twitching.

"Yes, I fed them to you when you were five. When it was appropriate for stories to end in 'happily ever after.' That doesn't happen in real life, you know, and certainly not with celebrities and their groupies."

"Technically, I'm not a groupie," I protested. "I'm a fan."

"Fan your delusions away. You are showing signs of being a groupie, all right. Believe me, I know the difference."

"And how would you know it?"

Mothers are hardly qualified to sit in judgement on things like this. At least, mine certainly isn't. She could see that I was annoyed, but backing down is not really her thing.

"Why can't you be a little more regular? Like Deepali?" she asked.

Regular? Mom's choice of vocabulary made it sound like she was talking about Deepali's bowel movements. Still, it was my turn to react. "Firstly, I think you mean *normal* and not *regular*—"

"Okay, you know that's not what I meant," she mumbled.

"And secondly, Deepali? *Normal?* Seriously, Mom. You know how much I love that girl 'cause she's always got my back, but she's anything but *normal*."

Deepali is not just the hottest girl in St. Xavier's; she's a legend. The high-school editorial committee decided to dedicate the yearbook to her, even though another student is the daughter of an award-winning actress. Mind you, the committee is made up almost entirely of boys and a few sycophantic girls who will do anything to rub shoulders with any variety of celebrity. But that's not all. Deepali is also the most unsaintly girl to ever have been enrolled at St. Xavier's School of Pristine Catholic Values. At that point, she had three boyfriends—Vik, Jaggi, and Dev—all at the same time. I've never been able to understand how she two-timed...sorry, three-timed them with such dexterity. She said it was never a problem—that their different personalities meant that they chose different schedules.

That's why Deepali wanted to experiment with kissing a girl. So that she could master the right kiss for her boys and know what it felt like during the process. At least that's what she said.

"Whatever happened to the idea of eternal love for one man? Like Sita?" I asked her.

"Sita-shmeeta," she replied nonchalantly. "If you are going to go mytho on me, at least pick Draupadi. She had it right with the one-to-five ratio." Of course, Deepali had to prove her intellectual commitment to feminism by referring to the one female character in Hindu mythology who was married to five husbands as opposed to the more typical situation in which male characters have multiple wives.

Deepali's boyfriends knew about each other, but they didn't really seem to care. Including Dev. They took what they got, and she loved the attention. So, when she received texts from them a gazillion times each day, she responded instantly. Deepali said she could sense it each time one of her boyfriends was going to text her. That she and all three of her boyfriends had textual chemistry. Would they even fall for this kind of stupidity? Especially Dev...that part irritated me. I couldn't put my finger on why. But then Deepali cannot understand the logic behind my having a crush on a celebrity in lieu of a real boyfriend. She has always been in Mom's camp on that particular subject.

"You stick with your textual chemistry. What Ali and I have is contextual chemistry—in the context of worthy love objects, he is definitely worth stalking," I had said to Deepali when I unleashed my summer plans—to be there in the front row and then backstage at every Ali Zafar concert when he toured the country that summer—upon her. What ensued, of course, was our usual banter regarding my borderline obsession, which I viewed as simply love for, Ali Zafar.

Deepali looked at me as though I were stark raving mad. "You know, stalking is considered a crime in most parts of the world."

See, that was the thing about Deepali. She had opinions about things. Strong ones. And they forced me to sit up and think. Another check mark on the list of things I love her for.

"I'm not a maniac, Deepali!"

"Actually, you might be. There's a Dr. Mirno from the Chinese University in Hong Kong who has defined three different kinds of mental disorders that prompt a person to become a stalker, erotomania being one of them."

"Eroto-what?"

"Erotomania. A situation in which a crazy fan stalks the object of his or her obsession, typically a celebrity."

There is no denying that Deepali is incredibly intelligent, but only in the sense of trivial pursuit (and by that I don't mean the board game that goes by the same name). She collects trivia the same way Mom collects shopping coupons—pack rats, both of them. But spend five minutes each day talking to Deepali, and you'll never have to read a newspaper in your life. Even though most of the trivia she picks up is from Facebook or gossip magazines, it always comes with special insight. Insight and opinion. Could there be a better BFF?

"Erotomania," Deepali repeated, delighted with her analysis. "That's my diagnosis, Ilz."

Deepali had to be the most well-informed person on the planet. She knew stuff...so much stuff, both meaningful and inconsequential. And she thought about it...deeply, a quality that I had huge admiration for, but if you didn't know her well, you'd never have guessed she was remotely cerebral. She was always a sucker for male attention, though not in a creepy way. It was almost like she'd use her feminine charms to lure them and then deploy her intellect to outwit them in seconds. In some ways, I wanted to be Deepali when I grew up.

I winced, now recognizing the truth in her words.

"It's a condition that lasts, on average, for nineteen months. It doesn't usually turn dangerous. Although how boring is that? A crime of passion would be so much more romantic."

"Deepali, I know you like living on the edge, but aren't you getting a bit carried away?"

"I'm just trying to rationalize why you are in love with someone you haven't even met."

"I *have* met him. Remember, at Phoenix Mills?"

But Deepali wasn't interested in my attempt to justify my stance.

"What if he turns out to be incredibly unhygienic?" she said, staring into space.

"If I could get that up close and personal, it would make my day," I replied wistfully.

"Or pathologically immature?"

"Hey, it's not like I am a member of the geriatrics society myself."

"Well, if age is not an issue, what's wrong with Justin Bieber?"

"What? With that hair flick and uncracked voice? Deepali, please!"

But she was dismissive. "The voice has cracked long ago, Ilz! The

guy is over twenty. Puberty is a done deal. I actually thought the hair
flick was cute, although that's gone too. Now he gels his hair back so
that it stands upright. Spikey."

It sounded quite punk to me. But seriously, I am not the kind who
is interested in firangi pop idols.

"So you prefer to hang around mosquito-infested concert venues all
summer, chasing Ali Zafar just because he's non-firangi?" she
challenged.

Actually, I like the idea of local talent. It was close to home. Like
Dev, he was even closer to home. Ugh, no! Dev belonged to Deepali,
and Deepali *was* home. Snap out of it, Ila!

"It's the ultimate attempt at aman ki asha, no?" I asked with an air
of self-importance.

"Give me a royal break," she said, rolling her eyes and fishing out her
phone from her purse. "There you go echoing your mother again. Only
she'd be willing to put up with an idea as crazy as that. Antiquated is
what I call the idea of South-Asian solidarity. Embrace the world. This is
the era of globalization." She was hurriedly texting one of her
boyfriends. Which one, I wondered?

I stared at her blankly, trying to collect my thoughts. She was right.
Friendly relations with the neighboring country was not the topmost
priority for most seventeen-year-old Mumbaikars, but I had to stand my
ground somehow. I certainly wasn't going to take the charge of being
called antiquated lying down.

"Come on, Mom's never said anything like that to me."

"She doesn't *have* to," Deepali responded. "My point being that I
have never met anyone who unconsciously aims to please her mother
more than you. Every time you utter a sentence, you end it with 'Right,
Mom?'"

She wasn't far from the truth. I have always hankered for Mom's
attention. And in the last year or so, I have realized that a sure-fire way of
getting her attention is to battle her on anything possible. Yet, I invari-
ably rue my actions because the moment I get her attention, I wish she
would back off.

Mom's a journalist, a single one at that. At any given time, you'll
find her buried in her laptop, ferociously documenting her opinion on a

burning issue for some big-shot publication or the other. When she's not working on news stories, she writes screenplays—something that she claims is the ideal stress-buster. If you try to get a word in edgeways, she makes you feel guilty for disrupting her creative time. Because Mom works freelance, she's home by the time I return from school. "It's the only way to pay the bills and keep a teenage daughter in check," she says triumphantly.

As I tell her quite honestly, I don't know what there is to be so triumphant about. It must be pretty lonely to sit around at home and type all day. Reality bites, and Mom scowls in self-defense, trying to ignore the sting in my statement. Still, that was her doing. She threw Pops out about seven years ago, I think. I can't tell you the exact story because both have their own version. Neither is that interesting, frankly...I mean, it wasn't like their marriage imploded because of a massive drama involving another lover; nor did one of them suddenly threaten the other with an axe or a poisoned smoothie. Mom always had a standard poetic response: "We were like two ships that pass at night." Whatever that means. Pops would say he'd get back to me with a clearer answer "some day when it's easier for you to understand." I think what he really means is some day when it's easier for him to explain.

Whatever. I mean, it's not like I have had any more or less of a dysfunctional upbringing than any other girl my age. Mom and Pops get along like a house on fire. Of course, they have their share of fights, mostly involving issues like what field of study I should pursue in college (like that's under their control!), or why (in Pops's opinion) I should stay away from the influence of Mom's BFF, Aunty Maleeka, or the relevance of emotional intelligence. Such situations typically end with Mom calling Pops a 'psychologically ambivalent narcissist' before throwing him out of the house. But then, is that really any different from other households? Deepali's parents argue so much that her father might as well take up permanent residence in the guest room. Is that what you'd define as a 'functional' family situation? As far as divorcees go, my parents are awesome buddies, which is why I don't get the ships at night thing.

But Deepali is not wrong in what she says—underneath it all, I idolize Mom and will do anything for her attention. Deep down, I know there's no one else I'd rather be like, though I don't yearn to have the lonely, typing life.

A firm opinion is critical to success. "Mom is not *so* antiquated," I said.

"What are you saying? She won't touch anything mod like Satya Paul. She only wears traditionally embroidered saris. And she calls Mumbai, Bombay."

'That doesn't really prove anything," I said, exasperated. "Everyone from her generation calls Mumbai, Bombay."

Deepali flicked back her long hair in an ultra-mod, fashion-model manner. And in full view of a group of cute guys over at the next table, none of whom she was three-timing.

"What I am trying to prove is Aunty Veena's lack of willingness to accept what is contemporary," she said.

Something inside urged me to stand up for my kin. "How can you say that? You know this is a lady who ran away from a conservative household to go study in America of her own will."

"Yes, but it's not like she ended up in Berkeley, land of the free and home of the talkative. She went to Williams College in Massachusetts, for gosh sakes. You can't get more conservative than that."

"Williams College? That's a top-notch place," came a male voice from behind us. "And pretty damned liberal from what I hear." Oof! It was Dev, Deepali's Boyfriend #3. He pulled up a chair between us, turned it so that the back of the chair was facing forward, and swung his leg over the sides of it, folding his arms over the back. In an instant, my stomach was a tropical storm of butterflies.

"Hey, B," Dev said, flashing his characteristic crooked smile at me.

Hey, B? That tone of voice, that twinkle of the eye...what on earth did he mean by that? Was it a euphemism for a 'hey, babe'? The thought took me back to that magical moment at Phoenix Mills when the Divine had orchestrated my eyes to meet those of Ali Zafar. Was this a signal from the Divine telling me to move on from Ali Zafar? I quickly shook myself out of it. What a ridiculous notion that Dev, or anyone for that matter, could compare to Ali Zafar, even for a moment!

"B?" I asked quizzically.

"B as in BFF," he responded.

"Since when did I become your BFF?" I asked, the pitch of my voice an octave higher than it should be.

"Hey, any BFF of Deepali is a BFF of mine." He winked at me and turned towards Deepali, who hardly seemed to notice his appearance. "Right, D?"

Oh gosh, D! I felt myself turn bright red, this time out of pure embarrassment at the inappropriateness of my feelings rather than the feelings themselves. Why, oh why, could I not shake this?

"D-shmee. Don't tell me you are thinking of Williams College?" Deepali said.

"Actually, I am," Dev said. He glanced over towards a group of guys hovering at the edge of the canteen. "See my bro there? He's just announced that he's going to be following in our dad's footsteps by going to Amherst College. I need to create some healthy rivalry in the household, so Williams College might just be the answer."

"Williams College, sure!" Deepali said. "The ideal college for the Bombay Punjus of every generation. First Veena Isham, now Dev Mehra!"

Was Dev closer to home than I had imagined? Regardless, this time, Deepali was missing the point. Williams College is a liberal arts school, and Mom is a woman who has always defined her own existence. For her, the whole experience was about the fact that she broke the shackles of a Punjabi household and ran away to America, not about the guiding political principles of her college peers.

"What I am trying to illustrate is that you unconsciously parrot her every thought. You think your father is a jerk just because your mom told you he's one."

Not entirely true. Pops was anything but a jerk. Still, I defended Mom.

"Well, she's not usually wrong when it comes to men," I said to Deepali, digging my nails into my jeans.

Dev looked over at me. Something in his face spelled out that he was clearly interested in this idea. He opened his mouth to say something but then abruptly decided to close it again.

Deepali rolled her eyes. "Well, if she's not wrong about men, then let's see what she has to say about Dev."

"About Dev? What?" We glanced at each other and then at her, equally confused. She on the other hand, displayed a smug, knowing expression. She shot her eyes from me to Dev and then back to me again, like she was watching a tennis match. Then she burst into giggles.

"What I meant was, let's see what she has to say about his potential for getting into Williams College.

"But as regards your Ali Zafar obsession and how that relates to Aunty Veena's judgement, I rest my case," she said. "It's ironic, though, that this comes from someone who argues with her mother about being a groupie in the first place. Maybe this obsession will be help you stand up for yourself after all.'

Dev puckered up his cheek to one side at the mention of Ali Zafar. For an odd moment, he kind of even looked like him. Oh, stop it, Ila! Nobody looks like Ali Zafar except Ali Zafar!

But Deepali had a point. I suppose any seventeen-year-old girl who has a crush on a pop idol needs to get her mother off her back. I needed to figure out how. Maybe *that* should be the focus of my perfect summer project.

chapter
two

AS I SAT THERE WAITING for Mom to come home, I couldn't help fixating on Dev's crooked smile and the way he had swung his leg over the side of the chair in the canteen. Did he really want to apply to Williams College? Was there a chance that Mom could counsel him? What would she think about him? And what would Pops think?

Pops! He had such a mixed reaction to Mom's argumentative nature, which he insisted was part of her Williams College training. Not that he detested debating or liberal views but sometimes...often...increasingly...he needed a break. That's exactly what he said the day he moved out.

"Ila, your parents have nothing but your best interest at heart. But right now, I am finding your mother a bit too much to handle, and she finds me to be a little too much of a jerk. Everyone needs a break from time to time, though, and sometimes, a separation might be the answer."

The answer to what exactly? You see, even though he moved out, it's not like I saw him any less. In fact, he seemed to be even more present at events that he had blown off before the separation—family dinners, Sunday lunch, pooja, havan. It's just that he retired to a different apartment in the evenings. It's definitely one way to escape Mom's too-much-to-deal-with personality.

Tough...would he have the same reaction to Dev? Ugh...why could I not shake this Dev thing? What would Deepali think of me if she knew I was thinking about all this? I needed to focus on Ali Zafar and being a groupie. Pops didn't give a hoot about my teen pop idol crush, unlike Mom who was sure to be grumpy.

Mom is always grumpy in the afternoons. As a freelance journalist, she lives from deadline to deadline, aiming to finish her work before I get home from school. The problem is, she never really manages to. I figure that if she stuck to her articles, maybe she'd have a shot at finishing it, but half of the time she gets stuck with writing screenplays and movie pitches, in an attempt to charm a producer one day. Yup, that's right—Mom wants to be in the entertainment business. Not Bollywood, per se, but digital platforms like Netflix and Hulu. She wants to change the face of Indian media from boring, weepy soaps to on-the-edge comedies and dramas that HBO broadcasts in its home country, America.

I am all for the idea of Mom making it big in the Netflix industry, but it is a bit of a pipe dream, and she should know that before her daughter points it out to her. Gosh, now I am talking like my Naani.

My bigger problem is that, as she sits proofreading her copy for the nth time during the long hours of the late afternoon, she snaps at anyone that intrudes into her space. That would be either me or Sakkubai, our ancient Marathi house manager who has been with the family since Mom was around my age. Sakkubai has stuck to Mom through her trials and tribulations and, in some ways, she's more of a mother to her than Naani ever was. This means that the moment Mom gives her attitude, Sakkubai gives it right back to her, usually for an extended duration, in Marathi, at a relatively high decibel level. It's the poisoned dart that never fails to silence Mom.

Our household has way more female energy than the average apartment in Mumbai is designed to handle (which is one reason why Pops might have willingly left when he did), so I typically make myself scarce until the evening junk food snack time—the bhel puri hour, six o'clock —by which Mom has more or less switched off for the day.

I decided to wait until after dinner before I dropped the groupie bomb. I knew that by then she'd have showered and settled down to a good book or some TV show.

I tiptoed my way to the veranda to find Mom and her nostalgia sprawled out on the couch with her crossword puzzle, the early tunes of Lata Mangeshkar echoing in the background.

See, this is the thing with Mom. Nobody really cares if there is a difference between the 'early' and then 'mature' vocal talent of the lady who is known as the Nightingale of India. Yet, Mom insists that Lata lost the innocence in her voice after 1976. "By then, the nightingale had already seen the light of day," she says. Now Deepali, Queen of Trivia, has actually insisted on more than one occasion that nightingales also sing during the day, but Mom says that's beside the point. She refuses to hear any of it—neither the discussion on nightingales, nor somebody debating her views on Lata's post-1976 tunes. Sheesh! See what I have to deal with?

Anyway, back to the scene at the homestead. It was the perfect time to test the waters.

"Ali Zafar comes to town in a few weeks, and I am going to his concert," I announced over Lata's songbird melody.

Mom looked up from her paper, her glasses perched on the tip of her nose in a granny stance. "What was that?"

"Ali Zafar comes to town..." I began repeating like a broken record.

"Yes, I heard you the first time, and the answer is no," she said, returning to her crossword.

Yeah? You heard? Then why did you ask?

Her reaction was predictable; so was the fact that she could give no logical reason to support her statement. I decided to press further.

"Mom, I didn't ask you a question; I made an announcement."

"In this house, there will be no announcements," she said without looking up.

"Why not?"

"Because..."

"Because?"

No response.

"Mom, I asked you a question."

"What do you want me to say?" A frown sat on her brows although her eyes were still focused on the crossword.

"Anything that could possibly support your decision to *not* support my decision to go to Ali Zafar's concert," I replied.

"It's inappropriate," she said, scrunching up her face.

"I am seventeen, Mom! Besides, how is Ali inappropriate? The guy is known for his squeaky-clean persona. He's not like Lady Gaga, half naked and devouring human flesh on stage."

Mom grunted from behind her paper. I decided to take it up a notch.

"What's inappropriate is the fact that you are so out of touch with the appropriateness of Ali Zafar's brand of pop culture."

Match point. Mom crushed her paper down on to the table. "Let me tell you what's inappropriate."

"Okay, I'm waiting," I said, knowing full well that keeping my cool would only irk her.

Mom shot me her death stare. Her Punjabi genes never failed to take over when she was under duress.

"Do you know how dangerous rock concerts are? With druggies and potheads who eve tease young girls for entertainment? There have been five incidents at those this year."

Eve teasers. How I hated those guys. Not just for their acts of public sexual harassment but also for the fact that their actions had become a topic that fed my mother's paranoia.

"Three, actually," I corrected her. "And none of them at rock concerts."

I daresay Mom had reason to be concerned, but that wasn't reason enough for me to cede power by acknowledging her valid worry.

"No decent girl goes to rock concerts," she said imperiously.

"Well, that's a bummer, because this decent girl already bought the tickets."

"You what? When? With what money?" She sat up tall, her head perfectly aligned with her spine.

A flicker of excitement tingled down my spine. I could not, of course, tell her the truth—that Deepali had purchased the tickets for me online during math class. "Let's just say it was a present."

Mom slammed her hand down on the table so hard that her glasses slid further down her nose. "There will be no presents in my house."

I pictured Deepali in my head and rolled my eyes like her. "There will be no announcements, there will be no presents...Will there ever be anything reasonable or fun around here?"

My so-called 'abhorrent teenage behavior' apparently infuriated Mom all the more, and she took off her glasses and began to wring her hands in frustrated agony. "Listen, young lady, when I was your age, nobody gave me concert tickets for presents."

"That's because you didn't have any concerts. And lord knows you needed them. Both the concerts and the presents."

Ouch! I bit my tongue.

But it was true—Mom hadn't been given enough presents in her life. Her parents typically favored their two sons, and Pops had dumped her (Or the other way around? Like I said, both of them have their own version.) way too soon by Indian standards. Even in their limited time together, he had never lavished her with presents the way Deepali's dad showered her mother with gifts despite their many disagreements. And it isn't like she is high maintenance or anything. In Mumbai, it's hard to get lower on the maintenance charts than Veena Isham—she takes what she gets, and that is not necessarily a good thing.

———

Separated parents. They are a breed unto themselves. Deepali never gets it when I say so, but the fact is, her parents are as separated as mine are. Deepali's parents don't talk to each other for days on end, though they live in the same house, and, like I said, her dad has been stuck in the guest room for ages now. You tell me that's not bizarre. Mine live separately yet chat weekly, sometimes daily. I've always thought it's the way things should be. And they have been. I'd always had a great relationship with Pops, and frankly that was good with Mom who readily admitted that she was the less nurturing of the two parents. That along with the fact that she was ever ready to ask for Pops' help in getting through to me when I refused to respond to her. And he would willingly comply. Oh Pops! I couldn't understand his motives for letting go of Mom so easily.

Poor Mom. She annoys me, but she's got a good heart. Her main problem, as I see it, is that she has no one else to focus on besides me.

"Mom, did you never have a teenage crush?"

Mom got up from the couch and began pacing up and down the length of the veranda with deliberate, pronounced steps. Not a good a sign. Then she stomped her way to the coffee machine and began messing around with the filter.

"It's eight thirty in the evening," I said. "You can't have coffee now. You'll be up all night."

Sometimes, in fact quite often now, Mom and I reverse roles, and I find myself admonishing her for habits from which she should be abstaining.

"Does it matter? You are planning to keep me up with worry all night anyway," she shot back gruffly. "Let's hope the caffeine overpowers my anxiety."

Anxiety. A standard Isham trait that perhaps runs in the whole ancestral line. Naani, Mom, and I are like three generations of the same person who walk around the planet with a galloping heartbeat and sweaty palms. The bad thing about anxiety is that it prevents blood from rushing to parts of the brain that are responsible for thinking, so the moment it hits, our regular intelligence (which, mind you, is up there) is rendered utterly useless. I've often wondered if anxiety is hereditary because both Naani and Mom have a knack for taking what starts out as anxiety and turning it into obsession.

What are they obsessed about? Stupid things, of course, like what time I will be home or what people will say if I don't eat enough, and so forth. And because they are busy processing this anxiety-turned-obsession thing most of the time, they aren't able to process the good stuff, which is why we appear to be either crabby or confused. Quite unlike someone like Deepali who's always Ms. Congeniality.

"What are you so worried about?" I whined. "Do you really think I'm off to get myself eve teased?"

"Ila, it's not the eve teasing that I worry about so much."

"Thanks a lot, Mom. That's really reassuring," I retorted.

Mom muttered something to herself.

"What are you worried about? The dope?"

"No, I know you are not stupid enough to go down that road."

"Then what?"

She swung around from the coffee machine and slapped the back of her left hand into the palm of her right one.

"What worries me, Ila, is that you are way too obsessive."

"Obsessive?" I repeated, gasping at her words. Of all the things I guessed she might say, this wasn't one. *Me?* Obsessive? What about *her?* Deepali would have a field day analyzing my mom when I report this back to her.

"Obsessive. This obsession with Ali Zafar is downright...scary. If I give an inch now, lord knows what kind of yard you'll extend it to later."

"Jeez, Mom. Can you please say that in plain English?"

"You are pushing it too far. Ali Zafar is not the man you are going to marry, Ila. Wake up and smell the coffee." She waved a Nespresso pod in my face.

"Mom, don't you think this is a case of the pot calling the kettle black?" I retorted.

"What pot?" she grunted. She gave up on the coffee and made her way back to the couch.

"You pot, me kettle. I think *you* are actually way too obsessive."

"Are you calling me a pot?"

"I'm just saying—"

"Because I'm not a pot. And I am not obsessive."

"No offense, Mom, but that's exactly what you are, and you unleash all your obsessive tendencies on me. And I think the PMS just makes it worse."

"Don't talk to me about PMS," she snapped. "I avoided PMS-ing all that time you were going through puberty. I am entitled to a few outbursts now and then," she said and rejected my tantrum in favor of her crossword puzzle.

chapter
three

MOM WASN'T the only one concerned about my obsession with Ali Zafar. Somehow, she had gotten to Pops too. He tried to second her emotion using allegory, but he wasn't very good at it.

"Sometimes you might want to take this Ali Zafar situation by the shoulders and shake it real hard," Pops said, gripping the air in front of him to demonstrate just how hard he wanted to shake it.

We were seated at our usual Sunday brunch table at Britannia, me having my chicken frankie and Mom and Pops sharing the beri pulao. Yup, sharing. They had always been like that—before and after the separation. Deepali would scoff at the idea when I told her it was an *amicable separation.*

"Seriously? If you are going to be amicable then what's the point of separating? They're just lovebirds caught in a bit of a flap," Deepali insisted.

Did she have a point? I deeply trusted her innate sense; it might be one reason why I wasn't so fussed about the separation. Another might be that while separating was their choice, staying amicable was something they did to keep me calm and well-adjusted. Or at least that's what I supposed. Admittedly though, they seemed to enjoy their amicability, even though Mom did always seem to throw in every so often that Pops was a jerk. And Pops couldn't help vexing her by pointing out how she had absolutely no sense of humor. Still, even though I knew it no other way, I guess it would be hard for somebody on the outside looking in to understand why a separated couple would be as amicable as my parents.

"As if to say, this is anything but your real life." Pops continued. "Wake up and smell the coffee!"

See, that's how separated Mom and Pops were. They might not be together anymore, but they continued to use the same expressions, especially when it came to chiding me. Especially regarding things like shaking Ali Zafar...or the Ali Zafar situ by the shoulders!

"That sounds harsh," I replied to Pops, sulking.

"Yes sure, it can be. It's the kind of thing my father used to do with me."

"I find that hard to picture," Mom piped in, "Your father was among the gentlest of souls on this planet. He barely knew any curse words when we first met."

"What do curse words have to do with this?" he asked.

"Just that cursing is a verbal display of violence," she said, chomping on a piece of carrot pickle, completely non-plussed.

Pops furrowed his brow deeper. "I don't get it."

"Weren't you just talking about shaking Ila by the shoulders?"

"Metaphorically, yes! You should know..."

Mom looked at him quizzically with a mouthful of carrot pickle. "Know what?"

"Well, you are the queen of metaphors, aren't you?"

"Trying to be punny?"

"See what I mean? Case in point." Pops grinned.

Okay, now we were getting to their usual levels of ridiculousness. Time for me to interject.

"Dial it down, people," I said, annoyed. "And can we please stick to the point here? Ali Zafar is supposed to be a pleasant topic for me."

"Yes, baby girl, but here's the thing," Pops responded, stroking back his hair three times with both hands. "A pleasant topic can only stay pleasant as long as you have it under control."

"I couldn't agree more," Mom said, back to her carrot pickle.

Interesting take from Mom! Typically, she would find any excuse to disagree with Pops.

"Care to elaborate, Pops?" I asked, intentionally ignoring Mom, but she jumped in with a response before Pops even had a chance to process the thought.

"When the pleasant thing becomes an obsession, it begins to control you rather than letting you control it, and that can lead to things getting totally out of control."

Pops stared at her blankly, as though trying to make sense of her words. C'mon, Pops, giddy-up!

"Yes, that can lead to things getting totally out of control."

See, that's the other thing about him. He has ADD, but he won't admit to it. Instead he'll do things like repeating the last sentence that he heard in an attempt to prove that he's actually paying attention.

"Out of control, as in total chaos," Mom clarified.

"Chaos," Pops echoed.

Not that he's slow on the uptake...on the contrary, Pops is a super smart human being, but sometimes I can totally see why Mom gets so exasperated by him.

"I don't understand what you folks are on about," I said. "How does a simple fixation lead to chaos?"

"Well, the right person to ask would be Mrs. M," Pops replied.

By Mrs. M, he was referring to Naani, aka my maternal grand-mother. For some reason, he never referred to her by her first name or by anything more maritally respectful, like Ma or Mummy. Mom shot him a scowl. She was always visibly irked when Pops made any mention of her mother. She had a lot of traits that drove Mom nuts, but whenever he decided to point them out, it was like she felt compelled to defend her.

"Interesting," I said, my curiosity piqued. "What does Naani have to say about all this?"

No response. Both of them made a point of focusing on chewing their biriyani.

"C'mon, what's the point of introducing ideas if you don't flesh them out?" I said, citing one of Mom's classic phrases. "Do I need to go ask her myself?"

Mom now turned to scowl at me. Pops turned to her with a nod of his head. "Show her, Veena."

"Show me what?"

Mom glared at Pops, red-faced, and slammed her palm down on the table. Ooh, if looks could kill!

"*Mom*, show me what?" I insisted.

Without another word, she whipped out her cell phone and opened it up to a WhatsApp chat between her and Naani. All this while continuing to shoot daggers at Pops.

I snatched the phone and began to scroll through Mom and Naani's typo-ridden text chat.

Naani - u r hell bent on frittering away relationships which you have no right to commit to without approval in the first place. So much for your silly obsessive tendencies over the years now causing a downfall in the respectable institution of marriage. an.y way pl back off from any obsessive action that is causing distress to JJ

Mom - You've got it wrong Mummy

Naani - DOn't be arrogant if have been misunderstood please explain ur self. don't send insolent messages.

"Insolent messages?" I asked, amused, scrolling down to the end of the chat to find nothing else.

"Yes," Mom said, grimacing, "Pointing out to her that she had it wrong was deemed to be insolent."

Pops, on the other hand, chuckled loudly, pleased as punch. "Naani doesn't hold back, does she? She's like a soldier with a machine gun, scattering bullets everywhere!"

I jumped to Mom's defense. "C'mon Pops, that's not fair! You're just enjoying the fact that Naani's giving Mom a dressing for being divorced! Why would you even share this with him, Mom?"

Mom's face softened at my response. "It's okay, Ilz," she said. "I'm used to it from both of them. Neither have any social skills. And besides, Pops doesn't really have any other form of entertainment."

"Ila," Pops said, "I admit that observing your grandmother's shenanigans is more enjoyable than watching Netflix. It's funny to see her defend me so whole-heartedly these days, considering that she was always against me marrying your mother in the first place, but the main takeaway I wanted you to get from this text exchange was about the whole 'obsessive tendencies' thing. Even Naani sees it as a fault, and with due respect to your mother, it would be better if this didn't turn into a like-mother-like daughter thing!"

Oh, there we go again! First Deepali, now Pops! When were the people in my life going to drop these accusations about me—and Mom —being obsessive? And what was with Mom? Why was she sitting there so quiet and glum, not even defending herself? Could it be that she actually saw some truth in what they said? Mom?

Note to self: ask her about this later, when Pops is not around.

chapter
four

"YAAR, I've got some scoop for you!"

Deepali burst into the school library, hyperventilating like she had just eaten her own weight in Cadbury Gems. Her face was flushed, and her eyes had the look of a deranged animal.

"It runs in the family," she said, her voice shrill with excitement. "Your family."

"What are you talking about?" I was curious.

"The stalking and the obsessiveness," she replied.

"Shhh!" hissed a geeky girl from three tables away. I acknowledged her annoyance by mouthing a 'sorry,' but Deepali didn't even spare a glance.

"Take a look at this, babe," she shrieked and slapped a yellowed newspaper—its edges frayed with time—onto the table. The daily had been opened to the center spread, and its headline danced across my vision: "BOMBAY GIRL'S BRUSH WITH STARDOM: WHAM, BAM AND THANK YOU, MA'AM." As I tried to focus on the thing that had been thrust into my face, I saw a photo of the 1980s' pop idol, George Michael of Wham! fame, standing with his arm around a girl who looked startlingly like...me!

My head spun as I stared at my twin. I had never met any 80's pop stars, let alone posed with one. And I'd never be caught dead dressed in a blazer with shoulder pads or with hair that big.

I searched for the caption. "Veena Vij travels all the way to London to meet pop star George Michael."

Veena Vij? As in my mother? As I peered harder at the image, it became quite clear. It was Mom, age seventeen, with George Michael, who was arguably one of the biggest stars of the time.

"Apparently she was head over heels in love with him and followed him all the way to Vern-ville, UK," Deepali said, throwing her head back so that her long, black hair cascaded all over the chair. She positioned her feet up on the table, crossing her arms behind her head.

"Vern-ville?"

"In Bushey, the place all of London's 'vernacular' types come from," Deepali replied imperiously.

Deepali doesn't get that you cannot literally extract (her rendition of) Maharashtra's socio-economic make-up and apply it to another country. There are no 'vernaculars' to speak of in England. But still, I got her point. Spasms of horror and delight shot through my body.

"Where did you find this?" My voice was shaking with excitement at the proof of Mom's obsession and my niggling suspicion that my obsessive genes had come from her.

Deepali laughed cynically. "I've been looking out for you, friend. I found your mom's partner in crime."

A thousand guesses flowed through my brain in the next few seconds.

"Aunty Maleeka?"

Of course. If anybody could convince my mom to step outside of her box, it was Aunty Maleeka. She was bold, daring, and broke every tradition one can possibly break in an extremely traditional environment. Mom, who had psychoanalyzed her for years, was of the opinion that Aunty Maleeka's rebellious streak was born out of the fact that both her parents came from extremely conservative families. Her father was from a devout Bohri Muslim family, while her mother had hardcore Sindhi roots. All who heard of the union bet on the possibility of it ending in divorce. Alas, the marriage really didn't have enough of a chance to test the waters. Aunty Maleeka's father passed away when she was barely two. She and Mom had been firm friends since then.

Aunty Maleeka is to Mom kind of like what Deepali is to me. Truth be told, I think we all need a Deepali or Aunty Maleeka in our lives, especially those of us who choose to walk the straight and narrow path. Aunty Maleeka always brought out the wild and wanton side of Mom. It made perfect sense that she would be her partner in the crime of teen pop-idol passion. But I needed to find out more about this particular escapade.

——

The bus ride to Aunty Maleeka's took forever. She lived on the fourth floor of DhanDev Mahal, a building overlooking Oval Maidan and inhabited entirely by Sindhis.

When we entered her flat, Aunty Maleeka was lounging in an African-print kaftan, listening to Dire Straits accompanied by a bottle of white wine. It was 4 p.m. Mitzy, her pet cock-a-doodle (and by that, I mean a dog who is a cross between a cocker spaniel and a poodle) was sprawled on her lap and would occasionally lick her wine glass. Aunty Maleeka didn't seem to mind.

"Welcome to the house of fun, girls. Can I offer you a glass of Pinot Gris?" she asked.

Aunty Maleeka offers me a drink every time I see her, though she knows I am well under the legal drinking age. It's this kind of thing that pisses off Pops. Mom just brushes it aside, knowing full well that I am more than capable of handling Aunty Maleeka. That gets Pops even more inflamed.

"Thanks, but I still have a few years to go," I replied.

"What difference does that make? We were all under the legal drinking age once. The only person it ever stopped was your mother."

I could sense Deepali's eyes lighting up. She loved loose-lipped banter, especially the kind that might nurture what she was convinced was the dormant rebel in me.

"That's a good thing, no?" I said indignantly.

"Goodness is relative," Aunt Maleeka replied, sticking her chest out and accentuating her boobs. She did that as a matter of habit, usually when pausing to churn a thought in her head. "You can be as good as you want, but being a prude is no good at all."

Quite right. I couldn't remember a day that Mom had been anything but a prude. But that wasn't why we were there. I cleared my throat.

"Aunty Maleeka, this newspaper article about Mom and George Michael that you gave Deepali...Can you please tell me more about it?"

"I let the cat out of the bag, huh?" Aunty Maleeka said, bursting into giggles. "I thought you knew about that ages ago. It was the biggest story of our senior school years."

Deepali grinned triumphantly. She had uncovered the secret over a casual chat with Aunty Maleeka at Silloo's beauty parlor the previous morning while they both were getting a manicure.

"Can you please go a little slower?" I said. "What story are you referring to?"

Aunty Maleeka gulped down half of her wine in one go. "You know, this is not too bad for an afternoon cap. Sure you girls won't try some?"

"Aunty Maleeka, please." My annoyance must have showed on my face.

"Okay, okay. The news was sensational. Your mother was a Wham! groupie who dragged me all the way to George Michael's house. Mind you, I did *not* get my fair share of fame out of the whole thing."

Deepali piped up from the background. "There you go, Ilz. Didn't I tell you she's a classified erotomaniacal stalker?"

"Mom is the last person in the world who could possibly stalk anything," I said indignantly.

"Veena Isham might be, but Veena Vij was not," Aunty Maleeka said, giggling hysterically as the wine worked its magic. "You, my dear, didn't know her in her younger years."

"You *know* she's a stalker at heart, Ilz," Deepali butted in. "She'd stop whatever she's doing to stalk you at a moment's notice."

I chose to ignore that last statement. I needed to understand Mom's behavioral patterns before giving Deepali the opportunity to analyze them.

"What exactly was she like back then?" I was partly curious and partly suspicious.

Aunty Maleeka took my question a little too personally—a sure sign of too much wine. She sat up straight, evidently annoyed. "*Back then?* Hey, how old do you think I am?"

Deepali jumped to my rescue. "Youth is definitely on your side, Aunty Maleeka. You know what these Ishams are like. For all their high-falutin English boli, they are just not very good with words."

Aunty Maleeka shrugged and then began her story: "Veena was obsessed with George Michael. And when I say obsessed, I mean crazy obsessed. She had posters of him all over her room, covering up the gorgeous blue floral wallpaper your grandmother had imported from some Laura Ashley shop in England. She even had a poster plastered on the ceiling right above her bed so that she could look at it as soon as she woke up every morning."

I was flabbergasted. Was this really my mother she was talking about? The lady who yelled at me for 'massacring' my walls with pictures of Ali Zafar?

"She was so in love with him that she'd take it personally when any of us pointed at his earrings to prove he was gay. She entertained the craziest dreams of chasing him down one day. All of us told her she had a screw loose, but then she actually did it."

"How did she mange to do it?" I asked, incredulous.

"By following his cat."

Deepali seized the opportunity to chime in. "Confirmed psychopathy. I'd be concerned about the gene pool, Ilz."

"Shut up, Deepali," I snapped, turning back to Aunty Maleeka. "Tell me more."

"We were both in London the summer after our eleventh standard. I was on vacation with my family. Veena had won some summer scholarship; she's such a brainiac, you know. But she's also kind of sneaky at times. I am convinced she won that scholarship just so she could go to England and stalk George Michael."

I waved my hands impatiently, signaling for her to go on. "She was a classic groupie for the entire time she was there. Two months! She'd go to the Wham! management office every day to pry out details about George Michael, but they wouldn't give anything away. Then, after reading some celebrity pop magazine, she figured out the street his mother lived on and forced me to get on a train with her to Bushey, a shitty English suburban town two hours away from Central London."

"Naani let her do that?" I asked, my mouth half open. It didn't sound like anything my conservative grandmother would stand for.

"Oh, she didn't know," Aunty Maleeka said, chuckling. "Your mother was a master at not telling the whole truth, if you know what I mean! Gosh, you mean you don't know all this already?"

Well, I'll be damned. My mother, who berated me for every little untruth I ever attempted to throw into the mix, was being exposed as a master in the art of deception.

"What happened when you got to this Bushey place?"

"Well, that was particularly annoying. We got to his street, but Veena hadn't done her homework right. She didn't know the street number."

"So?"

"So we sat there waiting. And waiting. And waiting. After nearly two hours, I was fed up and wanted to go home."

By this time, I could hardly keep myself from wriggling in my chair with excitement. A complete contrast to Deepali, who sat as calm as a sedated dog. Aunty Maleeka chuckled as she plodded her way down memory lane in between sips of wine. "There were three cats on the street. As we sat twiddling our thumbs, Veena suddenly had this eureka moment. George Michael's cat was called Xylo, a pretty weird name for a cat, if you ask me. So she started calling out to all the cats in the street. *Xylo, Xylo.* This brown-and-white tabby responded, so she got all excited. She was convinced it was his cat. Veena made me wait with her until the bloody cat decided to go home. Then she followed it right to the doorstep, rang the bell, and had this long chat with Mrs. Panos."

"Mrs. Panos?"

"George Michael's mother." Aunty Maleeka winked at Deepali who winked right back.

"Erotomania!" she said, clapping in glee.

I was more interested in the outcome. "Did she get to meet him?" I asked.

"Nope. Well, not on that day anyway. But Veena wouldn't let that poor Greek lady go."

"What Greek lady?" I was confused.

"Mrs. Panayiotou!" Aunty Maleeka shrieked.

"So George Michael isn't English?" I said.

"Arre, dhakkan," Deepali interrupted. "When have you ever heard of a Brit named Mrs. Panoayioutou?"

I turned red at being called a dhakkan in front of Aunty Maleeka.

"Anyway, Veena kept saying to Mrs. Panos in an overly sing-song voice: 'I am a poor little Indian girl who's come all the way from Bombay just to see him.' The only way dear Mother Michael could get her off her back was by telling Veena where in London her son hung out. Your mom does have a knack for persuasion."

I broke into a grin. "So she *did* find him eventually?"

Aunty Maleeka was beginning to write me off as even more of a dhakkan than she originally thought. "Of course, she did. How'd you think that picture was printed in the *Mid-Day* after she got back home? It became the talk of the town, and she became Bombay's own little celebrity."

I didn't know whether to be disgusted or inspired. As much as I wanted to despise Mom for her double standards, all I could think of was the sheer genius she had shown to successfully hunt her pop idol down. I idolized her even more. Perhaps I had inherited her genes. There was hope yet that I might track down Ali Zafar.

Deepali saw it differently. As we rode the bus back home, she switched to her shrink mode.

"I can see clearly now the rain has gone!" she squealed, dodging a phone call from Vik, Deepali's Boyfriend # 1.

She swung around the vertical bus rail with the agility of a pole dancer. The drama of the moment caught the eye of a middle-aged man seated relatively close by who, up until then, had been focusing on his iPhone. She proceeded to talk to me while stealing glances at him out of the corner of her eye. Deepali's ability to multitask never ceased to amaze me.

"Veena and Ila *both* insist on perfect English grammar, Veena and Ila *both* crush on pop idols, Veena and Ila are *both* erotomaniacal stalkers with a Type A personality."

When your best friend harps on about a personality trait, it is probably worth taking a few moments to reflect on her words.

"Do I really have a Type A personality?" I asked, knowing full well the answer to the question before I had even finished asking. Irreverent floozy though she was, Deepali was spot on about everything she decided to psychoanalyze. One day she would make the perfect shrink. I so respected the fact that she had a career path ahead of her when I was so far from even getting my shit together.

"The thing is, you've got to watch that obsessive gene before it gets the better of you," she said, texting love messages into her phone while sticking out her chest for her admirer in the bus. "Aunty Veena, on the other hand, needs to get a life. And you might just be the person to help her."

"How do you mean?" My curiosity was piqued.

"Think about it. Your mom has no hubby, no boyfriend even. How boring is that? She's incredibly attractive, you know. Forget one, she could have *multiple* men at her age."

I wanted to scold Deepali. Three-timing might come easy to her, but it wasn't necessarily Mom's thing. Deepali was quick to read my mind.

"Yeah, probably one boyfriend would work just fine for her."

She typed a text on her phone with intense concentration. "Deepali," I said.

No answer. "Deepali!" Still nothing.

"Listen to me, yaar!" I tried again.

Deepali finally looked up at me, giggling. "He said he'd do something to beat him!"

"Who? What?" I asked though I didn't really care.

"Vik. He said he'd beat up that super-hot dude staring at me on the bus. I love it when they get competitive."

One of Deepali's annoying traits is drawing her admirers into situations where they belittle each other. She does this purely for her own entertainment. Sometimes I think Deepali must be the most bored person on the planet, but those boys still chase after her like she is some movie star. Still, it's a skill that I could never hope to develop, so I respected her tenacity in honing it over and over again.

The bus had arrived at our stop. We walked down to the end of the road to the Mahalakshmi roundabout, which is where we always part ways. I take the Race Course Road towards Parel, and Deepali takes a left towards Nepean Sea Road.

"I thought you thought she was in love with Pops."

"Yes, yes, she is, and this is the way to prove it!"

What the heck did Deepali mean by that? But before I could dig in, she began to unleash a flow of creative thoughts.

"You know, only you could fix her up," Deepali said, snapping out of textual chemistry mode.

"Oh?" I wasn't really paying attention.

"Plain and simple. You are just as obsessive as she is, so instead of obsessing about Ali Zafar this summer, you need to get yourself a new project. And this is the perfect one."

Now I was intrigued. "You mean set her up on a date?"

"Not one, but several."

"Mom, on *a* date, let alone *dates*? Puhhleez, that would never happen. She'd run miles to escape that kind of situation."

"Exactly. That's why you won't tell her."

"So you mean a blind date?" It was an interesting idea, but interesting only as an idea. Mom would never agree to it.

"It's all about strategy and planning," Deepali said.

I could tell from the way she jangled her bangles that she was getting excited by the idea. "You'll have to pose as Aunty Veena initially...You and I together, of course. You can't do it alone."

"How the heck will we do that?" I was irritated by the stupidity of her suggestion.

"Simple. The Arranged Marriage dating app."

"You want to arrange a marriage for my mother?"

"Nah, dumbo. Since when do online matrimonial apps have anything to do with marriage?"

I examined her last statement, but I couldn't figure out why Deepali was calling *me* dumbo.

"It's about dating, Ilz. Can't you see? Dating doesn't happen in the Isham household."

Oof! Truth cuts like a knife. Still, I couldn't quite envision why anyone would list their profile on a marriage website if they weren't interested in getting married in the first place.

"The idea of marriage is so passé," Deepali said, throwing her arms out like Maria in *The Sound of Music*. "Dev says that Arranged Marriage is not about meeting Mr. Right. It's about meeting Mr. Right Now."

Dev! I hadn't thought about him all this time, which was probably a good thing. But at the mention of his name, I felt those butterflies having a field day in my stomach once again. That was definitely a bad thing! Seriously though, were any of Deepali's boyfriends qualified to pass judgement, given all of their seventeen years of singledom? Then again, he could have been frequenting Lagan.com in retaliation for being triple-timed. What else was he to do with the two-thirds of the time Deepali focused on the others? Why couldn't he fill in the time gaps by focusing over this way towards me? I had to check myself— there you go again, Ila. Stop it already!

"Not to worry, Ilz-capeelz," Deepali said.

For a moment I thought she was referring to Dev. But then I got out of my head and started listening to what she had to say.

"We are going to shuffle things up a bit. First, we give Aunty Veena a makeover. Spruce up her dress sense, shake up her routine, get her to graduate from mundane to modern."

I liked what I heard so far, but an app called Arranged Marriage just didn't seem appropriate.

"Let's go for an app that's more fun," I suggested.

"Well, what about Tinder?" Deepali asked.

"That's for millennials, Deepali!"

"Won't you believe it, there are plenty of old creeps in their forties and fifties on Tinder."

"And why would I want to set my mother up with an old creep?"

"Okay, Bumble, then! She can be in full power and choose who she wants to swipe right on and match with."

I liked the idea. Bumble was the only dating app that gave women the power to choose who they wanted to match with. But in reality, it was probably worth diversifying the chances with more than just two apps.

"Okay," I said reluctantly. "I suppose it's worth setting up profiles on all four apps."

"All four?" Deepali asked.

"Tinder, Bumble, Arranged Marriage and Grindr."

"Grindr is for the LGBTQ crew, hon. You are clearly not up on dating app knowhow."

No argument there. "Okay, okay, no Grindr. Let's just do the other three."

"Okay." Deepali rubbed her hands in glee. "Then we develop a date plan. Line up a man. Sorry...men. Why stop at one?"

I had to admit, it was marvelously sneaky—sneakily marvelous. I looked at the crowds of people jostling to get to the gates of Turf Club. All those men were potential power-walking dates for Mom. Which ones loved classic rock or Shankar–Ehsaan–Loy? Deepali's idea, if it took off well, was brilliant.

But how would we do this? Deepali was leaving for a vacation in Nainital in two-and-a-half weeks.

"Which is why we need to get rocking and rolling," she said firmly. "The three of us start tomorrow and have this thing wrapped up before I leave."

"The three of us?"

"You, me, and Dev."

"Dev? Why is Dev a part of this?"

Deepali cocked her head to the side in a completely matter-of-fact way.

"Because his writing skills are bloody good, and we need them to create a kick-butt profile. And also, because this is a great way for him to get to know Aunty Veena."

Seriously what was Deepali on about? Why the heck would Dev need to get to know Mom? To create the perfect profile?

"It's actually about getting to understand the inner workings of the kind of person that Williams College would want to accept," Deepali corrected me before I could question her. "Who better to understand than Veena Isham?"

Oh yeah, the Williams College counseling thing. "Deepali, that was then, and this is now. It's twenty-five years later!"

"Yup, and in these last twenty-five years, Williams College is still number one out of all the liberal-arts colleges in America. That says something, doesn't it? They probably have made many changes on the kind of person they choose to admit."

Okay, fine. When it came to Dev, I guess there was no harm in being somewhat charitable. Either that or it was a good excuse to justify his presence in my life. Plus, Deepali was right about his writing skills. And he was so much cuter than Ali Zafar.

Wait a minute...did I really just admit that? I turned my focus back to Ali Zafar. Yes, indeed, initially I had wanted to spend the summer stalking him but the whole thing had been thrown for a loop in recent days, partly because finding out about the whole George Michael thing shed light on how the whole plan may not be worth it after all. It wasn't like she'd ended up with anything more than a photograph in the paper —and frankly, one that simply made her look like a groupie. It was hardly flattering. Admittedly, as far as summer projects go, it did feel kinda creepy. This new plan was definitely more creative and interesting than becoming an Ali Zafar groupie.

But then there was this idea of Dev being involved. To be honest he'd been on my mind ever since I heard him say 'Hey B' in the canteen a few days before, with that crooked smile. And his leg swung over the side of the chair! Ugh...what was my problem? Dev was Deepali's—he had full license to be on *her* mind, not mine! Snap out of it Ila, I told myself.

So did I really want to do it? Let's see. Was it more interesting? Potentially, yes. Would I have fun doing it? Definitely. Could it be a tool to obtain some real power over my mother? Probably. And what about being forced to hang with the D&D duo all the time? Aka Dev and Deepali. Would it thrill me to see him or sicken me to see him in the presence of Deepali over and over again?

I'm not sure whether Deepali coerced me into the idea or whether I was a willing victim, but either way, I had made up my mind in a matter of moments. The next day, Deepali, Dev, and I would get right on it. Operation Mom, here we come!

chapter
five

OPERATION MOM, 15 DAYS TO GO - WE GOT THIS

Deepali and I took a walk through Phoenix Mills to brainstorm ideas for Operation Mom.

She came to a halt outside the Global Desi showroom. "The first thing we need to do is vamp," she said, using the shop window as a faux mirror as she smeared bright red lipstick over her luscious lips which made me jealous every time she pouted. Deepali had hardly uttered a prayer in her life, yet God had given her these massive, kiss-me lips. I, on the other hand, am a regular at praying, yet am blessed with thin, peeling lips that constantly beg for Chapstick. I wonder about God sometimes. Oh well, he has graced me with better language skills at least.

"I think you mean revamp."

Deepali gave me a dark look through her make-do looking glass.

"Re-vamping is taken for granted. The real challenge is in the vamping."

What was this? A scene out of Twilight? "How does one get serious about 'vamping'?"

"Vamping is all about Ess-Say."

"An essay?" What essay could she possibly want to write about this?

"Ess as in 'S' , Ayy as in 'A'". Sex appeal."

Mom and sex appeal would be on opposite poles if they were represented on a globe, I sniggered as I thought to myself.

"Exactly," Deepali said, reading my thoughts in the classic Deepali manner. "No offense, Ilz, but nobody on Tinder, Bumble or Arranged Marriage wants to have anything to do with a super conservative sati-savitri."

"Okay, I take your point about Mr. Right versus Mr. Right Now, but if the ultimate purpose of Arranged Marriage is to find brides—and I am fairly positive that was the intention of the founders—I cannot imagine why any of its members would choose to marry a vamp over a super conservative sati-savitri."

"Follow me," Deepali demanded and, without further ado, strode purposefully into the showroom and made her way to a mannequin dressed in a backless halter-neck kurta top. Deepali pulled out a *Cosmo* from her bag. On the cover was Bipasha Basu, Bollywood's top seductress, wearing the same top. Deepali waved the magazine in my face. "Vamp," she thundered. Then she opened to an inside spread of Aishwarya Rai, the pure and pristine previous Miss World, wearing an off-white sari with an orange border. "Sati-savitri. Get it?"

I got her message loud and clear. "Right. Bipasha gets vamp kudos over Aishwarya."

"Exactly! Ash might be the most beautiful woman on this side of the planet, but she doesn't give ass like Bips. That's why Bips ends up with hot dude after hot dude, but Aishwarya gets stuck with the Bachchan bores."

"C'mon, Abhishek Bachchan is cute."

"Cute, yes, in the sense of sweet little mama's boy. But who in their right mind would want to get stuck in the 'Godfather of Bollywood' household? C'mon, criminals probably have more fun in Tihar Jail. If Aunty Veena wants some fun in her life, vamping up is what she needs. Once she has the guy hooked, she can take the relationship anywhere she pleases. And don't you worry, my little Ilz," she said with firm determination, "We are going to fix all that. Come, let's check out Aunty Veena's wardrobe."

A shiver of nervous excitement ran down my spine.

"We can't do that. Mom will have a fit if she knows I've been messing with her stuff. As it is, she has an ulcer every time I borrow her makeup. Even when I try to do it on the sly, she notices."

But it was too late. Deepali had marched out of the store and was headed towards the entrance of the mall to summon a taxi to my place. I followed her meekly like a sheep follows its shepherd.

——

Deepali made a beeline for Mom's room as soon as we reached home. She flung the almirah doors wide open and ran her fingers across the row of perfectly folded saris that hung neatly on hangers with color-coordinated blouses and petticoats. Then, after a few grunts and groans, she took a step back and stood with her arms folded. She shook her head in utter disgust.

"Chihhh!"

Did my progenitor really evoke such strong negative reactions in my best friend?

"This is not going to work."

"What part?"

"None of it. Just look at all these saris—traditional, embroidered saris, temple saris."

"What's wrong with her temple saris? My mother's cousin, Gaga Maasi, gave them to her years ago for her boys' thread ceremonies."

"Figures," said Deepali nonchalantly. "With a name like *Gaga Maasi*, you can't expect your aunt to have any semblance of style. Seriously, despite all those names in the Maneka Gandhi Baby Names book, why do Punjus have to go for the most phonetically ridiculous ones they can find?"

Punjus! I hate it when Deepali is spot on about my tribe, which, frankly, is most of the time. Gaga Maasi, my mother's first cousin, was just one specimen of an entire line of unstylish Punjabi dames that typify my extended family. There is nothing about her—or frankly any of them—that could be even remotely associated with savoir faire. Style necessitates interest, and all these Punju women are interested in is singing and dancing at weddings, sangeet music parties, and Karva Chauth fasting functions. Yeah, don't get me started on Karva Chauth functions. Mom hasn't kept the married women's fast since her divorce, but she makes it a point to attend the big KC party each year so that she can pig out and cock a snook at the entire bitchy still-married suhaagan community.

I think part of the reason that our relatives are so unstylish is that they are just plain fat. Fatness is the Punju curse—we are doomed to be heavier than everyone else in the nation. Everyone knows and accepts it. Kaivalyadham, the yoga studio on Marine Drive, gives you a three-kilo leeway if you are Punju. I particularly despise the Punju dames in my extended family because I thought they would be supportive of Mom's decision; yet, they are the first to chide her for her choice to be single and to vociferously declare how her self-declared status is a bad thing for my upbringing. Poor Mom—she's always had to face the firing squad at every social opportunity. No wonder she pigs out in their faces while they fast. I think this is why she prefers staying at home to type rather than see them on occasions that offer less scope for proving points.

"Okay, Gaga Maasi is no style icon," I admitted. "But then, clearly, neither is Mom. Although she does have a few saris with polka dots."

Deepali shook her head with a tsk tsk. "Polka dots are so Minnie Mouse."

"Even pink or black ones?"

Deepali cocked her head to one side as she thought about it. "Nah, that's Aunty Perizaad meets ladybugs."

Okay, whatever. When it comes to fashion sense, I willingly defer to Deepali. Another check mark on the list of reasons to love her.

"You'll just have to take her shopping," she said, slamming the almirah doors shut. Then she turned around and flung herself on Mom's bed like a Bollywood actress in a song sequence.

"Shopping? Where?" I whined.

"Satya Paul or Global Desi. Preferably both."

I pictured Mom in a Satya Paul sari. She was no Bipasha, but if she agreed, she could look pretty hot in it. That said, she'd never wear their blouses.

"Deepali, Satya Paul saris have slinky blouses that end right under your boobs."

"That's what we need," Deepali said. She turned over on her back and gazed at her chest to see how much her boobs had flattened out as a result. Not much. Besides luscious lips, she was blessed with eternally perky boobs. No wonder guys wanted to date her left, right, and center.

"What are you saying? You know Mom makes an art of hiding her love handles and tiers of tummy fat with kurtas."

Deepali grunted and stared thoughtfully at the ceiling. "We need to get her to kick-boxing class."

"She does yoga. Isn't that good enough?"

"Has it got rid of the love handles?"

I shook my head.

"Well, there's the answer to your question."

I wasn't against the idea of Mom exercising. She wasn't fat, just chunky in all the wrong places. Like her relatives, she had the tendency to put on weight. But I also knew that she wouldn't go for just any exercise. It had to resonate with her mindset. I tried to explain this to Deepali.

"We need to find something invigorating, preferably with Punjabi or Latin music."

Deepali jerked upright. "I know!" she squealed, a lightbulb going off in her head. "Let's check out Baqar Hakim's spinning studio. I hear he caters to middle-aged housewives."

chapter
six

OPERATION MOM, 1 DOWN, 14 DAYS TO GO - TRIM
THE FAT

Going for a spin class at Baqar Hakim's Topspinners studio turned out to be one of the most surreal experiences of my entire seventeen years.

Summer vacation means that every day is a sleep-in day—the opportune time for teens to catch their well-deserved zzz's. Yet, Deepali hauled me out of bed early enough to make sure that we arrived there at the ungodly hour of 9:15 a.m. to find a line of Mercedes Benzes and BMWs in the parking lot with drivers standing around, puffing on beedis. I already felt like a pleb as I stepped off the rather less stylish red bus outside Alaknanda Building. Would I be even allowed to enter this establishment that catered to Mumbai's elite?

"Don't be ridiculous," Deepali said. "This is going to be totally jhakaas. Atmosphere, exercise and people watching, all at the same time."

She was right. The moment we entered the studio, our senses were assaulted by psychedelic lights, throbbing music, and the overpowering aroma of lavender that was intended to drown out the underlying tinge of body odor. In the class, there were two guys who looked like they had just walked out of *Fitness* magazine, a tall statuesque woman who looked like she had been peeled off the cover of *Vogue*, and seven or eight mildly overweight women trying desperately to look attractive in their designer exercise outfits. Everyone was perched atop the spin-cycles lined up along a mirrored wall. In many ways, it felt more like a night club than an exercise studio.

Suddenly, I became self-conscious. Would I even fit on the bike seats? Or would my butt cheeks just flare out and flop over them like the floppy ears of Mitzy, Aunty Maleeka's cock-a-doodle? Would the other spinners ogle me thinking, 'there spins a damsel from Amritsar with her wall-to-wall hips'?

While my angst was dancing to the tunes of Hindi pop, Baqar, the twenty-three-year-old all-India university cycling champion and 'spin-master', snapped his fingers in the face of my insecurity.

"Hey, Punju," he called out, grinning.

Drat. It was the hips. They were a sure giveaway.

"All you Punjabi girls come in looking like deer caught in head-lights," he said. "Not to worry, forty-five minutes on a spinning cycle will melt away your store of aloo parathas."

I felt myself turn bright red. Was it really that obvious? "Here's your bike." He directed me to a cycle with a seat that could not be more than one-fifth the size of my posterior. "And there's your inspiration," he said, pointing to the loudspeaker blasting bhangra pop.

Deepali needed no instruction and quickly hopped onto the bike—strategically placed between a guy who looked exactly like Suniel Shetty and another who looked like he could play Arnold Schwarzenegger's duplicate—three spots away. She skillfully avoided the glare of the stat-uesque bombshell.

The class started with a fast-pedaling session to "All is Well." All the ladies, regardless of their size, seemed quite used to it and began to pedal along merrily, Deepali included.

I, however, was another story. By the end of the first five minutes, I was huffing and puffing like there was no tomorrow. There was no way I could possibly carry this through for another forty minutes.

"And that brings us to the end of the warm-up," Baqar shouted glee-fully over the music.

The warm-up? He had to be joking. I looked pitifully towards Deepali, but she was already in the zone, swaying her bare tank-topped shoulders from side to side while spinning her legs like a hunted animal trying to escape a predator. I could see she was turning on her seductive charm to get Baqar's attention.

And like a puppy to a biscuit, he responded by shooting arrows of praise her way. "Arre, killer technique," he said with an equally killer smile.

Typical! To me, Deepali looked like a cross between a Bollywood dancer and a maniacal marathoner, but I guess guys like that kind of thing. I couldn't tell what she was more focused on—the actual spinning technique or on using it to seduce the spinmaster—but she looked up from her bike and shot him a dazzling smile, the kind you would see in a Close-Up toothpaste ad.

I, on the other hand, could barely hold myself together. The music had switched to "Laila oh Laila"; an indigo light drew circles on the floor to the beat of the rhythm. One of my favorite songs was going to complete waste as I desperately foraged for the will to keep my thighs from splitting apart.

"Make your resistance less." Baqar was shouting instructions into a microphone.

chapter
seven

I FUMBLED with a dial on the front of the bike. Ah, it became slightly easier.

"More less," Baqar said.

More or *less*?

As I prayed for the clock to move faster than my legs, the next forty minutes resonated with various Bollywood and bhangra tunes, strewn with instructions barked out by Baqar.

"Hill training, flat-road standing, bottoms up, bottoms down," he shouted. He instructed us to turn up our resistance level at every given opportunity. I promised myself never, *ever* again to complain about the dullness of my daily existence.

"Come on, Punju," Baqar hollered. "Challenge yourself. This is not a lazy daisy pedal in the park."

I upped the resistance on my spin bike for the nth time, gasping for a breath. Ascending from the Everest base camp could not possibly be worse than this.

"Speed it up!" Baqar yelled into my face. "No cheating allowed. Cheating slows you down and slowing down injects lactic acid into your muscles."

In situations like this, does anyone really care? As far as I was concerned, it was yet more liquid to add to the profuse stream of sweat that was edging its way through my wrinkles in 40-degree Celsius rivulets.

Clearly unhappy with what I perceived to be the highest level of spinning, Baqar began to mess with my brain again. He pressed a button on a remote control, causing the strobe lights attached to the ceiling to start spinning too. Then another light source threw out silhouettes of marathon runners on to the floor in front of our bikes. None of us had any choice but to stare at the moving pictures heaving this way and that, in sync with the high-energy tunes of the latest Salman Khan movie. The women looked incredibly focused even though their pedaling was not half as fast as the two men who looked doped enough to be Lance Armstrong. Deepali too looked like she was in a trance.

Then the psychedelic lights from the far-right corner of the room flung out geometric patterns that spun my head in tandem with the bike wheels spinning my lower body. Or vice versa—I couldn't quite tell. It was like *Chariots of Fire* on steroids.

What I didn't realize then was that all of this was a tactic. The spin-master had a deliberate motive to get into my head in the manner that a drug takes control of an addict. Moments thereafter, I lost all ability to sense pain, tension, or fatigue. Like Deepali, I too entered the zone. My prayers to the divine to quicken the clock to reach the forty-five-minute target faster than usual had long been abandoned. Yet, just as my leg muscles approached the level of numbness my brain had reached, the divine answered in the form of "Jhoole Lal" —a Punjabi ode to my Punjabi love handles.

Baqar was on a roll. He conducted all of our orchestral bike maneuvers in the dark like the master of a symphony. Every time the singer from Junoon shouted 'mast kalandar,' he signaled us to stand up from our seats, lean forward, and pedal harder. Twenty seconds later, we'd seat our butts down again. He repeated the pattern for the length of the song, and my fat jiggled every time I changed position. No doubt this was the magic of weight loss. How had Nusrat Fateh Ali Khan rocked to this tune over and over again on stage without losing his endless tiers of fat?

"This song trickles into each and every cell of your body to make you *fresh*," Baqar echoed over the music. "Feel your entire being re-energize from head to toe."

Finally, as the song ended, the spinmaster started to ease the pace. Everybody gradually decreased their resistance, and the music switched to a mellower tune.

I felt like a sweating horse, and I probably looked like one too. However, Deepali's visible form at the end of the class was another story. I looked over to see her body glistening with sweat droplets, like water on the scales of a freshly-caught fish. After the cool down, she stretched her legs to ease the tension off her muscles, mimicking the movements of the tall bombshell. Both looked absolutely gorgeous, like a pair of mermaids who had just risen up from the depths of the Arabian Sea. Even the mildly overweight housewives were filled with energy and raring to go after the class. And the two bodybuilder guys...let's not even go there.

I could barely mumble a 'thank you' by the end of the class, but Jhoole Lal had certainly freshened up Deepali. She flirted mercilessly with Baqar and competed with the bombshell for attention from her newly acquired spinning entourage of musclemen as I worked hard to gather my breath, belongings, and composure.

"So, I'll see you tomorrow, Punju?" Baqar said, giving me a thumbs up as I headed towards the door. "Don't stay away from me, or your thighs will be double the size when you return."

I smiled feebly and returned his gesture. It was a face-saver, of course. I had no intention of ever coming back.

Outside, I was so tired, I could barely keep up with Deepali who wanted to maintain her heart rate at a fat-burning level as she began to stride down Nepean Sea Road.

"Deepali, you are out of your mind if you think Mom is going to survive in there for five minutes, let alone an hour," I said as we skirted our way through the stream of foreign cars that were now revving up to take their memsahibs home.

"You're right," she responded, chugging an entire bottle of Gatorade in just three gulps. "Too much BO, no? Baqar really should improve the ventilation."

"No amount of ventilation or aromatherapy is going to be enough to rid that place of BO," I grunted. "I don't think that I have ever sweated so much in my life."

Deepali tsked while wiping her brow with the dramatic skill of a kathak dancer. "Horses sweat, men perspire, women glow."

"But seriously, it's not just about the smell," I continued. "Mom is never going to go for that high-powered exercise stuff. You heard how he kept calling me Punju?"

Deepali swung her jhola-style pocketbook upon her shoulder. "Arre, why do you always want to live in denial. Aunty Veena enjoys high-energy stuff that involves desi music. You know she'll love it."

Would she?

"Otherwise, just stick to the alternative."

"What's that?"

"Live with the *Punju* stereotype."

Perhaps. Deepali and I parted ways at the bus stop. As I rode the bus home, I could feel myself working up another 'glow' that had less to do with exercise and more to do with the temperature of the Mumbai summer day. Or perhaps sheer annoyance at the fact that Deepali was actually right. Truth be told, Mom *would* love Topspinners. She had always enjoyed high-intensity exercise—hiking, running, ashtanga yoga, all the things that I absolutely detested—not because she found it easy to do or was motivated enough to do it so regularly that it would actually keep her in shape, but because when she did, it gave her an odd sense of freedom, making her feel good. The combination of a high-calorie workout and the bhangra music was right up her alley. Whether it did anything to rid her of the love handles or not, she would be thrilled to spend the hour there. But Mom going to the spin class would entail me having to put up with the indignity of Baqar's comments about my Punju thighs again. Shoot! Was that worth it even for Mom? Surely there could be a way to achieve this goal without feeling like I had to be subjected to the crude judgement of someone who clearly didn't under-stand that my thighs had a better bond with gravity than most. Yeah, selfish though it was, I was going to vote against it.

Sometimes, I wonder how Mom and I share the same ancestors. She loves doing stuff and, given the choice, she would not sit idle for a minute. She said to me once that wasted moments eroded her brain. I, on the other hand, am quite happy to have my brain eroded. There's nothing I love more than downtime where I stare into space and do absolutely nothing. Or sleeping in until noon on weekends. It drives Mom crazy that I can sleep that much without even taking melatonin supplements. She's always stressing about the fact that I might be depressed, but she doesn't understand that I am just not a morning person, or an afternoon, evening, or night person, for that matter.

——

When I got home, Mom was standing in tree pose in the middle of the living room.

"Hello, baby girl," she said, stretching her arms towards the heavens. "Where've you been?"

"At a spin class," I replied, putting my things down.

"Spin? No wonder you are so pich pich," she said, breathing into her lower belly. By 'pich pich', she meant I looked disgustingly sticky with heat and sweat.

"Not half as pich pich as I was thirty minutes ago. Speaking of which, we should find you a kind of activity that will get you going pich pich too.

Mom wiggled her way into a yoga breath. "In, oohh, out, aahh."

"Mom!"

She repeated: "In, oohh, out, aahh."

"Like a housewives fitness class or something."

Mom continued her yogic breathing, using it as an excuse to take her time and be non-committal.

"I'm not a housewife; I'm a stay-at-home journalist," she said, positioning her arms out into mid-air with her last three fingers stretched out in the chin mudra.

"Still, a housewives-oriented fitness class might be better for you than some other kind of class, possibly filled with fitness freaks and muscle-toned hotties."

But Mom couldn't care less about what I was saying. She was way too focused on her pranayama.

"In, oohh, out, aahh."

It sounded like she was having a yoga orgasm, but this was not a thought that I wanted to share with my mother, so I left the room wondering which of the two, pranayama or endorphins, felt more like an orgasm.

Safely ensconced in my room, I plopped down on my bed and tried to come up with a plan of action to convince Mom to sign up for Topspinners though she had just completely ignored me in favor of her oohhs and aahhs.

I decided to stay positive by focusing on Operation Mom and made a list of the things I needed to talk Mom into in order to build up her sex appeal:

1. No more crosswords
2. No more traditional saris
3. A new tube of lipstick
4. A trendy new hairstyle.

Would she absolutely hate me for bringing this up? How was I going to approach her? And how was I going to do this in the two weeks we had left?

chapter
eight

OPERATION MOM, 2 DOWN, 13 DAYS TO GO - THERE ARE NO DESPERATE SITUATIONS, ONLY DESPERATE PEOPLE

"She is by far the most important piece of this," Deepali said over a paper cone of bhel puri down at the local bhelwalla stand. The *she* in question was my mom. "Primping her up is essential," Deepali continued.

How Deepali can think about primping while she is downing spicy bhel puri beats me. Frankly, how one can go for bhel puri at 10:30 in the morning beats me too, but that's another matter.

"Primping is all very well," I replied. "But we are running short of time. Shouldn't we also be looking for someone she can primp *for*?"

Deepali stopped chewing to think about it. "Not a bad idea—we should find someone totally primp-worthy. It'll be a simultaneous equation."

"Deepali, simultaneous equations have nothing to do with..." I began, but by this time, she was swinging her butt towards the building entrance. A flash of nervousness whizzed through me as I imagined Mom walking in on us scouring some online dating site.

"We can't," I said, grabbing Deepali by the shoulder. "Mom lurks around my room way too much. Let's go to your place instead."

But Deepali was never content to stay within the confines of her own home. Operation Mom had just given her an excuse for more excursions about town.

"My place is too boring," she whined.

"Okay, a neutral place, then. A cafe?"

"The Kalaghoda cafe?" Deepali said, excitedly tipping the final mouthful of bhel into her mouth with one hand while texting Boyfriend #2 with the other—another example of her physical and mental dexterity.

The pre-frontal cortex is charged with the responsibility of multi-tasking and attention, but the use of technology changes your brain structure. With the amount of time Deepali spends texting her boyfriends, it's a wonder that she has any pre-frontal cortex energy left for either multitasking or paying any attention to her admirers.

"No, it's too artsy. Mom's colleagues hang out there."

Deepali let out a whine of dismay, and her eyes welled up with tears.

I was flummoxed. Did I say something hurtful?

She flailed her arms as she swallowed her last bite of bhel and then scrunched her paper cone into a tight ball, squeezing it as though it were a stress ball.

"Teeekha!" she screamed. Just then, her phone buzzed, and she squealed again. This time because Jaggi, Boyfriend #2 had texted her.

I wasn't going to get anywhere with Deepali while she was preoccupied with the bhel puri and her boyfriends.

"I need to run some errands," I said. "Call me if you have ideas."

Deepali stopped texting and put her phone in her bag. She grinned at me, exposing bits of sev caught between her front teeth.

"India Cyber House!" she said, shooting wafts of bhel puri breath my way. "Open from ten in the morning to eleven-thirty in the evening. Dev says it's on Princess Street. I'll see you there after lunch."

"Dev?" I began.

"Yes, Dev!" She sharply interrupted. "He has a good sense about these things—primp-worthiness and simultaneous equations both. I've just asked him to meet us there."

An image of Dev's crooked smile flashed across my mind screen. I felt guilty for underestimating Deepali's ability to multitask.

——

Overwrought with insecurity, I approached India Cyber House internet cafe. The idea that someone known to me might actually discover me scouring the cheesy world of internet dating on the pretext of getting my mom a life was too much to handle. Trepidatious, I couldn't bring myself to actually step inside.

Fifteen minutes later, I was still pacing outside the internet cafe, waiting for my floozy mentor and the dude with the crooked smile. After another ten minutes, I spied Dev strolling down the street, his thumbs locked in his belt loops, a blue backpack strung over one shoulder, and his smile crookeder than ever.

"Hi, Ilz!" he shot me a smile, setting off something inside of me that no other smile had ever done. A momentary bliss to my anxiety! But then a different kind of anxiety took over. What was I to say to him? How was I to fill in the time without sounding or looking in the least bit coquettish or dumb?

"Er, hi, Dev!" I responded, carefully noting my pitch. "I guess Deepali is just taking her own sweet time."

"Well, that's Deepali for you. Not to worry though...hopefully my company isn't too boring," he laughed.

Boring? Heck no! I felt weak and became conscious of my fidgety fingers tugging at the ends of my t-shirt.

"Of course not," I laughed, completely missing the perfect pitch I had assigned myself.

Luckily, it was just a few more minutes before Deepali sauntered along in a pair of skin-tight jeans and massive Jackie O shades. With her tiny waist, big butt, and equally big hair, she looked like Sharmila Tagore straight out of a '70s flick.

"You're late," I snapped. "I've been here half an hour."

"Don't dhaap," Deepali retorted. "You couldn't have been *that* excited about finding your mother a man."

"I was here because of my sense of time, not excitement."

"Chillax," she brushed off my annoyance. "It's not like we need to meet an IIT application deadline or anything. Besides, Dev must have been good company, no?"

I opened my mouth and then decided to close it before I said something stupid. Dev raised his eyebrows, shrugged his shoulders, and turned his face to look away. What the heck was up with that?

"I sense Ila's nerves are a tad frayed."

Yeah, just a tad!

"What if somebody sees us?" I said, glancing around rabbit-eyed. "I mean if people see us browsing a dating site..."

Deepali took off her goggles and glared at me with an oh-you've-got-to-be-kidding expression. "Listen, I know paranoia is your specialty, but this is not the Kalaghoda café. It's a boring old internet parlor, remember? Everyone's here for the same old, same old. Here, I'll show you." She swung open the door to the café, revealing a line of men interspersed with the odd woman, all hunched over a row of desktop computers. Further afield was a seated area with comfy vinyl armchairs and low tables for the lap-toppers.

"You see these people?" Deepali pointed to a row of bespectacled geeks. "Why do you think they are here? Everyone comes for exactly the same thing."

Was Deepali nuts?

"I'm telling you," she continued, "they all come here to scour ArrangedMarriage.com. Either that or Indian-Passion.com," She turned to Dev. "You tell her, nah!"

He turned to me and flashed his crooked smile. Oh, my nerves! Were they nerves? No, a flutter. There was something about that smile that set my nerves a-flutter...

"Actually, Deepali is spot on," he said. "It's exactly why I suggested this place."

"Wait a minute, why do you even know about this place?" I asked raising my brow in suspicion. "Like do you come here to scour dating sites?"

Dev let out a loud chuckle. "Actually, I come here to use the printer for school projects. Arranged Marriage is not exactly my thing, but if it were, I'd just use the app on my phone rather than making a trip to cyber cafe...even if it is entertaining to look over the shoulders of others here."

I wasn't sure whether to be mortified at my utterly ridiculous question or relieved that he did not habitually come here to check out ArrangedMarriage.com, the website version of the Arranged Marriage dating app. And indian-passion.com, well, I didn't know exactly what that was, but I knew it was some kind of online dating site that didn't have an app. What I didn't understand was why anyone would go to an internet cafe to scour sites when you could just as easily swipe left and right in the comfort of your own home.

"At home, you have to contend with your wife. That problem gets eradicated with a trip to an internet cafe," Deepali said, staring at her nails as usual. "Besides, if you go for a website, then there is no chance of your wife illicitly checking your phone."

"Who told you that?"

"Dev did."

Dev looked over at me and broke into a sheepish smile. Darn, he was cute! Sheepish, but cute. He nodded in agreement. "It's sad but true."

"And Jaggi backed it up."

Of course! Deepali's boyfriends were her regular source of information besides Facebook. Jaggi, I didn't care about so much, but for some strange reason, it annoyed me that Dev would know these things.

"Ew—so tacky!" I said. "Why don't these dudes get a life?"

"Control your levels of prude," Deepali responded, unoffended.

Dev saw my expression and took it upon himself to offer some solace. "I totally get it, Ila. It completely sucks, but I figure that there is no upside in holding back this truth about the average older Indian man. Well...maybe not average...maybe this place represents the despicable few."

Whew! Maybe his views on the subject were a signal that he would not turn out this way in his married future! I glanced over at him to find his dark chocolate eyes piercing mine. A shudder went down my spine, unexpected yet pleasant. What was he thinking when he looked at me that way?

As we settled down in the laptop area, I turned my focus to the task and began to agonize over the reality of the project I had embarked upon.

"Seriously, Deepali, is this what my life has come to? Screening men on a dating app to set up them up with my mother?"

Deepali threw me a frustrated glance. "Yaar, we had agreed to finish this before I left for Nainital. If you are not planning to play ball, go back to your silly pop star, and we'll pick this up in October."

"What happens in October?" I was a little confused.

"Dandiya Raas stick dancing parties. We can check out the guys there. The scene at Jal Darshan Building is mind blowing."

I could imagine Mom's reaction if I mentioned Dandiya Raas. She had always been adamantly against them as she viewed them as Mumbai's deflowering hubs, but I kept my thoughts to myself and turned to Dev for his opinion. He shot me a smile—that irresistible, crooked smile.

"How'd you think your mom and dad met?" he interjected.

"Yeah," Deepali continued. "If marriages are made in heaven, Jal Darshan is heaven on Earth."

"I thought we had agreed that we weren't aiming for marriage," I said.

"We're not," Deepali replied earnestly. "But the JD scene is filled with nubile folks—you have to use the M-word to filter out those who don't make the cut."

I thought about what Deepali was saying. It was likely that people from Mom's generation would be unwilling to date for the sake of dating, but meeting up with the intention of finding a spouse was perfectly acceptable. But isn't it deceitful to come on strong and then ditch the person the moment you find out that they are interested in marriage? "Deepali, Dandiya Raases are infested with Gujjus."

Deepali looked offended. "And what is wrong with my community?"

"Nothing. But we are Punju."

"Babes, we are not setting up a twenty-one-year-old. Aunty Veena is approaching forty-five—an age at which most Punju men are in terrible shape, unless, of course, they are training for some mega Khalsa ordeal, but then that would bring with it a slew of other problems. Sorry Dev, TMI? A harsh look into your future reality?"

"TMI, for sure!" Dev said, looking confused. Whether he couldn't figure out what Deepali was trying to say or whether he was startled at the thought of devolving into terrible shape at some point in his undetermined future, I couldn't tell. That said, Deepali was right. Mom had already tried one Punju guy, and look how that ended up.

Deepali opened my laptop and handed it to Dev who began to type fiercely. The fact that his fingers were now touching my keyboard sent a particular rapture streaking through my body.

"Focus, Ila!" Deepali shrieked, snapping her fingers at me. "I know the view is good from where you are, but seriously!"

Did she really dare to say that? What the heck was wrong with this girl? Dev had turned quite pink.

"I agree with Deepali," he said. "Spreading the net far and wide is the best course of action."

"Yup," she responded. "Let's stick with Lagan.com. That way we can hand-pick the best lookers and get a good idea about their alcohol intake levels too."

I slumped back into the couch. The whole thing seemed kind of shallow. For an accomplished forty-five-year-old woman, surely we should be screening for things like intellect and common interests, but Deepali and Dev both had an entirely different philosophy. They believed that, like men, women were equally shallow at all ages. Men apparently don't care about intellect, especially a woman's, because it is scary and off-putting. Women, on the other hand, assuming they plan to marry a guy, most definitely care about the depths of his pockets. But when it comes to pure dating, her cares are out the window. Everything simply boils down to the hotness factor.

"Golden rule #1: Go straight for the looks," Deepali said.

"Where'd you get that from?"

"Jaggi, of course!"

Jaggi! I glanced over at Dev, dreading his reaction, but he didn't even wince. Instead, he glanced right back at me with a wink. What the heck did that mean? Did he even know about Deepali's other boyfriends? Or did he not care? Either way, it seemed wrong.

"And Dr Mirno, the Pakistani-Chinese doctor based in Hong Kong, remember?"

"I think so. Pakistani-Chinese—that's a hell of a combination."

"She's used to giving all sorts of psychological counsel."

"How do you know her?"

"Her TikTok's are totally dope."

Dev didn't seem the least bit interested in our banter. He carried on surfing and typing.

———

The three of us scoured ArrangedMarriage.com for a good half hour but couldn't find a single profile that sounded remotely appealing.

"Well, this has turned out to be a let-down," I said.

"You know, what we need is an app like Survivalist Singles, which is based in the USA," Dev said. "I wish they had more Mumbaikars on their website, but I suppose our urban residents are less interested in survival."

"Survivalist Singles?"

"A dating app targeted at doomsday preppers,"

I leaned towards Dev curiously. "What kind of nut job would create an app for people like that?"

"According to this, Andrea Burke from Cooperstown," he said, turning the screen my way to show me the profile of the founder on the masthead of Survivalist Singles.

Talk about being over the top. I was all for unique and compelling business opportunities, but the fact that someone would actually spend their time creating such a website and find a sizeable number of people willing to sign up was mind-boggling.

Deepali held up her left hand and stared at her nails.

"Ilz, c'mon. Some of us more sensitive people live in fear of the Mayan apocalypse," she said.

"That was five years ago!"

"Yes, but what if there's a revival?"

Dev looked up from the computer to gage my response. He lifted his long fingers from the keyboard and began tap-tapping them on his muscular forearm. Even though I was concentrating on his fingers, I could not escape those eyes. They pierced mine again, forcing me to look away in embarrassment. Still, he decided to help me out.

"I think what Ila means is that you can't revive a date."

"Hon, you can revive anything," Deepali scoffed. "That's the entire point of a revival. Think about it: a nuclear meltdown, an economic collapse, a hurricane, or a tsunami. The President of the United States versus some guy out in Iran. The world can end at any time."

If the world was to end, surely there would be more important things to plan for—like where your next meal would come from or how you'd keep warm at night—than a hot date. But Deepali was not one to listen to reason.

"Love is the most important aspect of Armageddon. How else do you repopulate the planet? You need love, not a handful of bhaajis growing in your backyard."

Okay, if I was going to be the frontrunner for Team Mom, then I needed to appeal for help. I sighed and pleaded with Deepali first and then Dev.

"Okay, how about just regular guys? I don't want to subject my mother to weirdo doomsday fanatics."

"Relax," Deepali said. She typed in something else and clicked enter. "It's not like they are all totally weird. See, here's an example." She opened the profile of a user who went by the screen name Mtexplorer2. He listed many conventional hobbies and interests like hiking, camping, and eating Mexican food, but also mentioned his extensive background with firearms for purposes of defense and hunting. The profile said he had an alternative water source, liked to collect gadgets that don't use electricity, and canned venison, so he'd have meat 'if the grid goes down and there are no freezers'.

I crossed my arms, vexed. "Dev, what do you think?"

Yeah, what did he think? I was suddenly interested in knowing all about his thoughts—practical, cerebral, ethereal, and otherwise.

"Well, does Aunty Veena like Mexican food? I guess I don't know her well enough."

I could see he was caught between a rock and a hard place—whether I was the rock and Deepali the hard place or the other way around, I could not tell.

"Firstly, this guy lives somewhere in Haryana, which is a little too far for a date for someone who resides in Mumbai," I said. "And secondly, how is a Haryanvi qualified to talk about Mexican food? And thirdly, does Mom really need to find a soulmate who is so focused on what to do if 'the grid goes down'? And really, when is the grid *up* there for it to go *down*? Shouldn't this guy think about turning vegetarian in case of doomsday?"

"How classically Isham of you to be so politically incorrect with your preconceived notions of Haryanvis!" Deepali said.

Okay, fine. She got me. I stared down at my nails, sheepish. "Anyway, it doesn't matter where he is. Let's keep looking."

She pointed to the part of his profile where he outlined his ideal date. "Mtexplorer2's idea of an attractive woman is someone who is physically fit and loves the outdoors. He says, 'I'm not looking for someone wearing a designer dress and purse. I want someone who looks wholesome, and a woman wearing a backpack in her profile picture is an automatic 10.'"

Deepali clapped gleefully. "It's a perfect Aunty Veena!"

Sometimes I think Deepali has really lost the plot. "Aren't you the one who pointed out that I should talk her into spinning because Mom is *not* physically fit?"

"Yes, but she's definitely into the non-designer purse or dress, backpack look. Like Dev here."

"I can definitely vouch for women with backpacks, he chuckled, pointing to his own. "What say, Ilz? Are the Ishams into backpacks?"

Backpacks. Who cared about those... all I could focus on were the wrinkles forming around Dev's mouth as he chuckled. His mouth...!

"Plus, I think it's kind of wild," Deepali said. She began to wave her arms around as if to draw an imaginary picture. Her gaze was fixed at the ceiling. "Imagine, a romantic night together in the outhouse, gazing up at the nuclear dust cloud blacking out the stars."

As far as I was concerned, it was time to go back to the search results.

"Let's look for someone better suited," I said peevishly. Judging by Dev's expression, it was clear that he agreed. Deepali just scowled and shrugged her shoulders.

"Next on the list is a guy who lists himself as Hariharan," Dev retorted. "His profile calls him 'a simple person, looking for a partner who should have simple living and high thinking and if she could serve my family as a daughter.'"

Dev shot me a questioning glance. I was put off by the fact that he hadn't bothered to even proofread his profile before posting it. "Man, this one sounds like he could do with some personality," I said.

"He must be intelligent, though. He went to IIT. And Aunty Veena loves the type of man with views on important things."

"Yaar, just because a guy went to IIT doesn't mean he can debate global issues. Far from it. True, it only has a two percent acceptance rate, but only after they have spent all of their high-school years mugging up. And what do they do after that? Go off to IIT and spend another four years refining their mugging-up skills into an art. Is it any wonder that IIT students and alumni are completely devoid of personality, humor, and physical skill?"

Dev stared at me, aghast. I couldn't tell whether he was impressed with or taken aback by my emphatic outpouring. Deepali eyed me skeptically as I continued my rant: "There is a massive difference between intelligent and intellectual. Mom definitely goes for the latter. If we have to go for an IIT-ian, at least he should be daring and different. Like Chetan Bhagat."

"Chetan Bhagat?" Dev nodded. "Interesting, yes."

What did he mean by 'interesting'? Everyone knew that the word 'interesting' was a euphemism for something negative. Oh gosh, had I just made a fool of myself?

"Boring," Deepali cut in. "He is married with two children. Plus, he's at least five years younger."

"Well, someone *like* him, then!" I said.

I swiveled my chair and threw up my hands in exasperation, flicking a pencil into the air. It sped through the space between me and the semi-bald man perched near the window with the trajectory of an arrow. Then, as if in a movie scene, it hit him right in the center of his bald pate before falling onto the floor.

Shoot!

Dev buried his face into my laptop, trying to look busy. My heart skipped a bit as he peeked over towards me somewhat unassumingly out of the corner of his eyes. He withdrew his glance as soon as his eye caught mine. What was that about? Deepali crouched under the low table to conceal a fit of giggles. Whether she was laughing at Dev, me, both of us, or the bald guy, I had no idea.

The man slowly picked up the pencil and turned around to look at us. I quickly tried to come up with a good excuse and grabbed a pencil sharpener that was peeping helpfully out of my bag.

"I am so sorry, Uncle," I stammered. "I meant to flick some shavings, but my fingers slipped and somehow...uh...by mistake, I flicked the entire pencil instead."

The man looked at me through rodent-like eyes, umbrellaed by a massive unibrow. His twitchy upper lip exposed a row of teeth that lent him the look of the squirrel in *Ice Age*.

"Actually, Staedtler's closed lid model is designed to hold them in," he said slowly.

I stared back at him blankly.

"The pencil shavings," he repeated. "Also, the velocity with which the pencil met its target would require some adjustment. $V = U + A$, where V is the velocity, U is the initial velocity, A is the acceleration, and T is the time taken."

I looked at him, dumbfounded. Deepali muffled a snort into her folded arms without looking up. Dev did a marvelous job of remaining expressionless.

"Er, I went to IIT too," he said sheepishly, his eyes narrowing in a way that he looked even more like a rodent than earlier.

I gasped. "IIT...er..."

"But I do like to read Ernest Hemingway and writings about Subhas Chandra Bose."

Dammit! He had been eavesdropping on our entire conversation— exactly what I had been afraid of. I fumbled, thinking hard about what to say next. Luckily, Dev came to my rescue. Deepali sidled back to the chair and clapped in excitement.

"Uncle, that's fabulous," he said, jumping up from his seat. "My friend and I are looking to set up my aunt on a date. She is of suitable second-marriageable age. Our requirements are clear and specific. Aunty has a penchant for engineers who read Hemingway, especially if they are from IIT. Thank you so much for your interest."

"Mention not. By the way, I'm Dilip," he replied, the left end of his unibrow beginning to twitch along with his upper lip.

Mention not! Talk about a vernacular response. That was it; I signaled Dev to cut if off right there, but Deepali took that as a cue to jump in.

"What's your favorite book, Dilip Uncle?" she asked unassumingly.

"*The Sun Also Rises.*"

'Perfect. And your favorite place for paranthas?"

"Sasi."

Then she burst into song: "Prima in Indus, Gateway of India..." I had no idea what she was singing. Uncle Dilip's expression turned from rodent-like to rodent-caught-in-mousetrap-like. She stopped mid-tune and raised her eyes expectantly at Dilip.

"Aha." He attempted a sheepish smile. "My favorite part of the song."

"Then sing it na, Uncleji," Deepali said coyly.

No response. In a flash, her expression turned from gleeful to venomous. "You don't know the lyrics, do you?" she lashed out at him. "You don't know the IIT song. For an IIT graduate, that's as good as a 2.0 GPA!"

The man opened his mouth to say something, but nothing emerged.

'Cat got your tongue?" Deepali said sardonically. She looked over at Dev and me and flicked her hair back. "See, I told you this place would be filled with dating-site scouring letches! Here's one who's just Googled a velocity equation while eavesdropping on our conversation, probably hoping to impress us with his IIT gimmickry. Just his lucky day that your pencil landed straight on his head...and he couldn't even pull that off properly. He forgot there was no T in the rubbish equation he was trying to sell us! And wouldn't a true IIT-ian factor in that the heavier the pencil, the slower it would travel but possibly cause more harm?"

The man was still grappling with how to explain himself when Deepali turned around to grab her bag and my arm. "Googling with far-sightedness doesn't equate to real knowledge from an IIT degree. C'mon, Ilz; close the laptop, Dev. It's time for an ice-cream."

Dev shook his head in amazement while I gathered my things feebly.

Deepali had shown her sheer genius once again. How she did it time and again never ceased to amaze me. Or Dev by the looks of it. She kicked the door open, showing off immaculately pedicured feet in open-toed sandals, and turned towards Friendly's Ice-Cream Parlor. I followed her like a meek little lamb, thrilled to call this smart girl my best friend.

——

"So, you paid enough attention to the equation to be able to tell that there was no T in it?" Dev asked as soon as we were a safe distance from the internet cafe.

Deepali gave a smug smile of satisfaction.

"And how do you know the IIT song?" I asked.

"I don't, stupid," she responded calmly.

I stopped dead in my tracks and stared at her in disbelief. Deepali knew exactly what was going through my head and turned around to explain.

"I was singing the Cathedral & John Connon school song, yaar. My dad went there. He still belts it out in the shower every morning, so I've had no choice but to learn it by osmosis. But Uncle Dilip has, clearly, neither been to IIT, nor to Cathedral."

I wanted to say something, but words failed me.

"Still, to his credit, the guy knows his Hemingway," Deepali said.

It was a ridiculous conversation to be having in the middle of a crowded Mumbai street. Or anywhere, actually, considering that Deepali is the last person in the world qualified to pass judgement about other people's knowledge of Hemingway.

Dev gaped at her, looking increasingly impressed by the second, yet disbelieving at the same time.

"Deepali, do you know any Hemingway book besides *The Sun Also Rises*?" he asked.

"Nope," she responded without a care in the world. "But I do know that he and Woody Allen were buddies."

"Er...you do know that Woody Allen and Ernest Hemingway lived in two entirely different eras, don't you?" he said, his brow raised.

"Really? Then how come he was in that Woody Allen movie?"

Before he could react, she slung her arm around my neck and burst into a giggle. "Relax, Dev, I'm joking. I just love getting Ila here riled up!"

We linked arms and began to walk down the street again with Dev following close behind. Above all, I loved Deepali's commitment to teaching me to take life less seriously. She always told me my Type A traits would probably amount to wrinkles on my forehead by the time I was in my mid-forties, and she might be right. It had certainly happened this way with Mom, and one would think I'd learn by example. When would I be able to shake off my obsession with being obsessive? How could I become more like Deepali and live in the moment?

"Sorry for being so uptight," I said sheepishly.

"No issues," she shrugged.

That's the other thing I really admire about Deepali, the fact that she doesn't get stressed. Unlike me who gets stressed about all sorts of little things, like whether I should select Hindi or Marathi on the ATM or what the best way to study Hemingway is.

"Deeps, have you actually read *The Sun Also Rises*?" Dev piped up from behind us. Deepali turned to a shop window to check out her reflection.

"Of course not! I rely entirely on CliffsNotes. No offense to you, Ila, or Hemingway, but who besides you guys would want to read a long, confounding tome?"

"What about all that stuff about IIT? The GPA and all?" he asked. "Where'd you learn that?"

"It's in Chetan Bhagat's *Five Point Someone*."

"So you actually read *that* book?"

Deepali shot him a glance. "Don't be silly, yaar. I read a movie review on *3 Idiots* that talked about the plot points Chetan had used in his original story." She adjusted her goggles right up against her eyes, making her look like an insect.

"Jeez, I rest my case!" he said, clearly impressed by her ability to think on her feet.

The thing with Deepali is that she is so bloody convincing. Even when she doesn't know the first thing about anything, she masterfully crafts such a bullshit story—*and* flutters her lashes while narrating it—that, it has anyone, guy or girl, eating out of her hand in minutes. No wonder everyone loves her. Gosh, Dev must be falling in love with her right in front of my eyes.

Her phone rang.

"Hi!" Deepali shrieked into the phone. "When did you get back? You know I've been *dying* to see you all this time."

From her excitement, I could tell it was Boyfriend #1, Pimply Vik, who had been away at a squash camp for barely forty-eight hours.

She continued, "...but then Jaggi finally convinced me to cast aside my sorrow and go for a walk. What to do, yaar. I had to at least try and get you out of my head for a few minutes. I'm with him now."

Of course, I had totally forgotten about Dev standing right behind us.

"Jaggi?" Dev asked, his brow raised.

"It's a term of endearment...she calls me that affectionately," I blabbed. It sounded ridiculous, but it was the first thing that came to my mind.

"Why Jaggi?" Dev asked, now looking mildly amused.

"Er, you know. Like she worships me...like Om Jai *Jagdish* Hare, hence Jaggi," I replied feebly.

Dev shook his head and smirked. He clearly wasn't buying this but chose not to engage further on the topic. At no point did he ask about the caller who had made Deepali so genuinely excited. Did he know? Was he complicit in her multiple boyfriend strategy? Or was there something I was missing instead? Instinct I had gained from all the years of experience I had with Deepali told me that Vik was the one she truly cared about.

I wished the floor would open up and suck me in. What was my life coming to? It was a warm evening during a summer vacation in my high-school years, and here I was, crushing big time on Deepali's Boyfriend #3. I should have spent the last few hours following Ali Zafar on Facebook; instead, my life was reduced to spending the day in an internet cafe in pursuit of middle-aged intellectual guys for my mother, assisted by my best friend's boyfriend who I was crushing on. Not to mention that I had been identified to her Boyfriend #1 as Jaggi, her Boyfriend #2.

chapter
nine

OPERATION MOM, 3 DOWN, 12 DAYS TO GO - DESPERATION IS A NECESSARY INGREDIENT FOR CREATIVITY

"Ila, did you set the milk for yogurt for tomorrow's trip to the Shiv temple?" Mom called out from down the hall.

I hadn't.

"I am so sorry, Mom. I forgot."

I could feel her frustration wafting down the corridor and into the kitchen where I was pottering around with a packet of Maggie noodles. "How long has it been since you declared that your post-pubescent scatterbrain days were over?" Mom wailed, wringing her hands in her signature action when frustrated.

"Er...five years?" I replied. No math needed.

"Is it so hard for you to remember just this one thing for me, then? Just one thing that you need to do every Sunday?"

Actually, it wasn't. Under normal circumstances, I would be quite sheepish about forgetting to do the one thing that Mom took seriously every week. However, on that particular day, I wasn't in the mood. I was too anxiety-ridden about all those profiles. Operation Mom was already giving me a headache! I kicked myself for volunteering to take on the responsibility in the first place. I love Mom and all, but sometimes she goes from being a regular parent to a religious fundamentalist. It's creepy. If the Shivling at Babulnath temple doesn't get doused with homemade yogurt at the peal of Monday morning temple bells, then we might as well join the band of doomsdayers.

Speaking of doomsdayers, scouring the dating apps had gotten Dev and me into a regular texting rapport, which was organized by Deepali, who had conveniently left us to it and disappeared to attend to her other boyfriends. I was thrilled to have an excuse for almost rhythmic communication with Dev, but I have to admit it made me nervous. I didn't want to get too into it (even though deep down inside, the idea was so appealing), nor did I want Deepali to get wind of how okay I was with her delegating this aspect of Operation Mom to me. I needed to step back and get some perspective before proceeding.

"So awkward," I said out loud, as I brought my Maggie into the dining room.

"What is?" Mom asked, suspicious.

"Oh, nothing!" I said, annoyed with myself for shouting in her presence. "School stuff, forget it."

"You know, I can't actually remember what it is that I ever forget." Mom scorched my noodles with a look of pure revulsion she directed at them. "You, on the other hand, have also forgotten that we are headed to Swati Snacks in precisely five minutes."

"Calm down, Mom! The Maggie is just an appetizer. Post-pubescent brains need food to think."

Mom scowled. Her mood lightened as soon as we got to Swati. I watched her stuff farsan into her mouth like a wild animal that had been deprived of food for a month. Since we are Punjus, Gujju fare is never served at home, so feasting at Swati has become a Sunday tradition. I am not much of a foodie, but Mom's active brain functions in terms of ingredients and spices. Knowing full well that the culinary experience was the highlight of her week, I knew I shouldn't ruin her binge session. Still, I couldn't resist.

"So, about your little stalking episode in the eighties," I said, readily opening up a Pandora's box of who-knows-what, "Thanks for letting that one slip."

Mom shot me a bewildered glance. She had been rendered speechless by the panki, the rice and yogurt pancake with green coriander chutney.

"A George Michael groupie, huh, Mom?" I continued, observing her carefully. "Not like anyone would sweep that kind of thing under the rug by mistake."

She stopped mid-bite and took a sip of her jal jeera drink, wincing as the sour liquid trickled down her throat. "Where did you hear about that?"

"I have my sources."

"Confirm your sources."

Normally I can't stand it when she goes all journalistic on me, but this time I was prepared.

"The *Mid-Day*—15 June, 1982."

Mom put down her drink and slowly wiped her mouth. I could see that her mind was racing. Her ears had turned bright red. "You talked to Maleeka, didn't you?"

What exactly had I given away?

"The mention of the *Mid-Day*," she continued. "That says it all."

Why is it that I choose to surround myself with mind readers—my best friend and my mother? Next, one of their dates would start psycho-analyzing me.

"What, like Aunty Maleeka is the only one who reads the *Mid-Day*?" I challenged.

"She probably doesn't read the tabloid, but she'd definitely have kept that particular copy for revenge," Mom said with a hint of a smile." But how did she get this into your hands when...."

"When?"

"When she wasn't supposed to...."

Uh huh! Wasn't supposed to! Clearly, I had successfully caught her off guard!

"Why? What's the big secret?"

"No secret! It's all just so ridiculous! Maleeka was really annoyed that they had carried a picture of me with George Michael in the *Mid-Day* with no reference to her at all. After all, I had forced her to spend hours with me while I figured out how to get to him. She felt it was a betrayal of our friendship."

My mother had just confirmed that she was a stalker. Hold that thought, I said to myself.

"It *is* a betrayal. Why didn't you include Aunty Maleeka in the story if you forced her to be a groupie with you?"

Mom slapped her panki down onto the silver thali plate, sending a spray of curried Gujarati soup flying in the direction of an unknown victim.

"I *did*. She got edited out of the story."

"By whom?"

"Savvy Merchant, the writer. She was my mother's friend. She's this high society type—writing stories that sensationalize people and things. When she found out through Mamma that I had met George Michael, she was all over me to get the story out, but she wasn't interested in the side parts, like Maleeka and Andrew Ridgeley."

Mom had transformed from an example-setting adult into an animated teenager. Her eyes were sparkling with excitement, and I could swear that the wrinkles on her forehead had vanished with that last statement.

"Who is Andrew Ridgeley?"

"George Michael's sidekick. His guitar player, the lesser known—and hottest—of the two guys in their band, Wham!"

Wham!—for all the creativity that goes into making music, why couldn't the band have come up with a less cheesy name?

"Mom, I am finding it hard to figure out if you enjoyed this or not."

"Are you kidding? I loved every moment of it," she replied, her eyes glazing over.

"So, you did let Aunty Maleeka down by appropriating her share of the glory?"

"Aiyaa, I didn't want to." Mom shook her head violently. "And I even suggested that she retaliate by asking the *Daily Bugle* to print her picture with Andrew Ridgeley."

"What even *is* the *Daily Bugle*?"

"That's exactly what everyone used to ask back then too. It was the tabloid created to rival the *Mid-Day*," Mom said, revealing her journalistic pride and competitiveness. "They printed her picture a week later. The problem was that it had such a lousy editorial reputation that no one bothered to look at it. And the fact that Andrew Ridgeley was George Michael's sidekick didn't really help things."

I felt like I was getting a history lesson in Mumbai's tabloid culture during the eighties. It was surreal. Aunty Maleeka's jubilation at unleashing the details of the George Michael story began to make sense now. She felt somewhat vindicated in highlighting how Mom had stolen the limelight from her during their teenage years.

"But it's all in the past!" Mom said. "Stupid, puerile nonsense that made us both look stupid and frankly made me the laughing stock for yours to come. So embarrassing!"

Atul Bhai, the restaurant manager, swung by our table with his customary follow-up. He's a nice enough guy, but with awful body odour. "Soo che, Veenaji? Anything more for the Isham ladies today?"

It was his way of letting us know that he wanted us out soon. We cut to the chase by ordering mango pudding for dessert.

Just then, my phone lit up with a text. It was Dev: *Time to create an online profile?*

"Who is that?" Mom asked without looking over at my phone.

"No one," I replied.

"No one means someone," she responded.

I was taken aback. "Can you stop being nosy? It's Dev, Deepali's boyfriend!"

"Cut it out," Mom said, signaling to Atul Bhai for a finger bowl. "If he's Deepali's boyfriend, he has no reason to text you."

Wasn't that the truth! Mom had no idea.

"Actually, he wants to talk to you," I said, frantically searching for words between mouthfuls of jal jeera. "He wants to get the lowdown on Williams College."

"Rubbish! It's all an excuse," she said. "He's into you, and you are into him too. I can see it written all over you."

"Eww! He's *Deepali's* boyfriend!" I retorted sharply, not clear on which part of all this was upsetting me.

Mom dipped her hands into the finger bowl that Atul Bhai had made the waiter produce.

"Right. Maybe Deepali planned it that way," Mom replied.

By now, I could feel that my ears were hot.

"Meaning what?" I shrieked.

Atul Bhai glared at us from the cash register.

It was clear that we had overstayed our welcome. We decided to take the discussion outside. Traffic was relatively scanty on Sunday afternoons, so Mom and I took the opportunity to walk home.

On the way, we passed Kalyan's, a local paan–bidi shop that stocks a handful of newspapers and film magazines. Mom bought a copy of the Sunday *Mid-Day* to talk me through the evolution of the tabloid from the eighties until now. No sooner had she opened to the second page than the bold letters of the story headline hit us right between the eyes: "DATING APP EXPERIENCE SPURS THEFT." The story was about some guy who catfished his way into a woman's home so he could steal jewelry.

"See this sensational headline?" Mom said, shaking the newspaper. "The story was probably written by one of Savvy Merchant's protégés. You'd be surprised how many people while away their afternoons reading gossipy stories like this. It's the reason why everyone loves the *Mid-Day*."

As we continued walking home, Mom focused on the decaying nature of tabloid journalism, but I was more interested in the story itself. Lunatics are entitled to do their thing, and to even have their thing splashed in the newspapers, but did the guy really have to be a dating app user? I gulped as I thought about our summer plan. Right then, however, Mom broke my train of thought.

"Listen, Ila, and listen hard," she said. "Regardless of what you tell me, that Ali Zafar thing is long over. It's clear to me that the object of your attention is now this Dev guy. I should know, I've been there—at your age, and now as a single woman so many years later, I sense these things immediately."

How utterly presumptuous of Mom! And to think that she could say such thing knowing that Deepali was my best friend!

"Mom! That's completely inappropriate. Deepali..."

"...is your best friend," Mum cut in. "And has been since you were five. She is extremely intelligent; she loves you and more than has your best interests at heart. I suspect that she too had planned a way to get you over your Ali Zafar fixation by introducing you to Dev."

"But why would she pretend he's her boyfriend rather than just directly introducing him to me?"

"Maybe she wasn't pretending earlier. Maybe it did start as a crush which is no longer working out. Deepali is an extremely smart young lady. I daresay Dev is smart, too, but I'll wager he's just not her type, and she is so fond of you that she's worried about him looking like a hand-me-down."

"I hadn't even thought of it that way."

"I know, but I'll bet you that she has. And she knows better than anyone how sensitive you can be."

Poor Deepali. Had she really been trying to do good by me all this time? And had I been foolish enough not to see it?

I suddenly went weak in the knees. Mom had picked up on this very basic truth. What was I to do now?

———

As I got ready for bed that night, I reflected on my conversation with Mom. She had zeroed in on my feelings for Dev—partly because she was my mother, and partly because, as a single woman, she was sensitive to these things. It was disturbing that she felt victimized by her singledom, like a character in a Tennessee Williams play come to life. I realized the dire necessity to overhaul Mom's situation—to pull her out of gloom and reignite the spark she seemed to have lost over the years.

"What if we found something else for you to obsess about?" I asked Mom when she came to kiss me goodnight.

"Like what?" She was curious.

"A man."

"A man? Why do I need a man to obsess about?"

Okay, given that I am Mom's impressionable seventeen-year-old daughter, I would rather not answer that question.

I didn't have to. Mom thankfully had answered the same question in her head.

"What I meant is, I have you, don't I?" she laughed.

"That's different; I'm your daughter. With Pops out of your life..."

"Let's not bring your father into this."

"My point exactly," I said. "Let's bring someone else into it."

Mom stared down at me contemplatively, rearranging my long, black tresses against the pillow. "Ila, seriously. You should focus less on rubbish and more on your schoolwork."

"I'm on summer vacation, remember? Besides, making sure that you are happy is God's work as far as I am concerned."

She was lost in thought.

"Seriously, consider dating someone."

"Dating?" she cried. "At my age?"

"What's age got to do with it?"

"Well, as you get older, that whole idea of falling in love is not so easy..."

"What's love got to do with it?"

Mom looked at me suspiciously. "Who are you, Tina Turner?"

I sighed, slamming my hands down on my thighs. "Seriously, Mom, there is something out there called a dating app."

"A dating app?" she said. "Nah, I stopped playing the dating game years ago."

"What better time to reinvent yourself, Mom?"

"My dear daughter," Mom said, planting a kiss on my cheek. "That ship has sailed."

"But, Mom!"

"Good night, hon," she said, switching off the corner light as she got up to leave. "Tomorrow, I'd like to hear more about this Dev guy."

How was I going to convince her to go on a date when I didn't even have the courage to ask her to change her sari selection or hairstyle? And, on top of that, where was I even to begin with the Dev situation?

chapter
ten

4 DOWN, 11 DAYS TO GO - THERE'S ALWAYS SOMEONE MORE SKINNY, MORE PIMPLY, & MORE DESPERATE THAN YOU

Deepali had designated Crawford Market as our morning rendezvous point because she had already planned to meet Vik there. There was something about the aroma of spices that she said turned her on. None of it made any sense to me. I mean, what's so sexy about worming your way through row upon row of crates stacked up with perfectly balanced multi-colored fruits and vegetables? It seems more like an obstacle course than a good place to go on a date.

She insisted it was Vik's idea. Apparently, his mother had given him a vegetable purchasing assignment. I marveled at the absurdity of the situation. What kind of rational-thinking mother entrusts her seventeen-year-old son with the task of buying vegetables? Deepali says that I can't help but be critical since I come from a Punjabi household where all domestic activity is relegated to women. This is without, of course, stopping to consider the fact that there are no men in my household these days. According to Deepali, Vik's mother is a progressive woman who is training her son to be a Renaissance man. Maybe she's right. Still, it didn't justify my intruding on her vegetable purchasing date at the local farmer's market. All I wanted was to meet Deepali somewhere outside of my home to discuss the state of my nerves about Operation Mom.

This time, I was late. Well, not late, but not as early as Deepali. You see, if there's one thing Deepali cannot resist, it's alphonso mangoes. I arrived to find her lurking by the mango seller, checking out a fresh peti that had been delivered that morning. Vik hadn't arrived yet, so I figured we had some time to talk. But all Deepali could focus on was the rows and rows of bright yellow mangoes tinged with a blush that indicated their ripeness.

"Ilz," she said, her face flushed with excitement. "The season is finally here, and it's looking pretty jhakaas!"

It was. This new crop of mangoes was decidedly bigger, juicer, and better looking than the measly ones that had been showing up in the markets for the last couple of weeks. The early fruits never quite cut it. You know you are in the thick of the season when the big, juicy ones show up. Alphonsos always remind me of Mom. I had never been bowled over by the fruit but, like Deepali, Mom couldn't resist them, and I have seen her devour up to three at a time. Aunty Maleeka had once told us how, as a kid, Mom used to eat nine a day and break out into the worst case of zits right through the summer. "We all loved aapos, but no one devoured them like Veena. We soon labelled her the leader of the Aam Junta."

I tried to draw Deepali away from the mango stall. "We need to talk about this Operation Mom stuff," I said. "And we need to talk about Dev."

"So talk," she said, holding up a large mango to her nose so she could inhale its delectable scent.

"Not with Vik around."

"I don't see him anywhere. Do you?"

"Firstly, this dating app thing is making me nervous. Mom's not going to play ball."

Deepali rolled her eyes and marched down the aisle to the next stall, which was stacked with a glorious array of vegetables of every shape and color imaginable. The vegetables were displayed according to color and perhaps worthiness—the lower shelves held leafy greens, above them were the solid green vegetables—green beans, cucumbers, and bitter gourd. Next level up were yellow lemons and squashes, and on the highest level was anything orange or red—tomatoes, carrots, and so on. The vegetable seller—a bald, squat man in a white tank top and blue pajama pants—was perched cross-legged on a middle tier shelf behind a massive traditional weighing scale. Framed on both sides by two huge bowls suspended at equal distances from the fulcrum, he was completely engrossed by a basket of a green beans that needed sorting. I was tempted to questions why his tomatoes were the highest on the veggie pecking order, but I didn't have the heart to ruin his concentration. I just followed Deepali quietly, as usual.

"I am so fed up with you and your insecurity," she said, vexed. "The two of you are inseparable."

"Me and Mom?"

"No, idiot! You and your insecurity!" She picked up a fine tomato from a neatly arranged stack on a hay-lined shelf and crinkled her eyes. "How's that for personification, Miss Geekier-than-Thou?"

Pretty weak, actually! But analyzing her poor attempt at poetic grammar was least on my mind. I wanted to focus on more pertinent matters.

"Look," I said, "my point is that Mom will never agree to meet some guy on a dating app."

Deepali waved her arms furiously. She tends to do that when she gets excited. Right then, it amounted to knocking over an entire line of tomatoes. Luckily, the vendor, who was still busy with his customer, didn't notice anything.

"Just because *she* freaked out doesn't mean *you* get cold feet! Your mother freaks out over something or other at least thrice a week," Deepali shrieked. "You should know; you live with her."

Of course, she does, and of course, I did, but I was not going to admit that.

"Must you turn this into a slinging-mud-at-Mom fest? Right here in the middle of Crawford Market?'

"Where everyone is so interested in listening to the finer details of what happens in the Isham household?" Deepali said, her voice dripping with sarcasm. "Besides, who's slinging mud, yaar? I love Aunty Veena, and I am happy to do her the service." She squeezed tomato juice right into my eye. Intentionally, of course.

I screeched instinctively, reaching up to wipe my eye. My elbow hit a pile of tomatoes and sent it tumbling down in a mini avalanche. The fruit and veggie vendor in the next stall, who until then had been fanning himself in front of his stand, stormed over.

"Kyaa bhai. Kayko idhar aakar sab kuch satyanaash karta hai?"

Thankfully, Deepali came to my rescue. "Sorry bhaiya, meri friend naa, thodi kaani hai. Maaf kar do isko."

I couldn't believe it. Deepali had told the fruit seller that I was blind in one eye!

"Kaani hai?" he asked, leaning over curiously.

"Haan," she replied demurely.

"Ingliss bolti hai?"

"Haan," Deepali continued.

Like it was even relevant what language I spoke! I gritted my teeth as I swooped down to gather the fallen tomatoes. I didn't know whether to be grateful or annoyed, but even as I was trying to rearrange them into the perfect pyramid that they had been set in earlier, I realized that my organizing and balancing skills were quite poor. A handful of tomatoes came tumbling down again, splattering bright red juice all over the front of my shirt.

"You are doing it all wrong, baby," the fruit seller snapped. So that's why he wanted to know if I could speak English. To use it as an excuse to practice his own language skills. Well, clearly my tomato-gathering skills—or should I say lack thereof—were providing him with ample opportunity.

"Sorry," I said sheepishly.

"You go, baby. I vill do," he said, brushing me aside.

More than anything, I hate being called 'baby.' It was bad enough that the building watchman and the school bus driver still referred to me this way, but at least they had witnessed my childhood. What business did a fruitwalla at Crawford Market have throwing these terms of endearment at me?

As usual, Deepali read my thoughts. "Respect, baby, respect. When's the last time someone showed you some of that?" she said, stifling her giggles at my less-than-respectable state as we exited the tomato stall.

"Go on," I said acerbically. "Cut me down to size."

"Ila, come on! Even an onlooker would be able to see that I just bailed you out of what could have been an awkward situation caused by Ila-brand clumsiness," she said, restraining more chuckles.

Of course. She's the illicit eater of tomatoes, yet I cause the accident and need to get bailed out. Welcome to my world.

"You called me kaaniya when you were responsible for trying to blind me with tomato juice in the first place," I said, trying to pick pieces of tomato skin off my shirt.

"Consider it a favor," Deepali said. "When one eye is debilitated, sometimes the truth becomes much clearer with the other eye."

"Where do you find this kind of cheesy, garbage talk?"

"Tulsidas."

Case in point. Even though Deepali professed to be unintellectual, she was way more well-read than anyone I know.

"Okay, look. We need to talk about Dev."

"What about him?" she asked suspiciously.

"Like are you really even interested in him? You actually seem fixated on Vik...and I don't know about the whole Jaggi thing."

Deepali scrunched up her faced. I had clearly caught her off guard with my line of thinking.

"Ilz, you have a point. Several, actually. Vik is the cutest thing on the planet, but the only way to test out the viability of Vik and I, is to put Jaggi in the mix. If I continue to pine for Vik when I'm with Jaggi, then that will speak for itself."

What? Where did that put Dev?

Before I could ask, her phone began to sing "Gangnam Style." Deepali is known in school for her ultra-unusual ringtones. She swooped down upon her cell phone like a bird to its prey. "Vik, babes, where are you? I've been waiting for an hour, and I'm *so* bored."

"Thanks," I muttered under my breath.

Before I could say anything else, her phone rang again. This time it was Jaggi.

"Jaggi, babes, what are you up to? How about an afternoon soiree at Bademiyaan to help shake the boredom of my day?"

Yup, Deepali's life was anything but boring. When Vik showed up from around the corner, I couldn't help but wonder why she even gave him the time of day. A tall, gangly creature with slovenly hair and even more pimples than the week before, he looked positively unkempt. But Deepali didn't care, she made a beeline for him. If anything, I was the shallow, superficial one.

"Hi, Deepali," he said in a dreary, drill sergeant tone.

"Hi, Vik!" Deepali squealed, throwing her arms around him.

He responded with a smile. Vik was significantly taller than Deepali —although he had the gumption to keep his hands away from her smooth, round rump, he could not take his eyes off of it. Deepali was well aware and loved every minute of the attention. I flash-forwarded into what would happen next—she'd milk the situation all morning under the guise of helping Vik choose vegetables for his mother. Then she'd give him the tiniest, but most suggestive, little peck on the cheek before sending him home, just in time for her rendezvous with Jaggi at Bademiyaan, during which she would be pining for Vik the whole time. Deepali was way above my level. Was it just her, or did Gujjus really have more sex appeal than Punjus?

Regardless, it was now time to write off the morning.

"Right, I'll be going home, then," I said. "Best of luck with the vegetables."

"Uh, where are you going, Ila?" Vik asked. Like he cared!

Deepali was too busy tousling Vik's already unruly mop. "Home," I replied. "Don't wanna stick around and be the kebab mein haddi."

"It's just as well," Deepali whispered loudly to Vik. "We don't want her cramping our style."

"I heard that," I said as I turned around to leave.

"You were meant to," Deepali retorted, then winked at me and grabbed Vik's hand. Then, she let it brush past her ample derriere—'by accident.'

Pimply Vik simply stood there, mouth slightly open, like a dumb fool.

chapter
eleven

OPERATION MOM, 5 DOWN, 10 DAYS TO GO -
UNLEASHING YOUR INNER ROMANI, PART 1

Mom has a deep love for all things Latin: Mexican food, mariachis, 'Feliz Navidad' during Christmas. I could never really understand the preference for Latin culture more than, say, Japanese or African or something closer to home, like Assamese. It wasn't until after she'd had a few too many glasses of Rioja at Aunty Maleeka's home one evening that I discovered her secret.

The building watchman had come upstairs to hand over Mom's glasses, which, unbeknownst to her, had fallen out of her purse when she arrived. Mom, aware of her inebriated state, dutifully avoided the watchman. But the moment he left, she followed him out into the lift lobby and broke into dance on the marbled floor—tap dance. Now, Mom doesn't exactly display the skill or grace of a seasoned dancer, so, for fear of embarrassment, I asked her to stop before one of the neighbors came out to complain about the disturbance to their peace.

"You might damage your feet by tap dancing without the right shoes," I hissed, thinking she might even damage the marble floor.

"This isn't tap, you dodo. It's flamenco!" Mom hollered back at me.

The watchman reappeared in the slow-moving lift, armed with a stick to see what catastrophe had struck. It was all Mom needed to mosey herself back into the flat where, used to Mom and her flamenco,

Aunty Maleeka sat flicking through her *Cosmo* without so much as a crinkle on her forehead. Safely ensconced in the comfort of Aunty Maleeka's living room, Mom decided to unleash the story of her past.

"When I was just fifteen, I went to a fortune teller who sat outside Chor Bazaar," Mom said, gazing dreamily into the distance. "He told me that he could see me in a dark-green dress, playing a Spanish wind instrument—a lady of the nobility teaching young children."

Now the one thing you should know about Mom is that, like 99 percent of the women in this country, she puts a lot of stock in psychics and what they have to say. She's accustomed to visiting every jyotishi possible to dissect any constellation pattern that might influence her day, but typically, they all talk about things that are proximal, both in terms of distance and time. None of them have ever connected her past, present, or future lives with anyone or anything abroad. The farthest she has ever ventured from her Punjabi self was when a naadi astrologer told her that she was a Tamilian in a past life and that her family temple is near Vijayawada. Needless to say, that was where he was from and where he wanted the darshan cash deposited.

"That one card reading by some chor at Chor Bazaar had more impact on your mom than any of the other jyotishis she has visited over the years," Aunty Maleeka chuckled. "Ever since that fortune teller told her she was Spanish in a past life, your mother has wanted to run away with a passionate Latin lover on a white horse."

"That sounds more like a description of Kalki returning in the Kalyug," I said, amused.

"Well, that's your mother for you," grunted Aunty Maleeka as she watched Mom stomp her feet and swish around her imaginary flared skirt. Then she sighed. "Look at her—such a free spirit. But her dinosaur-era values never fail to closet her wild side."

I couldn't agree more.

The events of that particular evening, several months ago now, spurred me to take note of an ad for a flamenco dance workshop in the *Times of India* when I got home from Crawford Market. Reina, the master artist of Salamanca Flamenco Academy, had arrived in Mumbai to grace the community with a three-hour masterclass for flamenco wannabes.

I was thrilled for Mom, of course. It struck at the core of what she defined as passion; plus, it was exercise. Surely this was a better way to get Mom sweating than spinning or doing static yoga. Besides, we'd have a chance to bond. I read the story in detail. It elucidated a theory that flamenco dancing had descended from kathak when, somewhere in time, a band of Spanish Romani people had travelled on foot to India to spend a considerable amount of time here. They had learned kathak and taken the art form back to Europe with them, and with the addition of shoes and swishy skirts and the elimination of the churidaar under the flowy kurta, their version of kathak metamorphosed into what we currently know as flamenco.

It was the perfect dance for Mom, one that expressed the uninhibited side of her soul. Unlike tango and salsa, which also exuded Latin passion, this was the one dance form that did not require a partner. Latin, passionate, yet centered on the self.

"Mom," I said, thrilled, "There's a Flamenco workshop happening tomorrow. Can we go?"

Mom looked stupefied. Judging by the expression on her face, it clearly was not what she was expecting to hear.

"Please? You said no to spinning. You *never* do stuff with me. This is perfect. Please?"

Her eyes lit up like diyas on a dark evening. That was all the answer I needed.

chapter
twelve

OPERATION MOM, 6 DOWN, 9 DAYS TO GO - UNLEASHING
YOUR INNER ROMANI, PART 2

Reina, the flamenco teacher, was Japanese. Why a Japanese
instructor would be teaching a Spanish dance form to a band of
Mumbaikars in Byculla, I have no idea, but then, who am I to question
the sanity of what happens in Mumbai? The class was filled with
mostly bawas and some gujjus too, the kind who have graduated from
Shiamak Davar's dance workshops. I couldn't help thinking that we
Ishams looked overly Punju (and by that, I mean owning Asha Parekh
hips. Ironically, Asha Parekh is Gujju) in the face of all these slim-trim,
Bollywood wannabes. But it was our free spirit that had brought us
here; I'd be damned if I was going to let my genetics or size rain on my
parade.

Flamenco might be for the free spirited, but the moment I stepped
into the class, it occurred to me that these dancers must have a huge
amount of discipline. Either that, or we were complete idiots. Every
participant stood to attention and was outfitted appropriately. Except,
of course, us.

"You'll need special kutsu for this class," Reina said, looking at us
disapprovingly.

"Kutsu?" I was confused.

"Shoes," Mom translated. Over the years, she had gathered an assortment of Cantonese, Japanese, and Korean vocabulary. "The kolha-puri chappals are not going to fly."

"What if we go barefoot?" I asked, unaware of the foolishness of my statement until muffled titters from the bawa and gujju bystanders began to undulate through the studio.

Reina shook her head politely. She was too kind to mock me to my face, even though I was convinced that's what she really wanted to do.

Mom had turned bright crimson. She probably didn't want to publicly acknowledge the fact that we were related by blood.

"Barefoot is no good," Reina proclaimed.

"Why not, if flamenco is a derivative of kathak?" I asked, going by the logic that kathak is always danced barefoot.

The muffled tittering quickly morphed to raucous guffawing.

I didn't understand what was so funny.

Luckily, Reina had brought several pairs of extra kutsu, which she gave to us to try. Apparently, we weren't the only losers who showed up to flamenco workshops without appropriate footwear.

"In flamenco, special kutsu is psycho," Reina said.

It's a blessing that Mom speaks Japanese. Apparently *psycho* is transliterated as *saiko* and, in Japanese, means 'the best.' "Shoes that are good for plantar-tacon," she continued.

All the bawas were perfectly coordinated and looked as if they had come straight out of dancing school. Hips in perfect opposition to arms. Elbows bent at 45-degree angles. Nose perfectly in line with chest perfectly in line with waist. And then there was me—perfectly unaligned, my tummy sticking out at one end and my butt at the other. My arms hurt so much that I could barely keep them up. My shoulders were slouched over my mid-section as I desperately tried to look at my feet to make sure they were in sync with those of everyone else in the class. I had never thought that my hips were too bad, but in comparison to the balletic bawas in the room, they stretched from wall to wall.

Gosh, was this a bad idea. It made my morning at Topspinners seem like a cakewalk; the darkened disco room in the spin studio prevented you from gaping at all your faults in excruciating detail.

Then, I looked at Mom. The first thing that struck me was that the flesh under her arms jiggled ferociously and was doing a dance of its own as she tap-tapped in accordance with Reina's instructions. It was my turn to be embarrassed. How could Mom not notice?

Then I realized, she *did* notice; she just didn't care. Mom was a flamenco savage. Fixated on her reflection in the mirror, she was following Reina's steps meticulously, as if her life depended upon it. It was pure meditation—no perception of sight, sound, or other people judging her. Just my mom, fine-tuning the mechanics of her free spirit.

At that moment, I admired her more than anything. When it came to doing something that she truly loved, Mom had zero inhibitions. She single-mindedly followed her passion like it was the only thing that mattered.

In that cloudburst moment, I realized that the workshop had worked wonders for Mom. Her face was cast in a serene smile, though her eyebrows were slightly crinkled with an intensity that only a mom with a mission can wield.

After the class, we headed to Mahalaxmi Juice Center for a mango lassi.

"Ilz, that was the most fun I've had in years," Mom said with blissful serenity. "Thanks so much for making me do this. Man, if only this were a regular class rather than a one-day workshop!"

A flutter of sadness crawled up my spine as she said that. I almost felt guilty that I couldn't provide Mom the experience for longer, as if I was responsible for its early end.

"Well, we have been invited for a six-week course in Salamanca," I said, recalling Reina's parting words (read 'sell job') to the class.

"Yes, on the condition that we take part in a performance at the end of it," Mom sniggered. "Imagine me performing."

Clearly, she had forgotten about her unabashed performance in Aunty Maleeka's lift lobby a few months ago. I was about to remind her, but when she leaned forward for her glass of juice, I caught a glimpse of her jiggly forearms. Perhaps encouraging Mom to perform in front of a live studio audience was not such a good idea. I wouldn't ever want to put her in a situation that might expose her flaws...emotional or physical. It was best perhaps to leave unto another lifetime what cannot be achieved in this one. Wasn't rebirth, after all, the true unique selling point of Hinduism?

chapter
thirteen

OPERATION MOM, 7 DOWN, 8 DAYS TO GO - DESPERATE
TIMES CALL FOR DESPERATE ANALOGIES

"What the...?" I practically shrieked when I saw Dev standing at the
door.

Firstly, I am not accustomed to boys showing up at my home. It's
against Isham tradition. Secondly, I was not accustomed to seeing one of
Deepali's boyfriends outside of a three-mile radius of her. It had
happened the other day when he showed up at the internet cafe before
she did, and now this! What was going on? Why would she send him
instead of having the decency to come herself? And thirdly, most importantly, it was...Dev! I had not had a chance yet to have the 'Dev' conversation with Deepali, and I wasn't sure how to address the whole
situation. But I quickly controlled myself before more of my unsettled
anxiety became apparent to my guest.

Dev was clearly taken aback by what he perceived to be my less than
warm welcome. "Er, bad time?" he asked.

"Never better!" I said, half meaning it—Mom was off to interview
someone, and Sakkubai had gone to the market. "Can I help you?"

"Deepali sent me," he replied calmly.

Duh, that was evident. She clearly wanted to extend the fight that I
had begun. I had called Deepali no less than twelve times and texted her
double that number of times in the last twenty-four hours to apologize

for my hissy fit at Crawford Market. Participating in the flamenco work-shop had put everything in a new light. Deepali was quite right that I needed to stop freaking out about Operation Mom. Veena Isham deserved more than the droll existence of a single mother, confined by the shackles of freelance journalism. And who was I to hold her back from what Deepali classified as her true potential, anyway?

I had spent the previous afternoon trying to create a profile for Mom for the dating apps but, within moments, I recognized that it was not something I was equipped to do on my own. It required a certain skill, a certain je ne sais quoi, *finesse*, in writing that only my buddy and mentor could create, but Deepali hadn't responded to a single one of my calls or texts. Was she too busy with her three boyfriends, or was she just super upset with me? I couldn't tell. Now she had sent one of her lackeys instead. Sure, we had talked about him helping us with his supe-rior English writing skills, and sure, he was darned cute to look at, but what was I to do with him without Deepali?

"Can I help you with something?" I asked again, awkwardly, showing him the way in.

"Actually, it's the other way around. I was thinking that perhaps *I* can help you." Dev winked at me with massive brown eyes that looked like two pools of chocolate inviting me in. His perfectly chiseled features stood out against his tanned face and shaggy mane. What was it with Deepali and ruffled-hair types? Dev was way better looking, however, than Vik—not a trace of acne on his gorgeous face. In fact, as far as looks go, he definitely got top marks out of all her boyfriends. Maybe it was the crooked smile...no it was more than that.

I suddenly became aware of the slightest tingle in my stomach. I couldn't tell whether I was more annoyed by the tingle or by the fact that it was related to one of Deepali's boyfriends. Grudgingly, I pushed the tingle aside.

"Why is Deepali MIA? Does she hate me that much?" I asked.

"You girls and your little love-spats," he said, making his way over to the side unit to examine our display of family photographs.

Deepali and I didn't have love-spats. We just had spats. "She's never sent one of her chhokra boys before," I said indignantly.

"Hey, never accuse a chhokra boy of being a chhokra boy until you know whose chhokra boy he is," Dev said, the corners of his mouth curving their way into that winning crooked smile.

What exactly does that mean?

"Deepali is an amazing girl," he said. "I totally enjoy hanging out with her, but I am not her chhokra boy."

"What you enjoy hanging out with is her bootylicious booty." I winced even as I heard myself uttering the foolish words. What was wrong with me?

As if to avoid commenting on my last statement, Dev picked up a photo of Mom, Pops, and me on a family vacation to Simla when I was five. "This is a great snap. Your dad is quite the looker. How's any date going to follow suit?"

Great. Now Deepali's chhokra had to be judgmental too! "Are you conveniently avoiding my question?" Yikes—what's wrong with you, girl? Drop it.

Dev laughed. "Listen, a guy is a guy, and Deepali is an attractive girl, but that's not why I like hanging out with her."

I stood there, dumbfounded. Okay, maybe I *had* been a little harsh.

"Sorry for the digression. Why are you really here?"

"I had texted you about writing up a dating profile for your mom, but I didn't hear back. Deepali mentioned that you might have a little writer's block."

If Deepali were here, she'd be judgmental too. Besides, there was that issue regarding his superior English skills. Frankly, he'd probably lend more value to the situation than Deepali. I led him to my room where my laptop was open to Tinder's profile creation page.

"It's just so hard," I sighed. "I have no idea what to say."

Dev sat at my desk and slung the baseball cap he was wearing over the corner of my chair. He peered at the computer screen. "Well, there's some value, I guess, in the old cliché—honesty is the best policy."

"Are you nuts?" I exclaimed. "I can't be honest. This is my mother we are talking about."

Dev's face broke out into a lopsided grin. Darn, was he cute! He took his book bag off his shoulder and put it down on the table before walking over to the wall filled with Ali Zafar posters. "No need, I'm on it. You need to create a really compelling online profile for Operation Mom."

I cringed, then shivered, then began to experience the strangest sensation, like the floor beneath me began to swing from side to side. All of a sudden, I was even more annoyed with Deepali. Not only had she ditched me and sent one of her chelas instead, but she had put me in an unnerving position where I didn't know what the relationship was between her and Dev. I found myself saying stupid things as though I'd just had three straight shots of tequila.

Dev sensed my angst.

"Relax, I actually think it's pretty cool," he said.

A ray of sunlight from the window caught his left side. Now he no longer looked cute—he looked hot, like some surfer type in one of those beach shows on TV.

"You do?"

Why was I speaking in monosyllables like an ineloquent idiot? Why was I even bothered about what Dev looked like against any kind of light? A tingling feeling appeared from nowhere.

"Absolutely," he replied, folding his hands behind his head. "I mean, I don't know your mom too well, but she seems like a pretty cool lady. She must be, being a Williams College grad and all. I think it's great that you want to set her up with someone."

"Great-shmate," I said, forcing myself to speak. "The problem is, she'll never agree to it, so I have to do this completely clandestinely. How on earth do you create a Tinder or Bumble profile that sounds appealing but doesn't reveal everything?"

"Like I said, you just need to be honest, even in a catfish profile," Dev said, grinning his lopsided grin again.

The tingle was becoming increasingly prominent and refused to be pushed away. It was interesting to hear a different perspective—Deepali would never advise me to be honest.

"Catfish profile?"

"A catfish is someone who has created an entirely fictitious identity for themselves online," Dev explained. "It's usually managed by a kitten fisher."

"A kitten fisher?"

"A witty friend who writes your fake profile...or texts."

"That would be you?"

"Well, both of us together, seeing as you will be doing the texting."

I wasn't sure how I felt about these feline fishing tendencies. I began to run the idea through my head, but I was interrupted by Dev gesturing towards my Ali Zafar posters. "Is it true that you have a crush on this guy and wanted to spend the summer stalking him?"

Maybe, but I wasn't going to admit to that.

"Or is it one of those classic phases?" he said, winking at me. Until recently, the only person who could make the butterflies in my being take flight had been Ali Zafar.

I figured I should avoid getting into a conversation that might embarrass me. "So, this profile?" I said.

"Sorry," Dev said, turning around to lean against the poster of Ali Zafar. "Here. You type, and I'll dictate."

"What are you going to dictate?" I was slightly annoyed. "You just pointed out that you don't even know my mom."

"No, but I do know *you*, and there's that age-old cliché—like mother, like daughter."

God, did that saying have a sneaky way of constantly worming its way into context! I rolled my eyes. "That *is* a cliché. I am nothing like my mom."

"Really? Deepali must have sent me to the wrong house, then." He walked over towards the window, the rays of the sun outlining his presence like some sort of halo around a boy-angel.

Ugh. What was I thinking? Focus, Ila. Get a grip!

"Okay, let's hear the counsel of the Great Dictator," I said, fumbling with a lame attempt at sarcasm.

Dev was not offended. He smiled to himself and cleared his throat. "We start with a name. It's the first thing people will see while browsing through a list of search results or getting an incoming message. It's got to stand out."

"It's got to stand out," I repeated like a foolish parrot.

Dev stared into the space in front of him with deep concentration. "You've only got one chance to make first contact, and there's a huge difference between CoolChic495 and SPANKMEHARDER."

Sticker shock or insult? Who the heck did this guy think he was?

"Just joking," he clarified, sensing my vexation. "I was just trying to draw an obvious example. Basically, you need to choose wisely, but not too wisely."

Dev spoke with great authority. And the more he did, the more regal he looked against the sunshine streaming in. I was completely intrigued by and curious as to his rationale.

"Firstly, what's 'too wisely,' and secondly, what's wrong with wisdom?" I asked.

"Most guys don't dig clever women."

Had Deepali trained him to say something like that?

Dev turned around to give me a piercing look. "Just to make it clear, *most* guys, not *all* guys," he said. "Some of us love a battle of the wits."

Those chocolate brown eyes...! Why would Deepali ever bother with the other two when she could just as well spend her time gazing into these pools of chocolate all day?

"Rest assured," he continued, "If you think you've come up with a really great username that makes you feel clever, there is a good chance that you may be the only person who gets it. Wit is great, but cramming it into your handle reeks of effort. So, no puns, obscure literary figures, or film references."

Half the profiles I had seen had film references. "So where do we even begin?" I asked.

"With something that describes you...your mom that is, in one or two words. Maybe a play on her name without being too smarmy."

Now I had to find an excuse to take my eyes off of him. I stared hard into my laptop screen, trying to ignore the tingle that had grown into a full-blown flutter. "Let's go back to the 'you dictate, I type,' please."

Dev cleared his throat and began. "Those who know me call me Venus because I am the brightest star of all those that dot the night sky."

I scrunched up my face. "Eww, and isn't that pure chikat?"

"Not if you follow it up with an honest opener," Dev said, closing his eyes to focus. "I am intelligent, I listen to rock and roll on Sunday afternoons, and when it comes to my kids, I love them to a fault."

His character sketch was so flawless, I had to stop typing. Had he read Mom's unwritten biography? He opened his eyes and flashed another one of his cute grins. "I can see that you are crazy about your mom. It must go the other way 'round too."

I flinched. It disturbed me somewhat that Deepali's good-looking chela had the ability to walk into my home on a Tuesday afternoon and read me like an open book. There might be benefits to having Deepali come here instead and cut me down to size.

"Mom has just one kid," I said. "Me."

"That's who I was referring to," Dev said, the unkempt fringe falling down the side of his face making him look even cuter.

I didn't get why he was talking in cryptic tones, though. "Dev, why wouldn't you just say *daughter*?"

"That'd give away that this is a females-only household."

"And what's wrong with that? Guys love women."

"Not when they are related to each other,' Dev said, moving his finger over his stubble. "Too many overlapping hormones. Plus, there might be creeps around."

I had a light-bulb moment. It's true that there was a lot of hormonal activity in our household, but I never imagined that we could be a turn-off to anyone. Or for that matter, a turn-on to a bunch of creeps.

"Of course, that's a superficial comment," Dev continued. "But then most guys are completely superficial when it comes to scoping out women."

This writing exercise was way more complicated than I had expected. What superficial fake picture of beauty was I to use for the profile? Dev suggested it wasn't a good idea to include a fake photo in the profile. For one thing, it tells the world that you are a liar. More importantly, it might send the message that you are not comfortable with yourself. But I couldn't use a real photo for obvious reasons. Mom looked extra-large in photos. Hang on a minute, maybe I could use a photo of her as a child. At least that'd be genuine.

"Yup, genuinely bad," he said clearly amused by the picture of Mom as a chubby five-year-old. "No guy wants to date someone because they were cute in 1975."

It occurred to me then that this was the first time in seven years that we had a guy in the household. Pops comes and goes often enough, but we were missing a man to give us his opinion 24/7. Now, many women might argue that they wouldn't want some guy coming in and peeing all over the toilet seat, but I have to say I was actually enjoying the banter with Dev.

Pretty much everything I know about anything is colored by Mom's or Deepali's opinion. With an input or two from Aunty Maleeka every once in a while. It's like we live as per a bible written by women for women. And when it comes to relationships, all rules seem to focus on what a man needs to change for a relationship to be successful. Rather one-dimensional, no? Mom didn't have a father or brother at hand to count on for advice. There was no 'male' in her life who could tip her off about what to look for and what red flags to avoid when venturing back into the world of dating. Yet, a man's opinion was critical. Online dating sites could arguably be candy stores for men who wanted a quick score. Thank you, Deepali! Thank you for sending Dev my way. There's an upside to everything.

"Why not put a picture of something that represents your mom?" he said, breaking my train of thought. "Like this one?"

It had taken Dev all of three Googling moments to come up with a picture of a sexy, red-haired woman dressed in white saree with a red border, playing a veena, all against a flaming red background.

"That is so not my mother!" I said.

"Of course, it isn't," Dev replied. "That's obvious to anyone who looks at it, but it represents her."

"With that red hair? I think not. She'd be better represented by a picture of something like...like...Venus...you know the brightest star in the sky."

Dev scrunched up his face immediately.

"Ila, I love the idea of using a star as the profile pic, but I think, in reality, it wouldn't generate many hits."

"Why not?" I asked, miffed by the idea that my idea might not be so great.

"Truth be told, a lot of guys on these sites are simply 'window shop-ping,' and they wouldn't even read the profile if the woman's picture wasn't appealing."

The idea of Mom being window-shopped. Perish the thought!

"Relax," Dev laughed, reading my mind. "There's nothing that cannot be fixed with a little bit of photoshop."

Another few moments, on Canva this time not Photoshop, he had replaced the sexy red-head's face with Mom's LinkedIn profile picture.

"Here you go, this picture will break that window-shopping habit and bring them straight inside the store. Guaranteed."

I wasn't sure how I felt about this whole shopping metaphor. When it came to Mom, the idea of being a store purchase hardly seemed more respectable than that of being a window display. Oh, whatever, I was overthinking it as usual and needed to let go! I decided to go with it. The profile was complete, and I had Dev to thank for it.

Then came the actual blurb. This was dicey territory. I suggested that we put in a few sentences that defined Mom's beliefs and values.

"Ila, the only thing that dating apps are fuller of than cleavage-revealing selfies is bias," said Dev with a serene expression that spoke of the wisdom of a thousand years.

I wondered how he knew all this.

"Dev, have you had some experience with dating apps?"

"Not exactly."

I looked at him suspiciously. How 'exact' does one need to be to swipe left and right?

"Put it this way, my parents are hell bent on me getting into IIT. Yup, one of their kids going off to America isn't enough; they want me to stay here and stay traditional. But I can't stand the idea. When I lock myself into my room for hours on end to study physics, I admit that I tend to surf physicality rather than physics," he said coyly.

"You check out women on what...Tinder? Bumble?" I asked, mildly upset at the idea.

"Er, it's what guys do," he grinned.

I blushed at my naivete. Of course they do.

We ruled out religion and politics. I was confused about how to define Mom's physical stats. Dev figured that mentioning ethnicity would effectively negate the need to include height and weight, and he felt that we should focus on hobbies and likes and dislikes.

"Be careful. Sharing an exhaustive list of every film, album, book, painting, sculpture, TV show, YouTube clip, and Homeric verse that she loves will make her look ultra-pretentious."

It was like I had embarked on a voyage of discovery that afternoon. I began to look at dating apps with an analytical eye. Never had I imagined that there were so many different ways to use one. A dating app could be treated like a sloppy basement dance party, or it could be used to strike up a conversation with someone, as though you ran into him at a bookstore. You could look for someone whose name you'd never remember, or search for someone whose name you'd want to change. But if you wanted a shot at either of these (or anything in between or beyond), you'd have to make sure you don't freak out and deter anyone who reads your profile. Regardless of Mom's ambitions in life, it probably wasn't a good idea to shout them to the internet. Rather, being frank and gender-neutral without being alarming was the way to go: for instance, "I'm divorced, and my child is still important to me."

———

It was almost time for Sakkubai to get home. One look at Dev standing in my bedroom, and she'd be hurling Marathi curses at him. It had happened once before when Harmless Harry (Hari, actually), a sweet Sindhi classmate, had come over to borrow my history notes. After seven minutes of vitriolic abuse, the poor guy ran away. Sakkubai promptly reported the incident to Mom who, needless to say, threw a fit. Mom is very old school about these things. How was I to relay the truth to Dev? I mean I couldn't very well say to him that he needed to leave because my mother was neurotic or that our ayaah was even more freaky and, frankly, she ruled the roost. Especially not after he had helped me create such an amazing profile. Besides, I didn't really want him to go.

When I caught him glancing at his watch, my heart sank. A twinge of mild agony surged through my insides. He was probably dying to get back to Deepali.

"Thanks for coming over," I said as he gathered up his book-bag. "I know you'd have had more fun hanging out with Deepali, but hopefully, you scored some brownie points."

"This *was* fun," he said, shooting me a sideways smile. "And I am thinking I definitely scored some brownie points."

Wait...brownie points for whom? It didn't seem like he was referring to Deepali. Was I overthinking this? The flutter in my stomach showed itself again. It scared the shit out of me.

chapter
fourteen

DESPERATION METER RISING

The moment Dev left, I frantically dialed Deepali again. No answer. Twenty minutes later, there was still no answer. Shoot! She was still miffed with me. Either that, or she was too busy with Vik or Jaggi. No, it was definitely the former. Knowing Deepali, there was no way she'd ignore my phone call for a guy.

I was at a complete loss for what to do. Venus now had a rocking dating app profile on all the four major sites, so I could sit back with my feet up until she (rather, I) got a response. Or, I could be proactive and start swiping right on Bumble to pick a guy to have Venus chat with. Suddenly, my mind was filled with vacuous thoughts. Where had Dev gone? Cancel that one—I didn't really care. What was Ali Zafar up to? Did it even matter to me anymore? I logged into Facebook to check.

There he was, staring cheekily into the camera for a perfectly Instagram photo, which had been touched up to show off his muscles, raw sex appeal, and wild, unkempt hair.

"Hmm...cute," I said out loud. The photo had 6,532 likes and 259 comments. Previously, I would have diligently read every single comment, pausing to like any specific one that I agreed with, or I'd refute it with an opinion of my own. Now, for the first time ever, I couldn't be bothered. Instead, I clicked on the music video of "Voh dekhney mein." For weeks now, every time I listened to it, I'd fanta-sized about being the 'ajeeb haseen' he croons to in the song. Today, I focused on the lyrics—her love for philosophy was just a phase.

A phase. I thought about what Dev had said earlier. Could my passion for Ali simply dissipate into nothingness, just like Mom's teenage passion for George Michael? It's true that thinking of Ali was not getting my hands clammy anymore. Had it all been in my head? Passionate love has got to be one of the most important things in a teenager's life. Deepali spends endless hours in love: talking, texting, flirting. All I ever do is spend hours on Facebook. While I stare dreamily at my posters all day, she has the real thing. Three of them—Vik, Jaggi, and...Dev!

Why were my palms so sweaty?

I saw Deepali's contact flash across my phone screen. Finally! I clicked on it instantly.

"What took you so long?" I asked, overly emotional.

"You needed to calm your heels," she replied, totally impassive.

Again, there is no such activity in the English culture, or any culture for that matter, as 'calming your heels.' Now that Deepali was back, I too returned to schoolteacher mode.

"The expression is 'cool your heels.' And it's not like my feet were on fire," I said.

"You're right. There was plenty else on fire."

I had an idea about what she meant, but now was not the time to ask.

"I needed your help, Deepali," I whined.

"And you got it."

"I got Dev's help, not yours."

"Yes, but you got it thanks to me."

"I just don't get it. You are so pissed off with me, yet you send your chela to do the job? What sense does that make?"

"None whatsoever on the face of it." Deepali giggled.

"Then?"

"Let's just say I have a few projects that I am working on that are incredibly important to me."

I certainly hoped she was talking about Operation Mom, but it couldn't be. Why would she send Dev?

"Who was going to help unblock you from your writer's block? Ali Zafar?" Deepali asked.

"What does Ali Zafar have to do with this?" I asked. I picked up a section of the newspaper lying on my desk, crumpled it up into a ball, and threw it at the wall.

"Absolutely nothing. It's what I keep saying."

"Your cryptic comments aren't helping."

"Ilz, understand what's important. I'm sorry we didn't get to the Dev conversation the other day. I admit, I felt a little awkward about the whole thing."

"Oh gosh, no..." I began. The last thing I wanted to do was to make her feel awkward. Deepali sensed my anxiety, always able to read me, and butted in.

"Calm down, Ilz. It's all good," she assured me.

"It is?"

"Yes, it is. So, as I was saying, *Dev* helped you get the job done."

His name set my insides a flutter again.

"Yes. And he did a great job of helping me create a profile that guys will find interesting and respond to."

"So, there," she said smugly. "Am I, or am I not, pretty smart in delegating?"

I got it. She wanted credit for Dev's contribution. "Okay, I'll give you that. Yes, you are incredibly smart, but why didn't you come too?"

"Because..."

"Yes?"

"Jaggi and Vik don't like him."

What was she going on about? Since when did either Jaggi or Vik even know that Deepali was hanging out with another guy?

More importantly, since when did Deepali start caring about what they thought?

"And if I'm going to end up with one of them, I need to start making some benching choices."

What? Did I hear that right? Was Deepali considering a downsize?

There was silence at the other end. I couldn't tell if she was thinking about what to say or how to say it.

"Let's just say that if they knew that I took Dev to your place to hang out with you, they would see it as an endorsement of him, and that would be totally the wrong message to send."

"But you do *like* him, don't you?" I asked cautiously.

Given what I thought Deepali had just said, it was a dumb question. I flinched even as I heard myself say the words. Yet, I was pressed to confirm.

"Of course not!"

"What's wrong with Dev?" I asked, now offended on his behalf.

"See, this is why it was awkward to bring this up. There is nothing wrong with Dev. He's a perfectly good guy. Too good, though, for me. Every time he's around, I delve into a huge inferiority complex, so I've decided to write him off."

Write him off? Deepali wasn't in love with Dev? Surely she wasn't serious.

She continued, "And then, there's that whole obsession with Williams College."

"Oh, for gosh sakes, Deepali! What do you have against Williams College?"

"Nothing. Just that I don't plan to leave the country, so if he's not going to be around, then there is really no long-term value." She paused. "I actually think you and he are ideal for each other."

I glanced outside to see a ray of sunshine lighting up the chirping of two birds perched on a tree branch framed by my window. Kind of like Deepali and me chirping away inside. There was something oddly suspect about what she was saying. Since when did Deepali care about anything longer term than the coming weekend? Still, if she was for real, I wasn't going to question it.

At that moment, all I could focus on was how Aunty Maleeka had once defined happiness: "Happiness is like peeing in your pants," she said. "Everyone can see it, but only you feel the warmth."

I could feel it now. It was liberating.

chapter
fifteen

OPERATION MOM, 7 DOWN, STILL 8 DAYS TO GO - DIVING
INTO THE DEEP

The profile had gone online barely an hour ago, but it took me a good
sixty minutes to work up the gumption to start Bumbling. Yes, indeed!
Bumble was my dating app of choice, with Venus (well, me) in full female
power mode. However, getting started on Operation Mom was easier said
than done. There were so many conflicting rules on the various YouTube
videos out there on dating app etiquette. Some said to start with a 'hey'
because it makes you accessible; others said to never start with a 'hey'
because it shows you are only willing to put in minimal effort. Which way
to go? As far as pictures were concerned, many profiles featured horrifi-
cally unappealing selfies. Unless you're Ali Zafar, selfies are never a good
call. But then the non-selfies, that wasn't so great either. Vikram, 59, with
big hair, swipe left; Hari, 46, with an unruly beard, swipe left; Gazdar, 51,
with a funky cowboy hat. I decided to check out his profile—"6'5",
nerdy, charming, audio snob, lover of music, drama-free-co-parent of the
sweetest little 4.5-year-old girl." Okay, so the audio snob part was a little
suspect, but the rest sounded okay, even though 'lover of music' really said
nothing about the music that he purportedly loved. But the part about
the drama-free co-parenting? No thank you, Venus was done with little
girls inside and outside of her home. Swipe left.

Mihir, 52—here was a profile with a selfie of him sitting in a hot tub! I cringed—does anyone even do that? Swipe left. Then I came across Bahadur Billy, 54, with perfectly chiseled features. Seriously? What idiot would pick a name like that, even for a dating pseudonym? Must be some cheapo I should ignore. But admittedly, he was quite cute for a 54-year-old in an uncle sort of way. His profile was somewhat interesting—"Recovering stock trader, 5'9" without heels. Let's share poor life choices. Shared happiness is double happiness." That last part sounded like something Dr. Mirno would say. Who the heck would want to date someone who makes poor life choices? I swiped right when I meant to swipe left. Oh no!

Before I could figure out how to fix the issue, or even whether it was possible, a message popped up on my feed. It was Bahadur Billy responding to my match request. Oh gosh, now what? It had only been a few minutes since I accidentally swiped right! Okay, I took three deep breaths and clicked on the message.

Bb: Speaking of stand-up comedy, will you watch Sorabh Pant next week?

Sorabh Pant was a regular at the Comedy Store in Lower Parel. He and this other guy, Vir Das, perform a series called 'Walking on Broken Das,' one of Mom's favorites. Stand-up comedy was the one thing she was willing to venture out into town for. Perhaps I should give Billy the time of day. My fingers trembled as I summoned up the courage to approach the keyboard.

Me (as Venus): Hello, Billy.

Bb: You can call me BB.

Me: Don't you like your real name?

Bb: Do you know my real name?

Me: William?

Bb: Where did you conjure that up from?

Me: Isn't Billy short for William?

Bb: No, no. Billy is Billee, as in cat. Bahadur Billy, as in Brave Cat.

I shook my head. How lame is that?

Me: Why call yourself Brave Cat?

Bb: It's a unique take on Punjab-da-sher.

He had immediately picked up on the Punjabi stuff. This didn't bode well.

Bb: I'm looking for a sherni.

This just gets better and better! In true Hindi film style, he was probably envisioning some oversized Punjabi woman with a parandi whiplashing her massive bottom. My bad for mentally balking at Dev's wisdom about ethnic honesty. How was I to throw BB off track now?

Me: I'm not actually Punjabi.

Bb: Really? Where are you from?

I had to think fast.

Me: Sikkim.

Bb: Well then, you must be one in a million.

Me: What do you mean?

Bb: There are not many people in Imphal. ;)

Okay, that does it. Any guy who doesn't have a basic sense of geography and is still pompous enough to show off his ignorance does not cut it.

Me: Good talking with you, BB, but I am going to pass on further communication.

Bb: What's your problem? We are just getting to know each other.

I took a deep breath and hit the block button. My first rejection. Was this a good thing? Weeding out the weirdos had to be a good thing. Just as I found my way back to the main screen, there was another message waiting. This one was from 'Lakda' in Indore. This time, I clicked on his profile to see what he was all about.

"Hello everyone... People say that each man changes with the passage of time and the infinitesimal struggles that he undergoes in this Life. My Philosophy: It's not time that changes us, it's our own Self Will, Determination and Desires. Desires make a better person. Being yourself is the Key to Success in Life. I am a Simple, Religious, Down-to-Earth person who was brought up with Modern Values and a Desire to Create my own Font."

It wasn't so much the name or fanciful description about Lakda that intrigued me. Or the fact that he capitalized qualities for emphasis. It was that final titbit—that he wanted to create his own font. I took a deep breath and decided to go for it.

Me: Your interest in typography. Is this a hobby?

L: You could say time-pass but, like many Low-Lying Thugs, I have great Aspirations to change the World.

Me: Low-lying thugs? Are you a criminal?

L: Actually, I just like to use those words to sound Criminally Attractive Online.

Criminally attractive. Interesting choice of adjective.

L: Which would be Infinitesimally more Appealing, were it to appear in its own Font.

Was this guy deranged or just plain bored? And what was with all that useless capitalization? There was no way I was setting him up with my mother. Yet, the conversation was kind of entertaining, so I continued.

Me: What's wrong with Times New Roman?

L: Times New Roman is the very definition of *Droll*.

Me: Arial?

L: That's everyone's Safety Font.

Me: And what's wrong with being safe?

L: Nothing, except it is a Lead Indicator of your Personality—that you like to follow the herd.

Me: You prefer to be a black sheep?

L: Actually, I was thinking more in terms of being a Leader.

Me: Interesting. What kind of font would a leader use?

L: And therein lies my Dilemma. I cannot find a ready-made font that Exhibits True Leadership Qualities. Hence my desire to create one.

A font with leadership qualities? The exchange was going from quirky to ridiculous. Why did I even bother to continue?

Me: Leadership is an admirable virtue, no doubt, but how does one even begin to think about creating a font that might portray leadership qualities?

L: Well, I have downloaded a software to help me begin Thinking.

Okay, now this was going nowhere. I was all for creativity and unique ideas, but creativity in fonts, useless capitalization, and typography using downloaded software is definitely one for the Loony Hall of Fame. Block.

A speech bubble popped up on my screen. It was yet another

message. Seriously? Had I not swiped left on all those profiles? Had I actually swiped right on all of them? I was completely embarrassed, but I figured making a tech mistake is hardly something to penalize yourself for when you are not familiar with how a dating app works. But these guys were sending texts barely seconds after I had swiped left—or was it right?—in their favor—did they not have a life? I clicked open the message to discover that this one was from 'Chhokra'. I decided to take a bolder approach.

Me: You've got to be kidding, right? No one calls themselves that on or offline.

Chhokra: You're right. Shud'v said, 'I'm Ali Zafar!'

Instantly, I knew it was Dev. Yikes, the tingling feeling came again! How did he know to message me on this account? It took me a good three minutes of focus to remember that he had suggested I set it up in the first place.

I took a minute to breathe and calm down.

Me: Why are you messaging me here?

Chhokra: Just wanted to check on your progress, babe.

Babe? Did he just call me babe? No one has the right to call me that!

Me: 'Babe' is a downright demeaning term.

Chhokra: Sorry. No offense intended. The thing is, judging by your profile picture you are *quite* the poster child for veena-playing single women. Smart, talented, and good looking.

I was stumped. How am I supposed to respond to something like that? I sat there, staring at the screen like a mute fool. The silence must have been obvious. Two minutes later, my cell phone rang. It was Dev.

"Sorry about that; I didn't mean to catch you off guard," he said.

"No, no, you didn't. I'm perfectly on guard, thanks."

I had just gone from being a mute fool to a blithering idiot!

"Relax, you needn't be on guard around me," Dev said. "Ever."

Sure, I had just asked for that. Sensing my apprehension, Dev took the edge off the awkwardness by asking me if I, or rather, if Venus, had received any enquiries. Without getting into too much detail, I proceeded to tell him about Bahadur Billy and Lakda.

"See what I mean about online names? How did the conversations go?"

"Fine," I lied. "I just need to explore a little more."

What I wanted to say was that the conversations sucked, and that I needed help weeding out the weirdoes from the genuine ones, but I couldn't tell him that. What would he think of me? As if reading my mind, he came back with a quick response.

"You know, there are a lot of crazies out there. If you need help identifying them, I'll be happy to chip in."

Of course I wanted him to help, but I didn't tell him that. "Thanks for the offer. I'm good right now, though," I said with deliberate-yet-fake reluctance. Why was it so hard to be honest?

"Okay, just putting it out there," he replied.

After pressing 'end call,' I stared blankly at the computer screen, wondering whether Venus would ever get a message from a guy like Dev. Someone who was smart, cute, and set Mom's heart throbbing. The thought was delightful and creepy at the same time.

I became aware that I was wringing my hands again. Forcing myself to stop, I got up from my desk and walked over to the window. In moments of boredom, I sometimes gaze at the zoo of humanity outside my window and use it as an excuse to ponder the meaning of life. I looked out now to witness the controlled chaos of Mumbai. The city has a sneaky way of appearing super-organized, like it's one big theatrical drama choreographed by God. People here are always in a hurry. Not because they want to make deadlines, but because they have a purpose. And it shows—they walk the walk and talk the talk so convincingly. It's a sharp contrast to what you'd find in Delhi with its 'chalta hai' attitude to life.

But how can you tell if it's true? Whether any of these busybodies actually have a purpose or whether it is an act they put on so the next person doesn't label them a loser? Learning how to dissect this is critical. Only then can you distill the honest from the phonies. If I could master this, maybe I could apply the skill to this new venture—online dating—I had embarked on? Why lead yourself into situations where you end up socializing futilely with psychos or sleaze balls?

A text from Deepali brought me back to the real world.

Deepali: What's up, babes?

Me: I need your help with Op Mom.

Deepali: Nt now, hon. With Vik.

I will never understand the workings of Deepali's head. First she texts me, then she blows me off.

Deepali: Dnt wnt him 2 feel neglected.

That was a first! I was sensing a different vibe from Deepali lately, a caring one. About Vik in particular, as opposed to Jaggi.

Me: Do I detect feelings?

Deepali: Of course nt.

Hmm. Really?

Deepali: Feelings = I want 2 b 'wanted'. So I need 2 make him feel 'needed'.

I think she was confused between what she wants and what she needs. Two minutes later, the phone rang. It was Deepali.

"I excused myself for a few moments. Make it snappy."

"Okay," I said. "I had two conversations just now with two different responders."

"Let me guess, neither of them led anywhere."

Where does Deepali get her sixth sense from? For all I knew, she had taken a course in spiritual communication.

"You were probably asking them over-inti stuff on day one."

"Translation, please?"

"Over-intellectual stuff. Isham style. It's off-putting."

Deepali was always pretty nimble when it came to pointing out my flaws.

"I was trying to get a conversation going. To break the ice," I snapped.

"Come on, Ilz. I know what you're like. Showing off your amazing intellectual skills, you need to put that on ice!"

I sighed. Deepali knew me better than I knew myself sometimes.

"Initial contact is a way to show a potential date that you'd like to talk to them. Go with a more casual conversation starter. Maybe you can comment on an item that you both share in your immediate surroundings."

"Like what?"

"Like, you know, the wobbly chair next to you," she suggested.

"But I don't have a wobbly chair next to me?" I said, confused.

"So make one up!" Her exasperation was overbearing.

"Really? That's the advice you have for me? What's wrong with 'How are you today?'"

"Uff! Boring. Shows that you are a strait-laced sati-savitri with zero personality. By focusing on something interesting you can both experience, you're removing any potential awkwardness with a canned comment."

"Deepali, is this what *you* do yourself with your three boyfriends?"

"Two. Dev is all yours, Ilz. In fact, why don't you ask him about this?"

What? Did I really hear that right? Deepali had openly admitted that Dev was "all mine"! I didn't know how to react, except stupidly!

"I can't do that!" I said. "What will he think of me?"

"He'll think you need help coming up with fake conversation starters," she replied coldly.

No, I couldn't do it, I couldn't call Dev for advice with this stuff. "Look, where are you coming up with all this advice?" I asked Deepali.

"From Dr. Mirno."

Great. So Dr. Mirno from Hong Kong had become my default Aunty Anne.

"Speaking of Dr. Mirno, would she know anything about double happiness?"

"Seriously Ila," Deepali said, "I want in on what you're smoking."

"What?"

"Anyway, I have to go now. Vik's back, and we're going to get busy."

"With what?"

"Use your imagination. Bye."

And so, I was back in the good company of Bumble and its busy bees. I figured I might as well take Dr Mirno's advice and try a different approach.

As I scrolled through the app, I began to think of Bumble's company mission to empower women by putting the control over the dating game into their hands. Poor Mom wasn't even aware of this, but what about Pops? What would he think if he knew I was actively empowering her without her even knowing it? It didn't matter—they were separated. Or did it? My feet suddenly turned cold.

chapter
sixteen

OPERATION MOM, 8 DOWN, 7 DAYS TO GO - YIKES! DOWN TO HALFTIME!

Bumble and anxiety aside, twenty-two hours later, not a single message had come through on Tinder. I paced up and down my room, worried that in my quest to be a female in power, I had come on too strong. I had been forceful and aggressive, swiping right—albeit accidentally—on all sorts of men on Bumble, while on Tinder, where the guys were in full power, no one had swiped right on Venus's profile. It had only been a day, and I was already having an internet dating dry spell. Deepali had warned me that once I got into it, Operation Mom would feed my obsessive nature.

Truth be told, I had spent the previous day with my phone by my side, pushing thoughts of Pops' reaction out of my head and waiting for a message from someone. Anyone. Maybe Dev's profile of Venus wasn't such a zinger, after all.

"Don't be stupid," Deepali said. "It's not the profile that's holding things back. It's your own fundas."

"What do you mean?"

"Just click on any profile, yaar. There's a zillion out there."

Deepali was right. There wasn't time to wait around like a damsel in distress. I needed to be proactive. I weeded through at least thirty profiles, which were either too boring or too whacko, before I finally arrived at one belonging to 'Adventurer.' Curiosity led me to explore further:

"I've got carpal tunnel in my left big toe, but it doesn't seem to affect my handwriting too much anymore. My best friend is a Burundian pygmy. His name is Mbaba-Mwanna-Waresa-Something, but I just call him Shorty. It's easier. We hang out all the time; although, when he gets mad at me, he punches me in the kneecaps and shoots me with a poison blow dart. We always laugh about that afterwards while I'm recovering in the hospital."

Not bad. I detected a sense of humor and no overly off-putting opinion or bias. What did he want in his date?

"I'm looking for somebody who is breathing and preferably not in any type of relationship, such as marriage, a cult, or prison. A woman who has a steady head on her shoulders, but not a steady shot when she's mad. As beautiful on the inside as she is in the dark. She has to have a sense of humor, especially when catching me in a lie, drunk, or out with the guys (or all the above). She must know how to bathe and do it regularly...with or without my assistance. She cannot be a blood relative (note to self: always check this first, not last) and must be of legal age. In Mumbai, not any town in North India."

Okay, this could be a go, I thought, intrigued and nervous. This guy sounded perfect on the one hand, but the comment about being beautiful in the dark gave me the heebie-jeebies. Then again, nobody's perfect. What would Deepali do in this situation? Oh, forget Deepali—I needed to learn how to take action.

On the count of three, I positioned myself at my laptop and morphed into Venus. Swipe right.

Venus: Hello?

I received a response in moments. Yay!

Adventurer: Hello? Is there anybody out there?

An opener from "Comfortably Numb." This was promising. Pink Floyd was one of Mom's all-time favorites. If Aunty Maleeka was to be believed, Mom had discovered their music in her teenage years, after she was done with her George Michael phase. Any guy who knew the lyrics to their songs deserved a chance. I summoned up the courage to play along.

Venus: Should I nod so you can hear me?

Adventurer: You are coming through in waves...

Time to switch out of Pink Floyd and employ Deepali's suggested tactic.

Venus: That might be because I am having a particularly hard time today because of the chair next to me.

Adventurer: The chair? Is it occupied by an undesirable character?

Venus: No, it's wobbly.

No answer. Two minutes went by. I shrank back from the laptop; this chair thing was probably a bad idea. Three minutes. Still nothing. Yikes, it was my fault. I had to do something.

Venus: I am sorry. Did I throw you off?

Adventurer: I didn't exactly know what to make of your last statement. My apologies.

Of course, you didn't. I should never have followed Deepali's rubbish advice from Dr. Mirno—a genuine doctor wouldn't spout their wisdom on Facebook. I needed to switch this around. As if choreographed by God, right then, I received a text from Deepali.

Deepali: Trouble?

Me: Majorly. The wobbly chair thing was crap advice.

Deepali: I was dhaaping! U took me seriously?

Dhaaping? Now she tells me! It's amazing how communicating by text incapacitates me. I honestly couldn't tell that she was joking.

Deepali: Fix it. Ask him wht he does fr fun.

I began to type in response to her command.

Venus: What do you do for fun?

Adventurer: I like to take pictures of people taking pictures of things. It really annoys them.

I copied his response back into a text to Deepali.

Deepali: Sounds gud. Favrt hotspots?

I did as told. Adventurer pinged back instantly.

Adventurer: I like going to fancy restaurants, such as Chez McDonalds, Bhelpuri Canteen, and Arbysaggio Ristorante.

Deepali was obviously keen on following up the conversation. She texted me three times in the span of a minute to figure out what was happening. But thanks to her, I was now easing into the situation.

Venus: Your favorite things?

Adventurer: To relax, I like unscrewing my favorite bottle of wine and sitting in front of my fake 'fireplace' on my bear skin rug, listening to the rain falling on the cardboard roof.

I guessed the guy was a survivalist.

Adventurer: The only survival skill I have is to continually create great literature to entertain mostly myself, but also anyone else who chooses to read.

Okay, perhaps, I just had survivalist on the brain!

Venus: Hmm. Speaking of reading, what was the last thing you read?

Adventurer: A sign that said, "One way; do not enter." Then I woke up in the hospital again. I REALLY need to pay more attention to road signs.

Deepali had been texting me with the savage regularity of a digital alarm clock. Finally, she could take it no more. The cell phone started shaking to the tune of "Vo dekhney mein." which I'd set as Deepali's ringtone. I was bursting with giggles when I answered.

"Oh, this must be good," she said excitedly.

I filled her in on the conversation thus far.

"This one's a keeper," Deepali decided after I'd finished. "Set up a date, now. No, yesterday."

"What if he doesn't pass the weirdo test?"

"You're right. We need to vet him in person. Let's ask him to come to some place we can see him."

"That's not going to work," I said, chewing on the end of a pencil. "He'd consider it a date, but Venus would be a no show, and that's going to reflect badly on her. If we like him, and she stands him up, he won't come a second time."

I scanned the walls of my room absent-mindedly. By force of habit, my eyes came to rest on a poster of Ali Zafar. I jolted upright as light bulb switched on in my brain. I knew what to do!

"Deepali, we could stalk him and spy on him without his knowing!"

A hearty chuckle emerged from the other end of the phone line.

"Brilliant! We can finally put the Isham skills to test."

"But how do I figure out where he lives without asking him directly?"

"I don't know." Deepali laughed, "Should we try following his cat?"

———

Before we embarked on the recce, I need to get my anxiety about Pops out of my system. I found him seated in his usual spot—on the back lawns of the Willingdon Club, shoving down a plate of bhel-puri and chai before his evening game of bridge in the cards room.

I wasn't sure how to exactly branch the topic, but I figured that there was no upside to beating around the bush.

"Pops," I began. "I need to know exactly how you'd feel about Mom dating again."

The spoonful of bhel-puri he was about to put into his mouth accidentally dropped into his chai instead...and the chai splattered all over the table and his shirt. That should have been my cue to end the subject once and for all.

"That bad, huh?"

"Not at all!" He said, indignantly wiping down his shirt with the napkin. "Just...where did this idea come from?"

"Mom needs an obsession—one that isn't me. I figured that maybe it's time she found one."

Pops looked over with a semi-hurt expression. "And what about me?"

Whoa! Had I just detected that separate apartments did not equate to *separated*?

"You guys are not exactly an item..."

"That's not what I meant!" he interrupted. It was either what I said or the way I said it, but Pops knew that there was a misapprehension of the subject matter that needed to be cleared up.

"What I meant was, why are you suggesting that she start dating again, in lieu of suggesting that I do?"

For real? C'mon Pops! I took a deep breath.

"Listen, you are super easy-going; you don't get in my business about things. Mom can't seem to stop herself. I think it would do her good to get a life, that's all."

He pursed his lips and shook his head from side to side.

"Yes, yes, she should have a life," he agreed.

"Was that a bad suggestion?"

"No, no, you are quite right. A life is the right thing for her."

I realized then that he was not going to treat this as anything but a competition.

"Pops, it's not like you shouldn't have a life as well—"

"No, no, I see your point about Veena," he cut me off. "Forget about me, I prefer to be lifeless."

"Pops, you are ANYTHING but lifeless!"

"Okay, well, whether I am lively or lifeless is immaterial," he said, chomping hard on his bhelpuri, a big frown line forming across his forehead. "I can determine all that in time. In fact, perhaps Veena getting out there in the world can help me determine that for myself."

Oh, great. If it wasn't competition, then what was this? Insecurity? But before I had a chance to ask him further, he just changed his stance.

"I think it's a brilliant idea!" He said suddenly bursting into a smile. "Yes, Veena should get a life."

"And..."

"And I will get a game of bridge."

"But, Pops—" I started.

"End of discussion, daughter dear. I do not want them to start shuffling without me. We'll pick this up later."

And with that, he got up and marched off to the card room, his shirt stained with green and brown chutney.

chapter
seventeen

OPERATION MOM, 9 DOWN, 6 DAYS TO GO - DESPERATION
IS THE MOTHER OF INVENTION

It had taken an entire afternoon of flirtation with barely any breaks
to figure out that Adventurer's real name was Fizz. By the end of it, I felt
like I had known him all my life. Fizz was a jazz aficionado looking for a
mature woman who had a keen interest in spirituality. Fizz didn't
exactly reveal his address, but he did say that, in the afternoons, he
frequented #22B of an ornate building in a Dadar enclave that houses
the largest concentration of Parsis in the city. No calculator needed to
do the math there. He was talking about Faramji Building in Dadar
Parsi Colony, the go-to place for Zoroastrian quirks and culture. But
whether he lived there or worked there, I couldn't tell.

Dadar Parsi Colony is always simmering with strife, racy rumors,
and shrieking women. I know because I have spent some time there in
the past. Mom has, on a couple of occasions, been assigned stories there.
Each time she was required to interview members of the community,
she dragged me along. Whether she needed some sort of alibi or if it was
to provide me with some cultural education, I don't know, but I had
certainly become somewhat accustomed to the ways of the colony.

Parsi women are a breed to be relished. When it comes to shrieking,
they possibly beat even Punju aunties. Regardless of vintage, Parsi
women are blessed with a booming voice box that often entertains an

entire block. Kind of like our household, whenever Naani visits or Aunty Maleeka comes over for a glass of wine. Maybe that's why I feel so comfortable in Parsi colonies.

Since it was a fine day, the bagh was littered with a bunch of Parsi aunties broadcasting their family quibbles and complaints into the environs. I braced myself to deal with the onslaught of noise attacking my auditory nerves as I approached.

"Why do they wear their nighties in the daytime?" Deepali asked with genuine interest.

I giggled at her naiveté. Deepali prided herself on her amazing fashion sense, but when it came to understanding the culture behind the fashion, she was way off the mark.

"They're not nighties," I said. "They're 'gowns,' worn throughout the day."

"Well, they look like nighties," Deepali said, twisting her face. "How come you are so tuned into Parsi fashion anyway?"

I opened my mouth to answer, but we were now in the center of the bagh. It wasn't worth competing with the decibel level around us. I pointed to the assorted variety of bawas and bawis standing at their windows, shouting to one another, and then pointed to my ear to indicate that I couldn't hear much.

It is a wonder that anyone could actually communicate amongst the high-pitched sounds of middle-aged female Parsis conversing in the bagh: "Kem chey, soo karech, aaje su randhiyu." You'd think that Deepali would be quite at home, given that all the shouting was happening in her mother tongue, but then culturally, bawas and Gujjus are nothing alike. These folks are more like my Punju clan. Take one look and you can see that investigating the daily doings or culinary agenda of their neighbors is more important to these men and women than the headline news in the day's paper.

"We haven't got all day," Deepali shouted above the din. "Let's track down our bawaji."

"Wait, how do you know Fizz is a bawaji?" I asked.

"Dhakkan, only bawas are allowed to live in Parsi colonies! Where've you been?"

Yes, where *had* I been? But why hadn't he just said he was Parsi?

Deepali certainly didn't care. "Where's Faramji Building?" She glanced around.

Our destination was on the ground floor of a low rise about five meters from the bagh. Deepali and I made our way to the window and positioned ourselves outside, where two aunties were discussing the best way to make akuri. One of them hollered to a hawker—a 'pauwalla' or bread man with his warm bakery paus in a wooden trunk strapped to a cycle—who was weaving his way around them.

"Ayy bhaiya, kadak pau," Aunty #1 summoned him to inspect his wares. Aunty #2 wanted a 'naram pau' and demanded thin slices from him. The pauwalla proceeded to slice up one little round mound after another while chatting away with his customers.

In the city of enterprise, even a UP-ite or Bihari pauwalla can rattle away in perfect Gujarati when required. When I remarked on it, Deepali corrected me: "It's not perfect Gujarati; it's perfect *Parsi* Gujarati."

Whatever the distinction might be, one thing's true for the pauwallas winding up at the bawas and bawis' doorsteps every day— chatting away in their native tongue made the 'aapro pauwalla' not just a welcome visitor, but almost an extension of every Parsi family. The Parsis may not be many things, but they are a friendly lot who instantly appropriate virtually every stranger as 'aapro' something-or-other. Knowing full well that the aunties would consider adopting us in no time, we made sure to keep our distance.

Strains of *Carmen* emanated from #22B. Given the purpose of our mission, the fact that it was opera rather than jazz was not promising.

"This can't be the right place," I said, concerned.

"Why not?" Deepali asked, chewing upon a piece of thick bread she had grabbed from the pauwalla.

"Why would a jazz aficionado be playing opera?"

"Maybe that's his mother listening?"

"Why would Fizz be living with his mother?"

Deepali looked at me quizzically. "I don't know. Why do *you*?"

The only way to figure it out was to peep inside. Deepali and I walked around to a window on the side of the building, as we didn't want to cross paths with the aunties. We craned our necks to look inside.

There on the sofa sat a crotchety looking, middle-aged man outfitted in a sudrah-kusti and a lehga that flapped loosely above his ankles. His thick eyebrows were knitted together in intense concentration. Three long strands of hair that looked more like whiskers sprouted from a large black mole on his left jaw. With eyes half closed, he was engrossed in the rhythm of the arias. A maid with a feather duster flitted about in the background.

Lips pursed, I glanced at Deepali. "There is no one around who could even vaguely qualify as his mother. Not a good sign."

"Perhaps the maid likes opera?" Deepali suggested. She swished her long, beautiful locks back behind her shoulders and shrugged.

Sometimes even Deepali resorts to utter stupidity. Sakkubai's musical horizons didn't expand beyond the latest Sharukh Khan movie. Fizz's maid could not be any different.

"Fine," she said. "There's only one way to find out. We're going in."

Was she stark, raving mad? "We are not!"

"How else are we to find out whether or not this really is Fizz?"

Now, I was nervous. "Let's forget the whole thing and go home."

"I didn't waste my entire morning to come here and find nothing," came the indignant reply.

She was serious. She smoothened out her top over her jeans and took a few steps towards the front of the building while I stood frozen. She stopped and turned around.

"Move it, hon. Whose mom is this operation for?"

Quite right. Get it together, Ila.

I took a deep breath, as if that would help prepare me for the anticipated humiliation. We passed the aunties whose conversation had moved on to berry pulao and entered the building through the front door. An overpowering odor of Parsi cooking assailed us immediately, as though all the residents were participating in a communal cook-off. Of course, I couldn't tell whether it was fish, fowl, or four-legged beasts being basted and broiled.

Apartment #22B had a gawdy umbrella stand parked next to the front door, which had a hideous knocker shaped like a cow with a massive ring running through its nostrils. It reminded me of my grandfather's dislike of women wearing nose rings—they looked like cattle, he said. Tempting though it was to use the knocker, ringing the doorbell would probably be more polite than banging loudly on the door in the middle of the afternoon. I don't know...I guess I just wasn't used to the idea of door knockers. We rang the bell three times before we heard the bawaji yell from inside: "Rosie, tame kem cho? Do I have to get you a hearing aid now?"

My heart went out to poor Rosie who had probably been deafened during the course of her employ with the bawaji. She opened the door to greet us, looking worn by the tribulations of life in the colony.

"Yes, tame kyana cho?" she said. After she had adjusted her glasses, she saw that we looked anything but Parsi. "Can I help you?"

Deepali saw me fumbling for words and jumped right in. "Su prabhat. We are here to see Uncle."

"And you are?"

"Mota mama's cousin's friend," she said without any hint of reluctance.

I clenched my fists behind my back to conceal my nervous response to Deepali's utter BS. Rosie stared at us blankly. Deepali had another go. "You know, from Colaba?"

"Cousin maane apro Tanaaz? Lal?"

"Haanji," Deepali replied gleefully.

It was sheer brilliance! How she came up with the impromptu nonsense remains a mystery, but I wasn't complaining. Rosie turned around and yelled out to her employer in Gujju. This was followed by a minute or two of incessant muttering. All I could decipher were the words "Taanu, baby."

Deepali, on the other hand, knew exactly what was going on. She jumped into the conversation with even more masterful BS that she spouted with the ease of a gymnast doing a backflip for the crowds. "We are here to talk about Tanaaz's special day," she said, switching to English for my benefit.

Rosie looked at us quizzically.

"Arre, you know what Taanu is like, na," Deepali said convincingly. "Always keeping secrets and trying to make sure we don't attach any importance to her. This time, we friends said she can't get away with it. We *must* make it special for her."

The bawaji shouted something to Rosie who figured that it was easier to let us do the talking directly. "Wait, just a minute," she said, closing the door. The music turned off, and, less than two minutes later, Rosie reappeared at the door to let us in. She showed us into a dusty old living room with the paint cracking on the walls. The windows were dressed in faded red and pink floral curtains, and the furniture looked like it had come straight off the set of a Merchant-Ivory film. Antiques of every kind crowded every bit of space on the dressers. The place was an open invitation for dust mites. Hardly the house you would expect Fizz, the cool jazz aficionado, to reside in.

We looked around for the bawaji, but he was nowhere in sight. Rosie seated us on the couch and offered us a glass of Duke's raspberry soda.

Deepali was revolted at the first sip and scrunched up her face: "What is this awful stuff?"

"Shh!" I glanced back, worried that someone might hear. "It's a signature drink for navjotes and weddings. Duke's makes it especially for the Parsi community."

But Deepali was not impressed. "Perfect recipe for making the guests throw up," she grumbled.

Five minutes later, the bawaji appeared from behind the curtains that fluttered across the threshold, separating the inner rooms from the living room. He was still wearing his lehga, but to look halfway decent, he had hastily put on a red-and-white checked shirt that could be mistaken for an Italian tablecloth. Deepali put her finger to her lips, indicating that I let her do the talking, which I was quite happy to do.

"Soo dikroo, Taanu sent friends to my home?" the bawaji said, obviously delighted to have company.

"Arre, Uncle," Deepali answered as though she were continuing a conversation from last week. "You know Taanu. She didn't send us. We came of our own accord, na."

"Arre, dikra, that part I know, but why are you here?"

"To talk about that only, no?"

Bawaji couldn't figure it out.

"What only, no?" he said in his sing-song tone, pushing his glasses back to the bridge of his nose.

The traffic noises increased suddenly and began competing with the rising din of cackling women in the compound outside.

"Arre, they are always taking it up to crescendo!" the bawaji complained. "Piercing my ear drums all the time. One day my head will explode."

The idea of the bawaji's exploding head splattered around this ultimate bawa living room didn't conjure very warm images. My train of thought was broken by the shrill whistle of a policeman.

"Every day! Every day, he does the same thing," the bawaji muttered. His face had gone from crotchety to downright cantankerous, like that of Rowan Atkinson in *Mr. Bean*.

He got up and made his way over to the window to examine the cause of the unmelodious cacophony at the traffic intersection. Then, with vocal energy that outdid all of the aunties in the colony, he yelled out to the policeman.

"Arre policewalla, tame shu kro cho? Is this a symphony or what?"

The policeman stopped to glance up at the hollering bawa. Obviously used to the complaint, he shot the bawaji a look of disdain and proceeded to pick up the whistling exactly where he'd left off. Bawaji grumbled further in Gujarati and slammed the window shut.

"He might eat your mother alive," Deepali hissed, grinning evilly.

Mother? Was she even *considering* the possibility?

"He might eat *us* alive right now if we don't get out right now," I hissed back. "Besides, we don't know that this is actually Fizz."

"We're about to find out."

"How?"

"Relax. I have this," Deepali said, turning back to Mr. Cantankerous, who was settling himself back on the couch. "Uncle, we need to prepare for Taanu's special day."

"What special day?" he asked. "Her birthday has already passed. One month ago."

"No, not that. I am talking about the other kind of special day."

But, of course, he had no idea what Deepali was alluding to.

Neither did I.

"You know, Uncle. She said that Fizz would know all about it."

"Kaun?"

"Fizz. You know, the guy on one of those dating apps?" Deepali said, piercing the poor bawaji with a stare so intense, I thought he might yelp in pain.

His face turned beetroot at the mention of the name. "What are you talking about?"

"That's just the thing, Uncle, I don't know what on earth she means by that or what that has to do with a special day. But she said that *you* would definitely know."

The bawaji's mole began to twitch, the three protruding whiskers doing their own operatic dance.

"How does Tanaaz know about Fizz?" he asked nervously.

I began to fidget with the edges of my kurta.

"She wouldn't tell me anything. At first, I thought she was talking about some kind of soft drink. Maybe the raspberry soda."

Twitch. Twitch. "Raspberry soda?"

"Well, come on, when you hear the word 'fizz.' what else are you going to think? But this internet thing..."

Twitch. Twitch. Twitch. The bawaji was getting more and more upset. He began to mutter some incomprehensible sentences under his breath. Deepali suddenly changed her stance. Her expression darkened as she stared him in the eye. "Achcha, I understand now." She nodded like she had just solved a crossword puzzle. "Fizz is your pet name."

All this while, I had been hoping that, somehow, this crackpot bawaji was just an innocent bystander who might somehow be related to Fizz. Alas, no such luck. His increasingly audible mutterings were a dead giveaway that this was the man himself.

At that moment, the traffic policeman's nagging whistle became so loud and insistent that it drowned out the noise from the surrounding car horns. The closed window did nothing to mask the unbecoming cacophony that aggravated all three of us, but most of all Fizz, who stormed out of the room like a tempest of wild horses, throwing open the front door so viciously that it banged against the wall.

"Come on," Deepali sprang up from the couch. "Time to make an exit."

I couldn't agree more.

We quickly gathered our things and ran out after him. The aunties were still standing by the front in the bagh. The bawaji marched right past them towards the traffic warden with the gait of a soldier charging towards the enemy in battle. All of the various onlookers stationed at different parts of the colony didn't bat an eyelid.

The traffic warden was stationed on a pedestal, but that didn't stop the bawaji from storming right up and yelling at him.

"Arre bad-tameez! Chapta khaayega? I told you before, is this a symphonee?"

The poor traffic policeman's whistle dropped from his mouth as he looked down at the mad bawa.

Aunty #1, who was standing close to us, sniggered as she slapped her palm on her forehead. "Faridun Dhotiwalla. You will never stop!"

Aunty #2 looked at us and said, "Dikra, where are you two from? I have not seen you before."

"Colaba," responded the quick-thinking Deepali.

"Colaba?" Aunty #2 was intrigued. "Related to Jeroo?"

"Yes, her favorite niece," Deepali responded smiling sweetly.

"What are your names?" she asked somewhat suspiciously.

"Mehr and Avaan. Bye Aunty, we have to go."

We dived out the eastern gate of the colony before Faridun had a chance to return.

———

"Do you know how dangerous that could have been?" I exclaimed, trying to catch my breath as we raced towards the bus stop.

"Relax, yaar! What's the worst a bawa can do?"

"Are you crazy? They are known to be nuts! What if he had called the cops or something?"

"What? To report that two girls had found out his secret online dating identity?"

She had a point. All along, Deepali had been playing him like a slide guitar, and he had eaten right out of her hands. The poor bawaji had looked so distraught at the mention of Fizz that the street traffic pande-monium was probably a welcome distraction.

Anyway, the good news was that we had discovered that he was a fraud. We could rule him OUT in large red letters. Deepali agreed. Mission accomplished.

There was no sign of a bus, and it was getting late, so we made the executive decision and decided to splurge on a cab. What sucks about Mumbai is that there are no autorickshaws allowed past Bandra. We piled into the first cab we hailed, a sorry excuse for a vehicle. Except for a thin strip of metal, the floor beneath our feet was completely missing, but that was the least of my worries. I was more concerned about the legitimacy of profiles on Lagan.com.

"Deepali, this doesn't bode well," I said. "What if all the other guys are liars too?"

"Let's weigh the odds. They aren't all going to be liars," she said.

"Still, don't you think this is a little risky? I mean today was okay, but what if the next guy turns out to be some other kind of weirdo…I mean is it safe for two teenagers to screen these types?"

Deepali cocked her head to one side as she thought about what I had said. "You are right. We should have a suitable partner-in-crime."

"Like who?"

"Aunty Maleeka."

I shook my head vehemently. The thought was ridiculous.

"You got a better idea?" she asked.

"Dev," I said with bated breath.

"Of course, I should have known," Deepali giggled. "I've created a monster. Goodbye Ali Zafar, hullo Dev!"

I felt my ears turn red. "Shut up, Deepali."

"Okay, hon," she teased. " I would love to indulge your fantasies of hanging out with Dev, but we are going to have to find another outlet for that. The meaning of a partner-in-crime in this context is someone who goes on a fake date to check this guy out first. There is no sense in Dev going, unless, of course, the guy is gay, which I guarantee he isn't."

It killed me that I was so desperate for an opportunity to see Dev, but in this case, I knew he couldn't really be of much help. But, Aunty Maleeka could hardly be trusted to take things seriously.

"What if she hits on the guy herself?" I said. "That'll take away any chance Mom has."

"Dhakkan, then you'd be doing both of them a favor. Any guy who goes for Aunty Maleeka is hardly date material for your mother."

As always, Deepali was spot on.

chapter
eighteen

OPERATION MOM, 10 DOWN, 5 DAYS TO GO -
DESPERATION IS MORE POWERFUL THAN INSPIRATION

"So, this is what you girls sneak around and do behind your mom's back," Aunty Maleeka said sternly when I filled her in on the details of Operation Mom. She and I were seated by the poolside of the CCI club, which was practically her second home. This was definitely not the reaction I was expecting. Of all people, I thought that Aunty Maleeka had my back in terms of my objectives to set up Mom.

"What I am saying is that your Mom might be divorced, but there is definitely an upside to everything. I wish I had a daughter to set me up too!"

The tube light that I am, it took me three whole sentences to realize that she was actually over the moon.

"Yes, if there is one life lesson you need to learn as you come of age, it's to be quicker on the uptake," Aunty Maleeka said, reading my mind. "Still, going online to find your mom a date, that's pretty jhakaas!'

She stuck her chest out so that the frills at the edge of her swimsuit caught the wind and began to flutter, further accentuating her boobs. On Mondays, Wednesdays and Fridays, she frequented the club's cards room for her regular game of bridge. On Tuesday and Thursday evenings, she swam fifty lengths at the pool, had a sauna, and then settled down to eat kebabs. The weekends were reserved for charity events and non-club activities.

"I should warn you, though. Your mother has a history of being favorably indisposed, or perhaps unfavorably disposed, towards Parsis," she said insouciantly.

"Oh, how so?" I asked.

"She thinks they are all either gay or crazy. She buys into that corny theory about how they are so inbred within the community that it's hard to find a specimen that's actually sane."

"Judging by Fizz the Adventurer, she might have a point there," I said, reflecting on our afternoon at Dadar Parsi Colony.

"Well, well, well. The apple certainly doesn't fall far from the tree, I see," Aunty Maleeka mocked. "'Being Judgmental'—By the Ishams. You people could write a book about it."

I think I've said it before, and I'll say it again: Aunty Maleeka is to Mom as Deepali is to me.

"I guess you can't blame her too much. Any occasion in which she *did* venture out of her box even slightly, her mother got on her case. Even in the JJ years."

That's my Pops she's referring to: Janak Jehan Isham, shortened to JJ.

When Aunty Maleeka makes such blanket statements about my family members, my instant reaction is to question whether there is even a modicum of truth in her words. But anyone who knows the Ishams knows that she understands us better than anyone else. Alas, Aunty Maleeka's analysis is bang on.

Mom once posed for a photo with Keanu Reeves, the actor who starred in the *Matrix* movies. Now, admittedly, I was pretty stoked that she was interviewing a known Hollywood actor. I mean how many times does a Mumbai-based couch potato journalist get to do that? Then she took a photo. She claims it was for me, but I think she took it just to prove to the world that she wasn't lying about how she'd spent the afternoon. When Naani saw the photo, the first thing she asked was: "Is his hand on your bum?" To which Mom promptly responded, "I wish." That led to a fight. Naani complained to Pops. Pops said he didn't really care. And then that led to a fight between Mom and Pops.

I was only ten when this happened, but seven years later, I am of the opinion that it would be cool to have the *Matrix* guy's hand on your butt. But what I don't know is whether Pops actually got upset about it, or whether Mom actually got upset that he didn't get upset. Honestly, I think it's the latter!

"Hi, Ila," a familiar voice said from behind me. I whipped myself around to see Dev looking even more like a boy-angel than he had the other day at home.

"De-ev," I said, my voice breaking for no apparent reason. I heard Aunty Maleeka half snort, half chuckle in the background, which made me turn an embarrassed shade of red. Didn't she understand that her general demeanor would make Dev, or anyone, frankly, question the company I choose to keep? However, he didn't seem to care.

"I'm Dev," he said, reaching out to shake hands with Aunty Maleeka.

"Oh, I know who you are," she replied. "I listen to these girls jabber a fair amount. One of Deepali's three amigos, huh?"

"Oh, no, he—" I began, but Aunty Maleeka cut me off mid-sentence.

"Do you guys really not care about her triple timing, or is it just fun to share?"

Yikes! I wanted the floor to open up and suck me in. Dev, of course, was completely good-natured about the whole thing.

"The best thing about hanging out with Deepali is getting to know the company she keeps," he said. He shifted his gaze to my eyes.

I began to melt instantly. In moments, I would be a puddle on the floor.

"Is that right?" Aunty Maleeka shrieked. She looked at me, her face pink with excitement. "Looks like your mom doesn't need to return the favor by setting up online dates for you, eh? And all this time I thought you had the hots for the film star, Ali whatever-the-heck."

"Zafar," I said brusquely, biting my lip.

"What's that?" Aunty Maleeka snorted, half interested.

"His name is Ali Zafar... and yes."

"Yes, what?"

"I do."

"You do what...you do?" she repeated, brushing down her fluttering frills. "You sound like you are taking a wedding vow."

"I do have the hots for him."

"Who? Dev?"

At this point, it might have actually been easier to be a puddle on the floor. Dev sensed my mortification and changed the topic.

"I won't keep you ladies. Ila, since you are here, I just wondered whether you might like to join me for an ice-cream? They are experimenting with some new flavors."

"Actually, I need to get home soon," I said weakly. "Perhaps another time?"

"Sure, no worries," he said, grinning his lopsided grin.

I tried hard to detect disappointment on his face, but I couldn't.

Never being one to read when it's appropriate to keep her mouth shut, Aunty Maleeka piped up: "Just go, na. Enjoy yourself."

I glared at her.

"What's the big deal?" she continued. "Your mom's not going to freak out if you're a tad late."

Dev, thankfully, came to my rescue. "Actually, I think Ila has stuff to do at home before her mom gets there."

Aunty Maleeka thought about it and nodded. Indeed, it made sense.

"Besides, I need to make tracks fairly soon. We'll do it another day." He winked at me and sauntered off towards the ice-cream bar. I couldn't help but admire the entire package—cute ass, hot bod, all wrapped together with threads of intelligence and chivalry!

"Did no one ever tell you not to stare a gift horse in the mouth?" That was Aunty Maleeka jerking me back to reality.

"Thanks, Aunty Maleeka," I said sheepishly, "but I hardly consider Dev a gift or a horse."

"Yet, you'll stand there gawking at him and assessing his value?" she smirked.

Not knowing exactly how to respond, I fumbled with the ends of my shirt. "You know that he and Deepali—"

"Oh, please. Give me a break. I wasn't born yesterday," she interrupted. "I know exactly when a guy has the hots for a girl. I have a radar about these things."

Feeling myself go completely red, I opened my mouth to say something, then promptly closed it like a goldfish.

"Yes, yes, I know. You have nothing to say. All you Isham women are the same. You live life in denial and have no idea how to respond to a guy's smoke signals," She snorted, fanning the heat off her face with a paper napkin. "Anyway, if you are going to scour online dating sites, Bumble and Tinder are not the way to go. They are filled with young and insular defeatists who are more concerned about what their mother or her money-grabbing jyotishi might think about the array of profiles on offer."

Why hadn't it ever occurred to me that Aunty Maleeka might know a thing or two about dating apps? All this time had gone waste when I could have gone straight to the source.

"What should I be looking at?"

"Something like OkCupid, which has awesome stats, or Truly Madly, which allows you to play interesting games with your matches."

"Interesting games?"

Aunty Maleeka was more focused on giving me a rundown of her favorite apps rather than delving into an analysis of their attributes.

"I like Frivil personally because the more attractive the people you pick, the better your popularity score becomes. And hey, you know I have no issues with being popular. But knowing Veena, she'd probably go for that one which only allows you meet well-educated types. What's it called? Oh yes, Woo. Or heck, Elite Singles where more than 80 percent of the users have bachelors or master's degrees in one thing or the other."

Then again, even if she does frequent all these dating apps, Aunty Maleeka is still single. Does that say more about her or the apps she frequents? I wasn't really sure.

Aunty Maleeka stood up from her deck chair and threw off her towel to expose her badonkadonk, perfectly outlined in her frilly, blue polka-dotted swimsuit. Really, such an exhibitionist!

"Anyway, lining up a blind date is not the issue. That's just a matter of posing as Venus to get the guy hooked," Aunty Maleeka said, getting ready to jump right in. "The real problem comes after that. How is one to get Veena to break her love affair with her laptop and agree to take the plunge? Just like your real problem is getting over your prissiness and getting yourself to that ice-cream shop to find that gift-horse."

"Aunty Maleeka!" I began, but by that time, she was already off into the deep end. I fumbled with the ends of my shirt for a few moments before springing up with a new determined feistiness. She was perfectly right—I need to respond to those smoke signals quickly, or else he might start blowing them in another direction.

———

I scoured the ice-cream parlor for Dev, but alas, he was nowhere to be seen. I hurried over to the bathroom in the hope that I might catch him on the way out.

"Miss, the use of facilities is only for patrons," I heard a stern voice from behind the counter. "Can you please order first? Chocolate? Vanilla?"

A wave of irritation ran through my torso. Of course, the ice-cream shop guy was right, but still, I didn't appreciate his attitude. I mean, who was being the patronizing one here? Without uttering a response, I turned around and marched out through the front door. I stood there in the parking lot for a few minutes, staring mindlessly at sidewalk vegetable sellers trying their best to negotiate a sale above the din of screeching day traffic. Oh, what the heck was I doing here anyway when I should be at home keeping an eye on Mom's dating profiles? Then I heard a familiar voice behind me.

"So, you decided to go for the experiment after all?"

Dev sprung into my line of sight like some long-lost prince in a fairy tale. I felt a familiar flutter make its reappearance in stomach.

"I...what?"

"Experiment with the ice-cream flavors," he laughed, with a massive wink, which sent me straight into addleheaded mode.

"That was a wink!" I teased him. "You winked!"

"As one does!" He did it again. "Now, can I get you that ice-cream?"

Could he *please* get me anything that could lull that flutter? I was worried about collapsing into a state of utter foolishness.

"No, no ice-cream for me today!"

There I went. Utter foolishness! Why go to an ice-cream shop if you don't want ice-cream?

"Truth be told, I figured you'd prefer the soft-serve at the CCI club."

Of course I would! Who doesn't love soft-serve? Wait how did *he* know that? It had to have come from Deepali.

"If you knew I love soft-serve, why did you ask me to come *here* with you?"

"I did," he said. He looked towards his feet with a somewhat sheepish expression. Cute but definitely sheepish.

"And?" I pressed him. "What flavor did you want to experiment with?"

"Nothing, really. A different kind of flavor perhaps." He broke into a grin. "I just want to be alone with you for a few moments."

He grabbed my hand and pulled me to the back of the parking lot, where we were almost completely hidden from view by a line of parked cars. Normally, I'd be concerned about the host of lecherous drivers peering our way, but I could see them huddled towards the street side, arguing over some kind of card game.

"Seriously?" I said to Dev. "That was so lame."

"I know," he said, turning to me. "But it's nice to be in a different venue, one that isn't infiltrated by your mom or Aunty Maleeka. Or Sakkubai. Next time, I'll just say, "Ilz, come meet me in the parking lot of the ice-cream parlor, I want to hold your hand.""

He had this way of catching me off guard! I took a breath, then pulled my hand away from his.

"You know Deepali is my best friend..." I started.

"I get it," he said slowly. "It's awkward, but you have to understand that Deepali and I are not an item. We never really were. Even if we thought for a moment that it was possible, that moment lasted for just five seconds."

I pushed my hands into my pockets; Dev slowly walked his hands up to my elbows, both of them this time. "I think it would be totally cool to hang with you for more than five seconds," he said. "Next time, I'll just say, 'Ila, I'm going to lose my mind if I can't hold your hand.'"

The flutter had turned into an entire army of butterflies, and they were hitting my sides hard. I didn't move; I just watched as his right hand made its way up to my face. A slight pang made its presence known, and I felt anxiety awaken in me at the idea that I should somehow misconstrue any of this. But then, as he laid his thumb on my lips, the flutter gave way to a serene joy. I couldn't pull away again. He leaned closer and closed his eyes. I began to close mine too. Right then, at that critical moment, my phone went off with a louder beep, beep, beep. For Pete's sake...why the heck had I not silenced it from the get-go?

I glanced over to scan the caller ID—it was Mom. Dammit! I had to take the call.

"Where are you, Ila?" I heard her voice. "I have been waiting forever."

And just like that, Mom killed the moment.

——

The fact that Mom hates going out is incredibly annoying. Mostly because when she is home, she tracks my every move. Quite some time ago, we made a deal to keep our location trackers on—"It's in the interest of safety," she convinced me. I am not so sure about that. I think it's mostly a tactic to deal with all of her alone time now that Pops is not in the house to keep her occupied.

From everything that Pops and Aunty Maleeka have told me, Mom used to be quite the social butterfly in her younger days. It baffles me as to why now she is at her happiest when she hides behind the safety of her computer screen, typing her way into fictitious bliss.

"We are writers," she said once. "We don't spend our time following the herds for superficial conversation on a Saturday afternoon. We stay in our imaginary world, creating stories that will get the herds to follow."

I don't know what imaginary world Mom is reveling in, but I can assure you that she is definitely alone. I can't stand being locked in the house day after day, all day long.

"What about the need to connect with your audience?" I asked her.

"That's why we have social media," she responded sagely.

But as antisocial as Mom is in real life, her social media personality is quite something. On the internet, she is incredibly articulate, prolific, and well known. Between Twitter and Facebook, her following is 65,000. I mean, I love hanging out on my social media networks—what teenager doesn't?—but I would never bother to reply to every Facebook comment and every tweet that comes my way.

I asked her about taking the time to reply to every comment once. Mom had explained with conviction, "If you do not make your audience feel that their word affects you, then why should they give your word a chance?"

That's what it's about. As a journalist whose opinion needs to be considered and a writer whose scripts need to be read, Mom takes her audiences very seriously. She spends her free time on Saturday afternoons meticulously going through her Twitter feed to respond to stupid questions, like "Why do you prefer to use Lucida Grande rather than a traditional font like Helvetica?" and "Will circling political vultures decide to eat Anna, Kejriwal, and Co. for breakfast?", to which someone else will post a classic comment, like "Corruption kis chidiye ka naam hai???"

And as if that's not bad enough, Mom will also sit and do the analytics on how effective her social media outreach is, whether her influence is going beyond her organic followers or whether her posts have gone viral. The greatest thing that happened to her recently was when she joined some kind of social media tracking tool that reported her influence score as shooting up over 100 percent in the span of a month.

"Perseverance paves the way for prosperity," she proclaimed, pleased as punch with her online victory. When Mom throws alliterations into her spoken language, you know she's in a good mood.

It's interesting to note how different my parents are when it comes to social media. Pops thinks of Facebook as an open mic for losers who love to wash their dirty linens in public.

"Yeah, that's because he is not exactly an open-minded person who will consider evolving," Mom had said cynically.

"Sure, both of us used to make fun of Facebook users, but then I realized that social media actually works for a writer, so I ate my humble pie and am more than happy to admit it. Your father, the other hand, was an investment banker for crying out loud! He refused to be a part of Facebook, even though it turned out to be the world's biggest IPO— every investment banker's dream." She licked her index finger and drew a circle in the air, an old trick to test the direction of air flow. "Which way do the winds of fortune blow? Had we the ability to own a few miserable shares of Facebook, we could have made a fortune."

Mom's online fame was kind of troubling, not for any reason other than the logistical problems it posed for Operation Mom. The fact that people already knew her made things problematic for us. Between Deepali, Dev, and me, we had managed to get a successful fake identity going on Lagan.com. Okay, not that the profile was fake, but there was no telling that Venus was actually Veena Isham, the successful journalist. Right after I got home from that fateful ice-cream parlor interlude, I had created profiles on Woo, Elite Singles, Truly Madly, and OkCupid, just like Aunty Maleeka had suggested. We had received several responses thus far, and nobody had connected the dots. I was quite happy with this—the last thing I wanted was for someone to approach Venus with preconceived notions about the kind of person she is, considering the amount of information by and about her floating around on the internet, but then I received a match request on Truly Madly that made me wonder if it was right to hide her identity.

I lay staring at the ceiling, contemplating which was more appealing —havaianas, kolhapuri chappals, or being barefoot in the park with Dev —when I heard a bell tinkle to indicate the match request. I held my phone up to my face. It was Dr. Yuva Dayalan, a Mysore style yoga practitioner from Chennai.

Dr. Yuva: Hello, Venus. You remind me of another yogini for whom I have great respect.

Impressive! A guy who knew the difference between when to use 'who' and 'whom.' I shuddered, recognizing my mother in me.

Venus: Really? What's she like?

Dr. Yuva: She has deep knowledge of yoga, a strong opinion on healthy living, and a magnetic influence over those she comes into contact with.

Venus: Who is this enchanting yogini?

Dr. Yuva: She is a Mumbai-based journalist called Veena Isham.

I almost fell off the bed in shock as I read and then re-read his words. We were done for! He could see right through us. For several moments, my paranoia refused to allow my rational mind to get a word in. Then, I began to come to myself. If this guy was for real, then regardless of whether he could see through the scam or not, it was probably a good thing that he was attracted to an online profile that looked and sounded like Mom, i.e., the real Venus. After all, the whole purpose of the exercise was to find a date for Mom. And the best kind of date was one who was genuinely interested in the person that she *really* was. I decided to explore further.

Venus: Hmm...Sounds vaguely familiar.

Dr. Yuva: She writes for the *Sunday Times*.

She writes, correct, but I didn't recall her having written anything in the *Sunday Times* about yoga.

Venus: Oh, yes. I think I have read her columns, but aren't they about local politics?

Dr. Yuva: Indeed.

Venus: Why do you call her a yogini, then?

Dr. Yuva: I have written to Veena Isham on many occasions to discuss the effectiveness of yoga and yoga kriyas. She is always responsive and her knowledge of Sanskrit, combined with her analytical skills, leads her to interpret the sutras in a manner that lends fresh perspective to what we already know and believe.

Wow! Mom as a thinker, appreciated for her thoughts! How great was that? Even better, she'd already engaged in an online conversation with this guy.

Venus: So, she is your online buddy?

Dr. Yuva: I suppose anyone with a regular Twitter correspondence with another person could be considered a pen-pal of sorts. Her penmanship is what's most impressive.

A pen-pal? What a seventies thing to say!

Venus: Tell me more. I am not very familiar with her stories.

Dr. Yuva: Well, it's partly her articles and partly her social media dialogue. I mean, the media is a very fickle thing, right? It finds subjects, fabricates stories about them, and puts them up on a pedestal, only so that people can throw rotten tomatoes at them.

A frisson of fear mixed with insecurity shot along my nerve pathways. Is this the impression that people had of my mother?

Dr. Yuva: But Ms. Isham is not like that.

I heaved a sigh of relief. The text continued:

Dr. Yuva: Her integrity shines through in every single conversation. She is the one journalist I read who always gives people and ideas a fair chance.

I was tickled pink—on behalf of Mom, of course. I wished I could share the conversation with her!

Venus: She sounds incredible, but you didn't tell me why I remind you of her. I am not a prolific journalist.

Dr. Yuva: Perhaps not, but I can see from your profile that you are a creative person. I see her kind of frankness in you, somehow. And also, that yoga holds deeper meaning for you than just being a series of postures to fill up an hour on a Saturday afternoon.

Wow, the profile had done the trick. I thanked Dev silently for the zillionth time.

Dr. Yuva: Would you be interested in pursuing a conversation?

Dr. Yuva certainly did not sound like a weirdo, but then neither did Fizz during the online conversation.

Venus: I have to attend to my daughter now. Perhaps we can continue talking tomorrow, same time.

I spent the next three hours studying Mom's Twitter feed. Dr. Yuva was listed as himself—Dr. Yuva Dayal. He'd had long conversations with Mom, amounting to several Twitter posts about the beneficial effects of jala neti and its comparative advantages over sutra neti. Wow, I never knew Mom had all this information inside that brain of hers!

My Ali Zafar ringtone sounded. It was Deepali.

"Hey," I said excitedly.

"Did you read something in *Cosmo*?"

"No, silly. I have been following a conversation between Mom and Dr. Yuva."

"And who is Dr. Yuva?"

"A yoga practitioner who teaches the Mysore style."

"Hmm...does he have anything to do with the Dayalan yoga championships?"

"Not likely."

"How do you know?"

"Championships are cheesy, and yoga is not a competitive sport. Anyone who thinks it is probably doesn't go deep enough into the art. Dr. Yuva is a master and has been practicing yoga for years and has been talking yoga with Mom on Twitter." I was brimming with excitement just at the thought of their exchange.

"And you are specifically interested in this guy because—?"

"Because he responded to Venus's profile. I am going through their conversation about the benefits of sutra neti to address sinus problems."

Now Deepali was excited too. "What are you saying, yaar? How does sutra neti work?"

Great, now she was getting more enthused about solving her boyfriend's sinus issues than about the date-ability of Dr. Yuva.

"Ilz, sutra neti?" she squealed.

I shrugged. In all fairness, Deepali had set me up with a lot of good stuff. The least I could do for her was to give her the sinus cleansing info.

"'It's a process by which you pass a catheter up your nostril and out of your mouth and then massage your sinus muscle with it to strengthen it,'" I said, reading directly off Mom's Twitter feed.

"Yuck, that sounds disgusting."

"Yeah, but it's very effective," I replied, still reading. "'The best way to actually chuck your inhalers for good.'"

"A real upchuck exercise! Do you know what else catheters are used for?"

"That may well be, but apparently they have been used for sutra neti forever."

Suddenly, I heard Deepali shriek at the other end of the phone line.

"Deepali, what happened?"

"It's even more disgusting than I thought. The guy is doing stuff that makes me want to retch."

"What? Who?"

"No offense, Ila dear," Deepali said, "But I am reluctant to count on *your* word as *the* word, so I have resorted to a quick Google search on sutra neti while we were talking."

"Great. Thanks a lot."

"No, thank you, Ilz. It led me to all sorts of super interesting links. I'm now watching a YouTube video on the process."

"Deepali, can we get back to the point?"

"The point being?"

"Dr. Yuva—"

"Ilz, I was right. He *is* the organizer of the Dayalan international yoga championships." She had Googled him before I could finish the sentence.

No way! I typed his name into search bar too. The very first item was an ad of the championships along with an image of Dr. Yuva squatting on the floor with one leg behind his head. I had to admit, he was quite good looking, even in that ridiculous pose. I didn't know whether to be disappointed that he had reduced yoga to a sport or thrilled that such a looker had shown interest in dating Venus.

"It's very promising that he is that flexible at his age," Deepali said. "But Aunty Veena is really and truly going to have to shape up."

"Maybe he will be interested in her beyond her physical appearance," I said, trying to think positive.

"It's not the appearance that worries me," Deepali replied. "Think about it, Ilz. A guy that flexible... She might have difficulty keeping up with him in bed."

It was my turn to shriek, "Deepali!"

Just because I had come to terms with the idea of setting my mother up on dates didn't mean that I was going to start planning her sex life— or, for that matter, to let Deepali do so.

"Arre, don't get so hassled, yaar," she said, failing in her attempt to sound offended. "It's just about taking action! Speaking of which, how are things going with Dev?"

"Dev?" I answered in a gruff tone. "Definitely no action there."

I was still annoyed with Mom for ruining what could have been an opportune moment. I had not seen Dev since then and was irritated by the thought of him being anywhere else but outside the ice-cream parlor with me!

"Really? I wouldn't have pegged abstinence to be his thing."

"It might not be," I responded. "It's just that Mom got in the way when I thought we might actually be getting together, and I have not really had any opportunity for action since!"

Deepali let out a loud squeal. "Aunty Veena doing what she does best. You see why she needs to get a boyfriend?"

"Yes," I sighed. "Speaking of that, I don't know about Dr. Yuva. He's a yogi. He might just be looking for a spiritually interested partner."

"Yeah, like Fizz the Adventurer." Deepali muttered. "Still, you never know. With that kind of flexibility, you know, his chakras are probably exploding with all kinds of kundalini."

"What the heck are you talking about?" I asked, confused.

"I don't know, but it just sounds like yogic tashan."

What she really didn't know was that the thought of Dev was making my own chakras want to explode with all kinds of kundalini.

"Stop talking nonsense and get back on track," I said. "How do we get to know Dr. Yuva better?"

"Isn't it obvious?"

It was. After I hung up, I looked into the mirror and leapt my way into a feeble excuse for a warrior pose. "Ila," I told myself out loud, "stop obsessing about Dev and start obsessing about the Dayalan yoga championships."

My reflection stared back at me in the mirror, making a serious attempt not to wobble.

chapter
nineteen

OPERATION MOM, 11 DOWN, 4 DAYS TO GO - IF YOU ARE
CURIOUS, YOU WILL LEARN; IF YOU ARE DESPERATE, YOU
WILL DISCOVER

The fact that yoga could be considered a spectator sport was beyond
the realms of my imagination—at least, until now. But then, there is
wisdom in that old cliché: every day is a new experience.

Deepali and I arrived at the National Sports Club of India complex
to witness what appeared to be a rehearsal for the Olympic Games of
yoga. The center of the stadium was abuzz with practitioners of every
kind keenly analyzing twists, turns, mulas, and bandhas. The contestants were lined up on one side, awaiting their turn to demonstrate their
yoga skills to a line-up of lungi-clad judges equipped with handheld
slates and chalk.

Deepali wriggled her way to the front so we could get a prime view
of all the goings-on. I followed dumbly, knowing that she would find us
the best seats possible. She did, in the second row.

As we settled down with some chili-flavored popcorn, a girl was
getting into position on the participants' yoga mat centerstage. Her
long, black hair was tied into a ponytail with a massive tikka adorning
her forehead, and she was dressed in a neon green leotard and shocking
pink yoga pants, making her look like some kind of model–actress who
had walked off the sets of a yogic Bollywood movie.

"Imphali or Nepali?" Deepali whispered to me, keenly observing the yogi's features.

I shrugged. She could be either.

"Yaar, do you know *anything*?" Deepali was laughing. "She's *neither*."

"And how do you know that?"

"Take a look at that outfit. It's so firang."

What did that have to do with anything? Firang yoga apparel was very much in vogue among Mumbai's die-hard yogis.

"Yeah, but who's going to wear a foreign outfit and stick a cham-keela tikka on their head? Only a foreigner would be that ridiculous."

Yes, the tikka was a ridiculous accessory for a competition that entailed twisting yourself into ridiculous poses. As I processed the thought, the compere made an announcement: "Next up, from Hong Kong, Chan-shing Tai, Wendy."

Hong Kong! It was a city so fast-paced that its inhabitants didn't even have the patience to let the next person finish their sentence. How does a place like that breed yogis?

Over the next fifteen minutes, Ms. Chan proceeded to flex herself into the most unimaginable poses. She stuck one leg behind her ear like Dr. Yuva had in the online photo and bent down to prostrate herself to the line-up of judges. Then, she positioned herself into a headstand, but no sooner had she lifted her legs, she folded them into a lotus position and lowered her thighs onto her elbows into something called the crow. Deepali and I looked on in awe as the audience cheered Ms. Chan's amazing yogic gymnastics, and the judges scribbled marks on their handheld slates.

"How do they do that stuff?" I asked, staring at her without blinking my eyes.

"I have no idea, but one thing is for sure. This dame should be in the Olympics." Deepali's eyes seemed ready to pop out of their sockets.

"Yoga is not an Olympic sport," I insisted.

"It should be," Deepali responded, chomping ferociously down her popcorn.

"In fact, it isn't a sport, period," I said, still in denial of these championships.

"Do you think she knows Dr. Mirno?" Deepali said, her eyes fixed on the chamkeela tikka.

"Deepali, how does your mind work?"

She didn't answer. By then, Deepali was too spellbound to even respond.

I have to admit that I too was enthralled by Ms. Chan's yogic acrobatics. It was as if we'd got a free opportunity to see a Cirque du Soleil rehearsal. One by one, in relatively rapid succession, we got to see the antics of Master Rajeev from Pune, Miss Nidhi from Mumbai, Swami Ramanathan from Kozikode, and Pundit Krishan from Jalandhar.

It was the next round that really knocked my socks off: yogic wisdom. It was an oral exam in which contestants were required to demonstrate their knowledge of yogic philosophy. Dr. Yuva was the chief examiner and had relinquished his dhoti in favor of white track pants and a Nike shirt that was so tight-fitting that he looked like some sort of a massive-chested, Popeye-just-ate-spinach-armed superhero. Hardly yogic. I couldn't take my eyes off his overly attractive form. Is this what they meant by tall, dark, and handsome?

Deepali nudged me. "Stop ogling. He's your mother's age," she chided.

Somehow, I couldn't picture the two of them together. Mom may be able to provide long discourses on Twitter, but her know-how of yoga was nowhere compared to this.

Dr. Yuva was clearly an authority on this subject and walked up and down the line of contestants, prodding each of them to spout their philosophical sapience.

"How does the yogic body breathe?" he asked, directing his gaze at Ms. Nidhi.

Questions on basic anatomy? Was he for real? But Ms. Nidhi's answer left me dumbfounded.

"We breathe through the nine openings," she responded.

"Absolutely correct," Dr. Yuva announced.

This was followed by a flurry of clapping by the audience. "There are nine openings in the body, and oxygen is taken in by each of them. Put your hands together, please, for Ms. Nidhi from Mumbai."

Deepali and I turned to each other in disbelief. He didn't just say that, did he? That there were nine openings in the body?

"The guy doesn't know how to count," Deepali whispered. Then her brow furrowed. "Wait, does he consider the nostrils to be one hole divided into two rather than two separate holes?"

I was grappling with the answer too. "Does the belly button count as an opening?"

"Nah, not unless yoga is okay with clogged holes," came the reply. "But seriously," Deepali continued, "was he talking about men or women? Because, you know, that there is a difference—"

"Deepali, let's not go there, please!"

A rustle of chatter had spread through the stadium. The others in the audience must have been equally confused about the nine holes. Dr. Yuva silenced them with an unexpected announcement: "For the next thirty minutes, we'd like to invite audience members to come and participate in a workshop. We will take you through a series of basic asanas that will make a difference in your daily life. Will those who wish to volunteer please assemble at the center?"

Deepali turned to me with a mischievous grin. I knew exactly what she was thinking.

"No way," I said before she could ask. "There's no way in hell I am going to embarrass myself in front of all these people."

She looked at me with puppy dog eyes. "Come on, Ilz. Don't be a wimp."

I tried to brush her off. "You and I are not exactly the putting-leg-behind-the-head variety."

"Don't be such a drip," she said indignantly. "It's not like they are going to make us do *that* kind of stuff. He said *basic* asanas."

"What do I need to learn basic asanas for?" I protested.

"To impress people."

"Which people?"

"Boys."

Sometimes even *Deepali's* knowledge of the male gender is dubious. Boys like watching cricket and football, not yoga shows. I could pretty much vouch for the fact that Dev didn't give a damn about yoga.

Neither did Vik or Jaggi, by the looks of it. But Deepali was not about to give in.

"Did you see how hot that Chan chick from Hong Kong looked? Imagine all she can do."

I reminded her that Ms. Chan's asana display was far from basic.

"Okay, sit here and sulk by yourself, then." She stood up, tossed her hair behind her shoulders, and stuck out her boobs defiantly. "I came here for yoga, and I'll be damned if I leave without getting some."

Deepali made her way through the aisle and marched down with the confidence of a statesman about to give a speech. I sighed, set down my popcorn, and got up to join her and about thirty others who were getting ready to participate.

I began to panic the moment Dr. Yuva began to bark out instructions. "Revisit your ocean breath," he said.

Revisit? How could I possibly revisit something I hadn't visited in the first place?

"Shut thighs tight," his voice boomed into my ear. He was standing right next to me.

"Shut thighs tight," he repeated for my benefit.

Okay, Mr. Yogic Wisdom. Just how tight does one have to shut their thighs here? It wasn't until I sneaked a glance at the others that I realized he was actually asking everybody to shut their *eyes* tight.

"Bring awareness inward," he continued. "Slowly assume mountain pose."

The only thing I could assume was an awareness of Dev, and that made me panic even more.

Do not panic, I said to myself. Do not think about Dev. Do NOT panic. Repeat aloud if necessary. No, *don't*!

The butterflies in my tummy subsided when he moved away to instruct others in postures to improve digestion.

"Poor digestion is the root of all sickness," he said. "Even if you don't do anything else, you must spend five minutes every day focusing on how to clean up the digestive system."

This was sure to benefit Mom, who had issues with gas. The shift from thinking about Dev to thinking about my gassy mother instead wasn't much help.

Dr. Yuva interrupted my thoughts. "We fill our day with unnecessary worry. Empty your mind. Get rid of all useless thoughts."

Does that mean getting rid of all thoughts or just the ones that are totally and utterly useless? Which of the following would qualify as thoughts worthy of being chucked: 'Is my mother's dating life really worth all this trouble?' or 'Can she get rid of her gas problems?' or 'I wonder if Ali Zafar does yoga—I should find out,' or 'What would Dev think if he knew that the online profile he created for Venus has led to this?' As I recognized the familiar flutter, I knew that the last thought wasn't about to be tossed out in a hurry.

After taking us through a series of twists that apparently wring the toxins out of your colon in the same way that water is wrung out of a wet kitchen cloth, he got down to the nitty-gritty of the gas issue with something called the pavanmukta asana, the wind free posture. All this time, he had been strolling among the volunteers, stopping to adjust people's postures when necessary. As if by divine intervention, Dr. Yuva arrived by my side just as I struggled to get into the foetal balance that would free my wind.

"More important than anything is to release the useless air that is old, that has been trapped inside your colon for a long, long time," his voice echoed in my ear.

First useless thoughts. Now useless air.

As we settled into shavasana, the last posture in the series, Dr. Yuva tried to remind the participants about the philosophy behind physical practice.

"It is these basic elements of yoga that sometimes lead people to ponder the meaning of life," he said, wandering over to the next person down the line.

I craned my neck to see how Deepali was doing on pondering the meaning of life and found her staring up at the sky with a blissful, yoga-drunk expression, the kind she has when she gets a good manicure at Silloo's. Deepali! If there ever was such a thing as a class-act human being, she defined it to the core. On the face of it, she appeared to be this unassuming, slightly girl, shallow to the core, but anyone who dug deeper could see that she was master of strategy—planning, devising, doing anything earthly possible to better the lives of those she cared for.

She had brought me here on the pretext of Operation Mom, but there was so much more to it. Deepali was actually interested in the mind-body benefits of yoga. She had been for a while, her exposure to yoga all thanks to Mom. Deepali wanted to get me into it too, but she also knew that I wanted to have nothing to do with any activity that piqued Mom's interests. No amount of convincing would get me to budge on that. But the best thing about Deepali is that she had somehow strategically planned my new infatuation. Who knows how or what, but she sure managed to get Dev into my head and Ali Zafar out of it in the bargain. Could she be any more class act?

I returned to my shavasana and smiled to myself.

And in this state, I made a few mental notes to self:

1. Put a lid on the idea of setting up Mom with Dr. Yuva. Communication by Twitter is really as far as this relationship should go.
2. Also put a lid on all those things you were going to get Mom to change—her hair, her obsession with plain-Jane saris, etc. The fact that you have not approached her about it yet means you never will.
3. Thank Deepali for forcing you to participate in the workshop so you could focus your yoga brain on Dev. It's the small things in life that matter.

chapter
twenty

OPERATION MOM, JUST 3 DAYS LEFT!

Thoughts of Dev had begun to interfere with the rational part of my brain: what was he doing right now? Was he back at CCI? Does he go there regularly? Did he make it back to the ice-cream parlor? I couldn't differentiate any more between the tingle, the flutter, the army of butterflies, and the times when my palms turned clammy. I felt like a big walking ball of emotion. I began to do peculiar, scatter-brained things, such as putting my socks in the fridge and leaving half-eaten apples in my closet. Sakkubai, annoyed beyond measure, began to cackle at me at the top of her voice. What was particularly annoying about all this was the fact that I recognized I was barely thinking about Ali Zafar anymore. The recognition of this fact annoyed me truly and madly—just like the name of that dating app. But, when I switched my thoughts to focus on Dev, I didn't care anymore.

Mom has a tool to help her with things like this. One of her fancy online fortune-tellers provides her with something called a biorhythm report to determine her intellectual, physical, and emotional levels. She uses it to plan whether to be more or less of a couch potato on any given day. In her case, it's usually more. At that point, I was so downright emotional that I contemplated subscribing to my own biorhythm report, but Mom shot down my suggestion, saying it's unnecessary at my age.

Were I to make a self-assessment, it would go something like this: on any given day, the levels of my intellectual efficiency would range between 70 and 85 percent of capacity, the physical levels in the 20s, and the emotional levels anywhere in between. As per the standard printouts I see on her reports (when I snoop), I'd say that categorizes me as 'silently lucid with less than desirable physical stamina.' But ever since Deepali and I embarked on Operation Mom, my biorhythm had swung 180 degrees. My stamina had improved immensely, and my emotional levels were threatening to go beyond the tipping point. I had Dev on my mind 24/7, and as far as Operation Mom was concerned, the project was coming along. The problem was, the one thing I took pride in—my intellect—had dropped to dangerously low levels.

I had wasted a precious twelve days hanging in limbo, waiting for any one of those godawful dating apps to be the answer to my prayers, and it had got me nowhere. All I had come across on the site were ultra-conservative types—Gujjus categorizing themselves as digambar or shwetamabar Jains; Punjus more gung-ho about connecting with the ideal gotra rather than with a soulmate; Sindhis from every conceivable province lost to Pakistan—Larkana, Shikarpur, Gujranwala; Andhra, Tamilian, Malayali, Kannadiga Brahmins; and Dyers Iyers and Iyengars out the wazoo. How was I ever to sort through the masses?

Had my brain been functioning at its regular efficiency, things would have been different. Common sense dictates that I should have known that if there was somebody who could shed some light on online dating—hell, had expertise in it—it was Aunty Maleeka. How could I not have seen this?

There was no further time to be wasted. Two days after she had embarrassed me in front of Dev at the CCI poolside, I embarked on my research. After a comparative analysis of the various dating sites that Aunty Maleeka had alerted me to, I made a few mental notes as to what I'd learned:

Elite Singles: Square. Filled with uncreative types who aren't yet ready to admit that they kind of want to get married. I mean, sure, star-tups are all about innovative and brilliant new ideas, but Elite Singles takes that point a bit too seriously. Does the world really need dating website and app for all the geniuses out there? It was more conservative and less weird than OkCupid.

Aisle: Really square. People who want to skip over all of the fun stuff and just get married, or have super serious relationships. The app was populated by women who believe that having short hair attracts negative energies and sexually frightened men who own nice crockery. Creating a profile could be downright daunting given the fact that it requires definitive partner preferences like "Passive or Aggressive." That doesn't fit the bill, not in the case of human beings anyway!

OkCupid: Kind of hipster/nerdy. Made up of 50 percent people who claim to be musicians or artists, but who actually make their money waiting tables, 20 percent hipster hotties who take themselves and their tattoos too seriously, 15 percent left-leaning preppy guys who decorate their bedrooms with pictures of stadiums, 10 percent inexplicable dodos, 4 percent dudes with kids, 1 percent people who are using it as a joke. The site is based in the US, but many of the Desi profiles list themselves as being Mumbai based.

Mumbai Craigslist: Not technically an app. It was instead a website—a scary one, filled with decrepit posers who were probably human traffickers, or maybe even axe-murderers, in real life. Aunty Maleeka had texted the link to this one as an afterthought. To me, it looked like a colossally bad idea.

OkCupid was definitely the way to go. I settled down to scrutinize the profiles on the app.

Three hours later, I came across a profile with the name Rahul G. I wanted to immediately reach out to Dev, but I resisted. I still hadn't heard from him since that day at the ice-cream parlor, and tempted though I was to call him, I didn't want to appear too eager. I decided to text Deepali instead.

Me: Come over ASAP. Found our next target.

As soon as Deepali arrived, we went to the building compound to get some fresh air. This in itself is a cherished concept in Mumbai. Our building is located in the backstreets of Saat Rasta. Depending upon which way the wind blows, there are two kinds of fresh air available—one that brings with it the stench of a local slum, and another that brings spores of the sulphuric pollution from the liners in the Arabian

Sea mixed with the traffic fumes of Mahalakshmi and Worli. At least going down meant we could escape the confines of the apartment and Sakkubai's nosiness. It provided a comfortable escape hatch to settle into a conversation with Rahul G.

Filled with puns, metaphors, and all sorts of innuendos that I couldn't figure out, his profile was hard to deconstruct. For example, he referred to himself as a "cat among the pigeons." I didn't know what that meant, but the beauty of digital existence is that you can look up just about anything at a moment's notice. All anyone needs to really learn these days is how to Google.

According to FreeDictionary.com, the phrase means "to do or say something that causes trouble and makes a lot of people angry or worried." Now, you'd think that people would be turned off by a negative descriptor. I certainly wasn't jumping for joy, but two things immediately came to mind:

1. One should be thankful for honesty on the internet, even if the truth is worrisome.
2. What kind of trouble did this cat cause?

I opened up my OkCupid app to find out. By now, I had become quite comfortable communicating with strangers online.

Rahul G: What I mean by that is that I am a romantic, but not an ordinary one.

Firstly, what does this have to do with cats, pigeons, or causing trouble? Was he saying that he upsets the women he dates? Secondly, what's 'ordinary' about a romantic? If anything, they are hard to find out of the realm of normalcy. Well, that's what Mom says, and frankly, I agree. I mean a guy like Dev is not your average Joe. Also, despite the initial signs, it still wasn't clear to me that he was actually a romantic. Deepali agreed too. I decided to grill him about it.

Venus: Does this mean you are an 'extraordinary' romantic?

Rahul G: I am a creative romantic.

I glanced nervously at Deepali. That could mean anything.

"Look at the bright side," she said, grinning mischievously. "He might be an actor."

Deepali perched herself on the edge of the compound wall and scowled at a bunch of kids playing hide-and-seek on the lawn. She doesn't like people who are more than three years her junior, especially the little kids who often come up to her and call her 'Aunty.'

"C'mon, Deeps, what would an actor be doing on a dating website?"

"Oh, please! What would a successful journalist with 60,000 followers on social media be doing on a dating website? People are lonely, you know."

I shuddered as I acknowledged the reality of the situation.

Where was Dev and why hadn't he called me? That said, 'creative' is a misleading word.

"Fifty percent of people who claim to be 'musicians' or 'artists' actually make their money doing odd jobs."

"Maybe he's a hipster hottie," she said, swinging her legs to and fro, reading from the extensive notes that I had made while researching the sites.

I responded instantly, like a programmed robot. "Twenty percent of hipster hotties take themselves and their tattoos too seriously."

Deepali looked at me suspiciously. "How do you know all this?"

"Aha," I replied imperiously. She had no idea that I had spent all morning researching Aunty Maleeka's recommended choice of dating apps. "The statistics on OkCupid are mind-blowing."

Deepali sighed at the pure geekiness of my statement, turned her head sideways, and glanced at me through the corner of her eye. "So, what about the other thirty percent?"

Without further ado, I elocuted the other stats.

Deepali's face broke into a massive grin. She slapped her hand down on her thigh. "How do I find the one percent who take it as a joke, Ilz?"

I shook my head at her forlornly.

"You kind of did. Dev claims to be part of that one percent."

She shrugged and didn't seem convinced. In the meantime, another message bubble popped up from Rahul G.

Rahul G: In the eighties, there was a very famous black-and-white photograph of two lovers kissing in Trafalgar Square in London. It was taken in a similar style to the photos of Robert Doisneux, but it wasn't his. Do you know the photo I refer to?

"I can't say I have..." I began typing, but Deepali stopped me abruptly.

"See, this is how you'll end up turning them away. You can't say things like that. It's a turn-off," she said, mildly annoyed.

"Okay, so what's a turn-on?"

Deepali snatched the laptop from me, hunched over the keyboard, and typed with intense concentration.

Venus (with Deepali typing now): I might.

Rahul G: I thought so. What fascinates most people about that photo is the fact that it is taken at Trafalgar Square, but can you guess what fascinates me most about it?

Venus: The passion seeping through the kiss?

Rahul G: But how does the photographer capture that?

Venus: By catching the lovers in the moment?

Rahul G: Through the pigeons!

Aha! Back to the pigeons. Deepali puckered her lips and continued.

Venus: The pigeons? Oh, that photo!

She still didn't recognize it, of course, but master multitasker that she was, she Googled it during the chat. However, she couldn't find anything.

Rahul G: There is something incredibly romantic, no, about the pigeons who are shocked into flight by the sudden display of passion by these lovers?

I got it then. The lovers were the proverbial cat. All this time I thought he was being metaphoric and idiomatic, but this was at least half literal—the part about the pigeons.

Deepali gazed at her nails, taking a momentary break, and then continued.

Venus: Isn't that just a function of the nervous personality of pigeons?

Rahul G: One pigeon might be nervous, but how can so many be?

Venus: Trafalgar Square is known for its congregation of nervous pigeons.

Rahul G: And lovers who will embrace in a mad, passionate kiss.

How could Deepali keep up? I had to read his sentences twice or three times to make sense of what he was trying to say and still couldn't understand. "Deepali, this guy is a loon," I said.

"Or just a bechaara who is in love with the idea of love," she laughed. "Give him a break, okay." She resumed typing.

Venus: Wouldn't Paris have been a more appropriate venue for the photograph?

Rahul G: No. Paris is the city of love, so any photo of Paris is resplendent with passion, regardless of its specific subject.

Deepali shot me a jubilant look. "Take note. Paris is resplendent with passion."

How did she stay on the same wavelength as this guy? "No, he said *photos of Paris* are resplendent with passion," I said.

Deepali snorted. "Same difference. The city has to be resplendent in the first place if the photo you take of it is going to be resplendent."

I thought about it for a moment. "Not necessarily. A lot depends upon the time of day, the lighting, and of course, Photoshop."

"Buddhu, don't get so techno. You're taking all the fun out of our plans."

"What plans?"

"To go to Paris."

"When are we going to Paris?" I asked indignantly.

"That's immaterial."

Correct. What was material was that there was a good chance of Paris coming to me (rather than me going to it) if only Dev would get it together and call me. Right then, we were encircled by a handful of kids who were looking for a place to hide.

"Shoo! You have the audacity to think I'm so large that you could hide behind me?" Deepali yelled at them.

The kids cast dark glances at her and emptied the space in a hurry.

I pointed to Rahul G's next message, which had just shown up on the screen.

Rahul G: London is far more compelling. In the eyes of the world, it is a dark and gloomy place with bad weather and unpalatable food.

Deepali, as usual, put a different spin on this.

Venus: I thought London is known to have better chicken tikka than you can get anywhere in India.

I looked at her, incredulous. She's vegetarian, but since when did that matter?

Rahul G: The fact that lovers can engage in so passionate a kiss that they shock the pigeons into flight is symbolic of the brutal uprooting of contemporary Britain. The flight of the pigeons heralds the reality of passion in the chaos of modern civilization.

Deepali stuck her nose into the screen to re-read his last message. "Okay, I don't know what he means, but it's definitely the kind of poetic philosophy that Aunty Veena is into."

She was right. Rahul G was definitely a creative romantic. Perfect, perhaps, for Mom. How could we orchestrate a meeting with him? As if by telepathic response, a message bubble appeared on the screen.

Rahul G: I live in the hope that one day I too will find my love among the city's pigeons. That's where you can find me on any given afternoon.

Venus: Trafalgar Square is a heck of a commute from Mumbai.

Rahul G: I go to the Gateway of India. It's replete with pigeons and the massive architecture of the monument juxtaposed against the seashore makes it all the more compelling.

Deepali looked up at me and smiled without uttering a word. I nodded in tacit agreement. Our next venue had been decided. Gateway of India, the following afternoon.

chapter
twenty-one

OPERATION MOM, 2 DAYS - DESPERATELY SEEKING SOLACE

Before I could focus on Rahul G or the Gateway of India, I needed to get the Dev thing out of my system. I had been thinking about him constantly, and I couldn't stand the fact that he hadn't called me. More than that, I couldn't stand the fact that his lack of interest so bothered me. I didn't want to appear too eager, but seriously, how long should I wait? I decided to nip it in the bud by making an unexpected appearance at his home. I knew he lived within walking distance from me, but I had no idea which building he was in. I opened up our class address book to figure out his exact address.

The lift man looked at me suspiciously as I rode the elevator up to the 10th floor of Dev's apartment building. Clearly, I was not part of the familiar crew.

"Baba's friend?" he asked. "Are you new?"

Well, that's an untoward thing to say! I chose not to dignify his question with a verbal response and nodded back at him instead. As I stepped out onto the landing, a bead of sweat took shape at my temple, and my palms resorted to a familiar clamminess. Ridiculous, Ila! This was hardly something to get nervous about. Plus, there was a fair chance that he wouldn't even be around.

The gods were on my side that day. Not only was Dev at home, but he opened the door when I rang the bell, donning a red baseball cap and a white tank top that showed off his very defined biceps. Damn!

"Ila!" He looked right into my eyes, genuinely surprised.

"Not quite what you were expecting, huh?" I proclaimed with obvious irritation.

"No, but this is pretty cool."

"Cool?" I retorted. "Cool as in excellent? Or cool as in thanda—cooling off?"

Dev was clearly taken aback at my less than convivial interaction. "Are you upset with me?"

"Yeah!"

He looked towards his feet, hissed, sucking in his bottom lip, and then nodded his head slowly as if to come to some sort of realization.

"Would you like to come inside?" he asked gently.

"No."

For the next minute or so, the two of us just stood there awkwardly without saying a thing. Then, Dev broke the silence.

"Ila, I—"

"You didn't call me!"

Dev clasped his hands and nestled them behind his head.

"When your mom called, you suddenly needed to make tracks," he insisted.

"So? Did you assume that was a great segue for me to cut out?"

"Kinda," he responded. "I thought that maybe it was the ideal excuse."

"For who?"

"For you, of course! It was my idea to take you to the ice-cream parlor, remember?"

No! Seriously? He thought I had wanted to back out of it? Ugh! Who should I be more annoyed with? Mom for ruining the moment, or Dev for misinterpreting my actions? He looked at me somewhat sheepishly now, a hint of a crooked smile forming at the edge of his mouth.

"Will you change your mind and come inside?" he asked.

Nope, not happening! I had showed up uninvited and could not make any more of a fool of myself than I already had. I crossed my arms and planted my feet more firmly into the ground. Dev took a deep breath, and, leaning against the threshold, he acquiesced.

"Okay, so if you were that pissed off about my not calling you, why didn't you just text me to say so?"

"Who said I was pissed off?" I argued.

"Well, what is this visit about then?" he shot back. "An irregular display of Drama-Queen-ism?"

"Hey, the role of Drama Queen is reserved for Deepali."

"My point exactly. I can't believe you could be so bent out of shape!"

"I could have been a lot more bent out of shape and done something really dumb—like squirting green chutney on your red baseball cap, for example—but that kind of behavior is best left for the crazies."

I cringed after I heard the words that I just spoke. Why did I *always* say the dumbest things in the presence of Dev?

"The crazies, yeah, weed them out!" Dev said indignantly. "Why ruin a perfectly decent baseball cap and spoil my day in the process."

"You're so full of yourself."

Dev shook his head and broke into a full smile. "Na-uh, I'm actually more full of you."

"Wait, what?" Dammit! That flutter again.

He regarded me closely. "I thought you were relieved to escape when your mom called. I thought maybe I had come on too strong...and okay, my bad. I realize that now. But hey, maybe it wasn't the wrong move after all. Maybe, it was more appealing than you want to let on."

Was it my imagination, or did something flicker in the depths of those chocolate pool eyes? The flutter in my abdomen started going nuts again. Still, I persisted with my indignant attitude.

"Don't be ridiculous," I said. "It's your lack of civility that I found offensive. It would merely have been polite for you to have reached out to me after you pulled me into the parking lot the other day."

"Polite? Is that why you refuse to come inside my home? To illustrate the perfect example of politeness?"

"Yes."

He took another deep breath and stared into the ceiling for a moment. Then, he took off his baseball cap. "Okay, I'll work on the politeness. Starting with this as a peace offering." Holding it in both hands, he forwarded it my way. "Like a begging bowl...begging forgiveness."

I wasn't going to go inside...not today, but I couldn't leave until I had one good shot. "You know that offering me your baseball cap is kind of a cop-out maneuver."

"What?"

"When you categorically told me the other day, 'Next time, I'll just say, Ila, I'm going to lose my mind if I can't hold your hand.'"

"You're right," he said. "No time for cop-out maneuvers."

And with that, he leaned forward, placed his baseball cap on my head, yanked me against him, and bent his head to kiss me. I melted right in, my mouth opening to his and our tongues meeting for the briefest moment before I pulled away. My emotions were going nuts— should I, shouldn't I? But I didn't want to think, so I uncrossed my arms and flung them around his defined biceps. All I could focus on were Dev's lips, which fell open as soon as I leaned in to kiss him back. His fingertips grazed the small of my back. He paused for a moment, and my eyes fluttered open. He smiled at me with his crooked smile. I smiled right back, and then he leaned in to kiss me again—sexy, sweet, and delightful all at the same time. How could all this have happened? And how the heck could I possibly go home and get my mind off this romantic interlude to focus on Operation Mom?

I didn't actually enter his apartment that day. I walked home reluctantly, inhaling the smell of Dev as I still clutched his baseball cap. My emotions a complete whirlwind, I tried to take stock of my feelings. Thinking about Dev had become a constant, persistent, and intrusive exercise that led me to acts of lunacy, like showing up at his home uninvited. But then, that led to this crazy episode on the landing. Was it good, bad, or just completely insane? To Dev's point earlier, maybe I wasn't the only one who needed to watch out for the crazies. Yet, no longer did I feel like I was at risk of being weeded out.

———

Triumphant and happy with the way the morning had turned out, I was ready to head to Gateway with Deepali. We called Aunty Maleeka to see if she'd go with us, but she said she was too busy schmoozing with celebrities that afternoon. Something about planning a Norah Jones concert for her Tata Cancer Relief Fund. On a regular afternoon, she'd invite me to join, and I'd probably take her up on it, but we both agreed that scoping out Rahul G had to be a higher priority.

"Look at it this way," she giggled. "We'll both be dedicating our afternoons to a good cause."

I suggested taking Dev with us, but Deepali wouldn't hear of it. "You see Dev on your own time, please."

"But he's offered to help me weed out the crazies," I insisted.

"The only crazy I'll need help weeding out is you," Deepali retorted as she stretched out a hand to observe her nails. "Somehow, I don't think he can help much with that, given he's responsible for it in the first place."

I stood there, gaping at her. I am still coming to grips with how to deal with statements like this.

Deepali complained all along the ride to Gateway. She can't stand crowds, and frankly, I don't blame her. When it's particularly hot and sticky outside, throwing yourself into the throng of humanity is the last thing you want to do. That said, I didn't mind much. Like many others, I love watching people; Gateway, being the favorite gathering spot for locals, was the ideal place to people-watch.

At some level, visiting Gateway takes me back to my happy place. On Sundays, when I was much younger and my parents were still together, Mom, Pops, and I would frequent the giant-balloon sellers to acquire one of their massive balloons that was sure to pop within the hour, most often resulting in me throwing a tantrum and crying a pool of tears. There was never an outing when we weren't attacked by beggars and by photographers who offered to commemorate our outing for a nominal sum, never a day when we wouldn't rub shoulders with over-inquisitive tourists—both Indian and foreign—but we didn't care. We'd indulge in the hubbub, delighting our taste buds with the artificial sweetness of candy floss while watching the boats depart the wharfs for Elephanta Island and Mandwa.

We'd even go during the monsoon when the rain subsided. The

water-laden winds would create a massive sea-swell against the wall running along the front of the Taj Mahal hotel. There was always a line-up of young boys who delighted in diving into the humungous waves. I'd want to follow suit, and when my parents refused to let me, it usually led to another hissy fit on my part.

To pacify me, Pops would take us for a ride in a Victoria—one of the gilded horse-drawn carriages that ply their trade along Apollo Bunder. Evening Victoria rides were the best, as we got to look at all the buildings lit up as we trot-trotted around Oval Maidan.

The day we had chosen to scope out Rahul G was particularly hot—a strong indicator that a monsoon was on its way. The area between Gateway and the Taj was infested with even more people than usual. Throngs of Chinese tourists had shown up on the classic Highlights of Mumbai tour. Their aim seemed to be to document the monument from every possible angle and get every single group member into every single photo.

"When I was younger, it was Japanese tourists," I said to Deepali. "Amazing how times have changed." I was surprised at myself—I sounded middle-aged and crabby.

By now, I was more focused on a particular channawalla who was upping his sales with a fake story about how, in 1911, Queen Mary keeled over and fainted at the sight of the awe-inspiring Gateway. Deepali turned out to be quite gullible.

"You've got to give them the benefit of the doubt, yaar," she said. "I mean, you can't tell what goes on in the head of these queen dames."

Queens or dames, Deepali? Make up your mind, they are two different titles. Stop inventing new vocabulary!

"Let me reassure you that there was no scope for fainting," I said, more than happy to launch into a history lesson. "King George V and Queen Mary didn't even see the real Gateway. They arrived here in 1911 and were greeted by a fake cardboard structure because the real thing wasn't fully built until 1924."

"Okay, so maybe that's why she fainted," Deepali said with an unduly serious look. "Because she was ultra-disappointed."

"Maybe," I replied. "Or maybe it was just that she couldn't deal with the reality of having arrived at a pigeon-infested mess." Looking around me, I felt I might faint too.

Our hero was all too obvious. He was the only person in sight who was wearing a trench coat in the heat of the afternoon sunshine. Granted, it was only a rain jacket, but even that could be too much for a 34-degree-Celsius day.

"Bechaara. Could do with some help with the wardrobe," Deepali said imperiously.

I could only guess that Rahul G had been influenced by the photograph at Trafalgar Square. The male model lover in it had no doubt been clad in something similar to ward off the cold.

You'd think the trench coat was his most distinguishing feature, but it wasn't. Positioned at the edge of the throngs and unmindful of the young hawkers tapping his shoulders every five minutes to entice him to buy chana and singh, or anything else they could possibly flog, he had a melancholy look about him. He stared intensely out into the ocean, at nothing in particular, his lips moving without uttering any sound. Deepali tried to make out his words, but she wasn't too good at lip reading.

"Who knows if he's actually saying something?" she said.

It seemed as if he was engaged in some kind of silent soliloquy to which only he was privy. Then suddenly, without any warning, he charged into the thick of the pigeons. They morphed from being an unruly throng of city birds gathering random pieces of chana from the ground to a chaotic cluster of dirty airborne feathers unleashing squawks of fear and possibly a few hundred forms of avian disease.

I looked at Deepali, startled. "This is what he calls romantic?"

"It's anything but, yaar!"

As the commotion subsided, one could see Rahul G emerge as a pleased apparition in the middle of all this, laughing at the pigeons as they dissipated into the skies. Suddenly, he began searching frantically around him, probably for the long-lost lover who he expected would show up out of the blue. No luck in sight, he hung his head and found his way back to the fringes of the crowd. There, he began to unleash a strange cooing sound as if to invite the pigeons back. And back they came.

After a few minutes of rest, he reenacted the entire performance from beginning to end. And again. And again. Bizarre though his actions were, we were clearly the only ones taken aback by them. Nobody else seemed to really care.

A young singhwalla noted our disbelief.

"He does this every day," he chuckled. "Rain or shine. He says he has a special relationship with the pigeons, and they understand his feelings."

Confirmed looney? The singhwalla definitely thought so. "Uska kuch to goodnight hua hai," he said, pointing to his head. "That coo-coo thing—he says that's his special language to talk to the pigeons." The singhwalla then proceeded to tell us how once, during a Saif–Kareena film shoot, the production crew had cleared away the pigeons. This so upset Rahul G that he stormed the set mid-shoot to coo-coo the pigeons back to what he felt was their rightful flocking ground.

I looked at Deepali and sighed. There really wasn't much to say.

"I'm leaving for Nainital in three days, Ilz," she said wearily. "We might need to put the project on hold till I get back."

I hung my head in despair as we rode the bus home. With all this help and input from Deepali and Dev, I was counting on finding someone for Mom. I had really hoped that migrating to OkCupid would be the answer to my prayers. But alas, we had expended huge amounts of energy without getting anywhere, and though I was getting places with Dev, Operation Mom seemed to be stuck at a stalemate. Perhaps it was time to change the name of the game from Operation Mom to Mission Impossible.

chapter
twenty-two

OPERATION MOM, JUST ONE DAY LEFT - LIFE BEGINS ON
THE OTHER SIDE OF DESPAIR

All I could focus on the next morning was the Rahul G episode and
the failure of Operation Mom. Even the thought of Dev wasn't enough
to distract me from my disappointment. I wanted desperately to cry on
someone's shoulder. Deepali and I had scheduled a game of badminton,
but that was a few hours into the day. Before that, she was busy with her
boyfriends. Besides, she'd had enough of my ranting all the way home
from the Taj. I called Aunty Maleeka instead.

"I told you not to expect anything, didn't I?" she said in a holier-
than-thou tone. "In retrospect, you have to consider the worth of pre-
screening the entire world before setting your mom up on a date."

"What, and risk her meeting a complete whack job?" I said. "That'd
be far worse, and I'd never forgive myself for it."

Aunty Maleeka softened a little at this. "No need to take the world
upon your shoulders. It's a pretty neat thing you are doing for your
mother. The problem is, you're treating it like an ICSE project."

"I just want to set her up," I wailed. "She's never going to learn to
chill out otherwise."

There was silence at the other end of the phone. I could sense that
she was in deep thought. "Don't worry," she said finally. "If it's a blind

date you want for her, a blind date you shall get. I'll go online and make it happen, and I'll make it happen before your Nainital deadline."

"But that's two days away!"

"Leave it to me," she insisted. "I can pull a rabbit out of a hat if I have to. Just give me the login details."

I wasn't sure Aunty Maleeka's rabbits were what Mom needed. If that were the case, she'd have been dating ages ago. But at that point, anything was worth a shot.

No sooner had I hung up the phone to wallow further than it rang again. What had she forgotten to say?

"I beg you, no loonies," I said sullenly.

"Er, bad time?" came a cute male teenage voice.

I must have been extra hormonal since the moment I recognized the caller, I practically burst into tears.

"Yes, sorry, I can't talk right now. Let me text you."

I hung up and thanked god for text messages. What a loser Dev would think I was if he heard my weepy voice. I shot out a quick summary of the Rahul G fiasco.

Dev: Sorry it's not going too well. I did try to warn you about those crazies. I didn't realize you'd got so into it so soon. On the Op Mom front, that is.

Neither did I, I thought. And I didn't realize I'd be so into *him* so soon either.

To make matters worse, Mom was acting rather strange. She seemed more irritable than usual. If I asked her a normal question, like "Do you plan to go to Amarsons on Saturday?" or "What time will you be home today?" she'd snap at me with the ferocity of a dog guarding its territory from an invader.

"Jesus, calm down already," I had said just that morning when she shot back at me for one of my random questions.

"Firstly, we are Hindu, and secondly, watch your tone, young missy," came the response. "I am sick of your sass."

I decided to unleash my frustrations on Deepali later that day over a game of badminton.

"I don't understand what sass she's referring to," I said.

"It's probably just menopause," Deepali replied coolly. "They all become like that at this age." She smashed the shuttlecock to the floor as if to say it was a done deal.

"She's only forty-five," I snapped, scooping up the shuttlecock and whacking it back at her ferociously. I didn't know who I was more annoyed with—Mom for snapping at me or Deepali for reducing the situation to middle-aged hormonal imbalance.

"Now's when it all begins. First hormones, then hot temper. Next will come the hot flashes," Deepali replied, ducking out of the way.

Menopause? Seriously? On one level, I thought Mom had been hot tempering and hot flashing all her life. Still, I didn't need this crap from Deepali.

"Mom's not hot flashing any more than you. It's summer, remember? There hasn't been any rain yet to cool things down," I had positioned myself in the middle of the court with my hands on my hips. "In fact, the weak monsoon is probably the culprit for hot flashes in the whole population. That does not mean all Indians are menopausing."

Deepali lifted her racket to serve. "Why take it so personally? You should see my mother. She's usually all doe eyed and soft, but of late, she's become so lethargic that she won't go anywhere. She's transformed into one mega lump on the butt of humanity. It's menopause, I'm convinced." She whacked the shuttlecock towards me.

Deepali was always so brutally honest about her mother, it was as though they weren't even related. I admired her for being able to look at the situation objectively.

I watched the shuttlecock soar through the air as it shot towards me. I had purchased it not too long ago, but it had become frayed and worn with use. I guess that's what happens with menopause too, and even though I was not convinced that it was the reason for Mom's outburst, I knew that the M word would make its presence known sooner or later. Sure, but what did that mean for Operation Mom?

——

I reached home to find Mom rummaging through my closet. I didn't question it at first—she has a habit of rearranging my clothes or scrutinizing the hem length of my skirts when I am not around. But that day, she was waiting to admonish me for something. Pangs of anxiety shot through me.

"Can I help you, Mom?" I asked, trying to look as innocent as possible.

"Funny you should ask," she responded gruffly. Then she turned around, folded her arms, and stared at me. "For what? For absolutely what, Ila?"

"Sorry, Mom. I don't follow."

"You certainly don't. That I accede to."

She hovered around my bedpost, twisting her left hand around her right wrist, a sure sign of stress.

"All my life I had imagined that you would follow me. I silently hoped for it even, but that clearly is not destined to be."

I examined her carefully. Where had this sudden drama sprung from?

"And maybe it's not entirely a bad thing," she continued, "for who is to say that I have the most admirable qualities on the planet? Now, I haven't asked you to enroll in a high-level academic summer course or anything, though that should perhaps have been the case. But to idle away your summer days in trivial pursuit?"

"Mom, what are you talking about?"

Mom pulled out my black-and-white tank top from the laundry basket, the one I had worn the day before during our jaunt down to Gateway. Oh no, was she getting on my case for wearing a tank top in public?

"Look, Ila, this interest you have developed in clothes and make-up..."

I looked at her suspiciously. "Yes?"

"It's a little out of character, isn't it?"

What was she getting at? Was she saying I shouldn't have an interest in clothes? She looked at me quizzically. I peered quizzically back at her, wishing she'd just say what she wanted to say.

"Is this about Ali Zafar again?" I asked, throwing my bag down in a huff. "Because, you know, I have not been doing much of that, lately."

"You haven't," Mom said with a sigh. For a moment, I thought she was relieved, but then she looked me straight in the eye with a piercing expression. "What *have* you been doing?"

Er, how was I to answer that? My silence was probably telling.

"Where were you?" she drilled.

"When?"

"Today."

"Today when?"

"Right now."

"Playing baddy with Deepali."

She wrinkled her forehead and made her stare sharper. "And yesterday?"

"Also with Deepali. We went to Gateway."

"What? Two girls alone in those eve-teasing crowds?"

"We weren't alone," I lied instantly.

"Who else did you have with you?"

"Aunty Maleeka," I said, making a note to call and give Aunty Maleeka a heads up about it right after Mom and I parted ways. "Besides we weren't really at Gateway. We went to the Taj." Oof, why was she forcing me to lie?

"Bookstore?" she asked.

"Cake shop." I shot back.

"Hmm. Like more sugar is going to help you stay trim."

"Speak for yourself, Mom," I snapped.

Mom stared at me with wide, enraged eyes. "Not a nice way to speak to your mother."

I scoffed. "Well, you seem to have a free reign to call me a fatso."

Mom shot me a startled look. "I didn't call you a fatso."

"You might as well have. That's what you meant," I said, sulking. "In case you hadn't noticed, I am the one who has been pushing for us to go to fitness classes—spinning, flamenco, and what not."

"Under normal circumstances, I might be happy that you want to stay fit or that you are taking an interest in clothes and make-up," Mom said, biting her lip as she paced up and down the room. Then she paused and turned to look me in the eye. "But are circumstances normal, Ila?"

I opened my mouth to say something, but nothing came out. Mom looked me straight in the eye with perhaps the most intense expression I have ever seen.

"Is there something you are not telling me?" she asked.

Yes. Most definitely. "No, of course not."

"Are you sure there is nothing abnormal going on?"

Would I tell her if there were? Probably not.

"Abnormal?" I repeated.

"Abnormal, deviant, errant?"

"For example," Mom continued, yanking up the lid of the laundry basket. "What's this?" She pulled out Dev's muted red baseball cap. My breath froze in my lungs and then rushed out in a sigh I couldn't contain as the recollection of the previous day's episode on the landing settled in. I'd brought his baseball cap home, and Sakkubai must have picked it up and put it in the washing.

"I was waiting for *you* to tell me about this," she said, "because, really, Ila Isham, that is all you needed to do."

"Sorry, Mom," I said, sheepishly looking at the floor. "I know you don't approve of boys in the house."

Mom looked at me thoughtfully. "You know, I am actually pleased to see you are hanging out with a real boy rather than a poster of Ali Zafar. I just don't approve of him being in the house alone with you."

"Oh, no, it's not like that," I said, turning bright red. "Dev just came over to help me with a...an internet situation. He must've forgotten it here."

Mom's face turned bright red at the words. She jumped at me like a she-tiger at its prey. "Internet? Internet what?"

"It was for Deepali. He's into her, you know, not me," I said, frantically trying to think of a halfway-believable story. Mom grunted disbelievingly.

"No, seriously!" I protested. "He wanted to buy her a gift and needed help."

Mom wrung her hands and said quietly: "I wasn't born yesterday, Ila."

Quite right, she wasn't. I had to do better.

"Seriously," I insisted. "We'd have gone to Akbarally's, but he wanted to get her something different, so we ended up researching...Amazon."

Lie upon lie!

Mom pursed her lips and resumed her pacing and wrist-wringing. "It doesn't add up. Your storytelling skills are not that great. What are you hiding?"

If only it was so easy for me to speak the truth. "Mom, I think you just need to chillax."

"I can't," she squawked. "There are way too many changes that women go through at this age."

Changes? Deepali was right. Mom was freaking out because of the 'big M'. It *had* reared its ugly head. I needed to show her support.

"I know, Mom. You are bound to be more irritable these days, I understand."

By this time, she was all riled up. "What are you talking about?"

"Menopause."

Mom looked at me, gobsmacked.

"Who said anything about menopause?" she exclaimed.

"Well, when you said *changes*, I thought..."

"I was referring to changes in *you*!"

"I am a girl, Mom, not a woman." I don't know why I was offended by the suggestion.

"In the Isham household, you are a girl; but in the eyes of a man, you are a woman," she said sternly. "I just don't want you to do anything stupid that you will regret. So, you need to be upfront with me. D'you hear?"

I stood there, staring at the floor, wondering how exactly we'd got there. Was she pissed about Dev? That in his eyes, I might be a woman? Was it, in fact, the mention of the M word that had vexed her? Or was she cranky that I had suggested that she was cranky because I had brought up the M word?

What I failed to realize as Mom marched out of the room huffing like a beleaguered steam engine was that it wasn't she, it was *I* who was missing the cues.

chapter
twenty-three

OPERATION MOM, JUST ONE DAY LEFT (CONTINUED) - SOMETIMES THAT'S ALL LIFE IS, ONE DESPERATE ACT AFTER ANOTHER!

"Wouldn't *you* be upset if someone called *you* fatso?" I asked Pops, seizing the opportunity to needle Mom. I was seated in the passenger seat of the car, so I didn't have to deal with her looking me in the eye.

"Which jackass called you that? Tell me now, and I'll have his head," Pops said, stepping on the accelerator. His perma-wrinkled forehead furrowed deeper into a frown as he considered the idea of some guy crapping all over his baby girl's happiness.

I don't think he actually means it, but Pops has a way of saying things that he thinks will make him sound extra macho. Mom insists it's a latent trait that has come alive since they broke up. She doesn't miss any opportunity to point out his shortcomings.

"Instant reaction!" Mom shrieked from the back seat. "Focus on the road. Do you want to kill us?"

Pops knows it's best to ignore her. It is the only way to keep the peace at home, and given that he doesn't exactly live with us, keeping the peace is imperative. That way, he's welcomed to visit at all times. Don't get me wrong. As I said before, Mom and Pops have a surprisingly amicable relationship for a divorced couple, but there are those few choice moments when he'll say something that makes her fly off the handle. Typically, this is followed by a massive argument, and subsequently, she throws him right out of the house. Sometimes, she doesn't let him come back for a month at a time, but then when she does, it's usually quite amicable again.

I decided to switch gears myself. "No, Pops, nobody called me that except for me."

"You called yourself a fatso?" Pops said, scratching his chin. "Where did you get that idea? You're not in the least bit fat."

"I'm not skinny," I pointed out.

"You're not supposed to be, baby girl."

"But I was once."

"Yeah, when you were six."

Pops makes it a point to avoid conversation about weight gain when Mom is around. It's a sure-fire way to piss her off. He says it's the case with all women. If you tell them they are fat, they get upset with you; if you tell them they are not, they go on about it anyway. I could tell, though, that he wasn't quite sure how to handle the topic with me. Pops generally gets confused between Ila 'his baby girl' and Ila 'the woman-in-progress'. Either way, it was a topic I wasn't going to let go of, but my reason was different. I wanted to annoy Mom for being mean to me earlier that day.

"Pops, the fact that I have gone from being skinny to not-skinny means that my next stop could well be fatso. We have a propensity, you know," I said.

Pops glanced at me, exasperated.

"On Mom's side of the family. Look at Naani. She went from being positively hot in her thirties, to fat in her forties, to obese in her fifties. And now Mom's heading that way too."

"Ila!" Mom snapped.

Ah, there it was, the answer to my provocation.

"Well, you refuse to come spinning or anything with me."

"What are you going on about? I came to flamenco class with you."

"That was a one-off workshop," I said petulantly. "You don't exactly go the extra mile to get off your couch."

I noted the forced silence from Pops and used it as an opportunity to read a text from Aunty Maleeka.

Aunty Maleeka: I have figured it out. Blind date set with Col Jhun-jhunvala. Coming now. Where are you?

No way. She'd figured it out in a matter of, what, four hours? And *Jhunjhunvala*? What was the need to establish pseudonyms?

Mom shot me a sarcastic eyebrow arch. "Seriously? Is this all about *me* becoming fat?"

"Yes."

"Nothing else?"

"No."

"Ila, please don't assume I can't read the fine print."

"What fine print?" I asked innocently.

"Do I really look like I was born yesterday?" she snarled. "You could at the very least come up with a better lie!"

"Lie? What lie?"

Pops pulled the car over to the side of the road, stopped the engine, and looked me in the eye as the sun beat down on the waves at Worli Seaface. I texted Aunty Maleeka our exact location.

"Sweetie pie, first of all, about your alleged fatness—"

"It's not alleged!" I barked at him.

"Look, you're not a fatty. Neither is your mom. Also..."

Also what? What else could possibly be more humiliating than this, especially at a time in life when I was getting her to transition? And what lie was she going on about?

"You have been acting kind of odd, of late," Pops said.

Odd? Me? What was he going on about? And who was he to comment, considering he was not even around most of the time? How did Pops have the audacity to call me odd? He had brown sideburn touch-ups that didn't exactly blend in with the rest of his salt-and-pepper head. What could be odder than that?

"Mom says..." he began.

"Did Mom prime you to say all this to me?" I accused. "Because apparently I am lying about her calling me a fatso?"

"No, no! That's not it. The thing is, Ila, we are concerned about *your* concern over...well, things like this weight issue and stuff. It's not like you at all. We are concerned about what it could possibly be leading to."

I looked at Pops in utter disbelief. Was he for real? What if I were a guy and wanted to train hard so I could have six pack abs like every other male model in sight? Somehow, I doubted he'd get on my case then.

"No, that's not it. Is there *someone* you need to impress?" he asked.

I opened my mouth but closed it as I couldn't find anything to say.

He broke the silence with a nervous laugh, attempting to crack a joke. "Apart from your old man, of course."

There I was, desperately trying to set my mother up on a date, and it had backfired into her thinking that I was trying to lose weight in order to impress some guy! I couldn't resist giggling. Pops wanted to laugh too; I could tell, but when he looked over at Mom—who was staring at me, alarmed—for permission to react, but he didn't get any. He stared at his shoes instead.

But the biggest question was how to get them off my back. I collected my thoughts, wondering what to say. A young hawker came to my rescue. He showed up at the car window flashing a copy of *Stardust*.

"Only fifty rupees, Sahib," he implored. "Ek copy toh le lo."

I glanced at the cover, which had a picture of Tina Ambani on a brown leather armchair, trying to look corporate, which she looked anything but. Then again, you can't really blame her for looking like a housewife. Deepali loves to rag on Punjus, but I couldn't help thinking that when Gujju women reach a certain age and level of fatness, they all begin to look the same. Wait a minute—Deepali was my answer! I smiled to myself as Pops shook his head to dismiss the boy.

"I am not chasing anyone. Well, not for myself," I proclaimed.

My parents stared at each other awkwardly, waiting for the other to speak first. Finally, Mom broke the silence.

"So, you *are* chasing someone?"

Did she know about Dev? I quickly shifted gears into the Deepali-Dev story I had just created as an alibi.

"No." I responded promptly.

"Well then, what exactly can we glean from your statement?"asked Mom.

"That I am actually helping Deepali."

"Deepali?" Pops clarified.

Mom thumped the flat of her palm against her forehead. "Why does that girl need to impress someone when she has already clearly impressed those good-for-nothing boys who keep chasing her?"

I took offense to that—Dev is not a good-for-nothing boy!

"That's the whole point, Mom." I said. "She's not impressed by their good-for-nothingness."

"Er, I know I have missed the recent developments, but seriously, what does this have to do with being fat?" Pops asked trepidatiously. It can't be easy being the only dude among a bunch of highly-strung, neurotic women. Or perhaps, it isn't easy being a guy among women.

"Don't you get it, Pops?" I said, looking at him like he had totally lost it. "You think I am concerned about weight gain, but Deepali is the one needs to get in shape. She's my best friend, so I need to support her. But, unlike Mom, I hate exercise, so I wanted her to come with me to support my attempt to support Deepali."

Pops bought the story. "You know, Veena, she's growing up. This is probably part of just some normal teenage development."

"No, it isn't. Normal teenagers don't use that method," she said, looking mysterious and petulant at the same time.

Why was she speaking in riddles? "What method?" I asked.

No answer came. My parents continued to stare at each other in silent communication. A few moments later, Mom broke the silence again.

"Ila, even if you are helping Deepali impress some guy, this *thing*... it's still not good enough."

"What do you mean? What *thing*?" I asked, exasperated.

"It's too much. And if she is the reason, well, then we are concerned about her safety," Mom said.

"Her safety? All she is doing is trying to lose weight."

Mom slapped her hands down on the top of the back seat, now addressing Pops. "This is rubbish. We need to talk to her parents, JJ."

What? Talk with Deepali's parents to express concern over her so-called fat issues, which I had just made up? The story, though fun at first, was not getting me anywhere except deeper into a black hole. Besides, even if Deepali was on board with it, her parents' involvement would complicate things—a lot.

"Is this stressing you out, Ilz?" Pop said, noting my silence.

Stressing me out? That's just putting it mildly. I decided to use the only option that came to my mind: change the direction of the conversation.

"A woman under stress is not immediately concerned with finding solutions to her problems. Rather, she seeks relief by expressing herself and takes comfort in being understood," I stated.

"What the...? Where'd you get that nonsense?" Pops asked.

"From Mom."

"Stupid question," he said, smiling at her through the rear-view mirror.

Mom sat there with folded arms and a cross expression. I smirked, knowing I had hit her weak spot. All this talk about stress was bound to stress her out further, so I decided to continue with my soliloquy.

"Stress can also arise out of the confusion created when one's mind overrides the heart's desire to choke the living daylights out of some jerk who desperately deserves it," I continued.

"Baby girl, what are you going on about?" Pops said.

Mom, on the other hand, had lost her cool. "My nerves have hit their highest point," she shrieked, then ran her hands through her hair before closing them in a clasp behind her neck. "This girl has done me in!"

There we go again—Kyunki Maa Bhi Abhi Scriptwriter Hai! She is a great TV soap scriptwriter and certainly knows how to act out the scenes herself.

I turned towards Mom. "Well?"

"Let's go home," she relented.

"Great idea," Pops said, turning the key in the ignition and looking into his side-view mirror.

Pops is not a bad driver by any means, unlike Mom who simply can't be trusted behind a wheel, but given his usual bout of attention deficits, he often doesn't pay attention to the finer details. No sooner had he begun to reverse the car than a blood-curdling scream practically shattered my ear drums. The car came to a screeching halt, and the odor of burning rubber from the car tires floated our way.

"What the—" he yelled, his neck turning sharply and squinting into the rear-view mirror.

"You almost killed me, JJ!" shrieked a familiar voice.

Aunty Maleeka stood at the trunk of the car, looking even more buxom than usual in a white, spaghetti-strapped maxi dress. In her hands was a yapping Mitzy, who looked more like an accessory than a dog. Though she had just deafened the entire neighborhood with her screams, she looked as if she didn't have a care in the world.

Mom shook her head with a 'tsk tsk.' It was her tell-all way of acknowledging that she'd had way too much experience with Aunty Maleeka's fake screams over the years and recognized that this was a ruse.

Not exactly someone who cherished his moments with Aunty Maleeka, Pops held his head in his hands. "Great!" he groaned. "Just when I thought I could exit the insanity."

"Maleeka, how did you know we were here?" Mom demanded.

Aunty Maleeka chuckled as she calmed Mitzy. "Didn't you tell them I was coming?" she said to me. "You guys are seriously too dysfunctional to even communicate."

Aunty Maleeka broke into uncouth laughter and glided to the side window nearest to where Mom was sitting. She continued, "You're so preoccupied with your arguments that you're using it as an excuse to kill poor Mitzy and me." She cuddled her pooch and planted a kiss on his ear. "Hai na, Mitzy?"

"Sorry, Maleeka, my bad," Pops said, gritting his teeth and staring into the steering wheel. "I should have been more careful."

Aunty Maleeka was unfazed. Any opportunity to converse with him was an opportunity to wind Mom up—it was a pastime she cherished. Mom rolled her eyes as Aunty Maleeka opened the car door and slid into the back seat alongside her.

Pops eyed Mitzy suspiciously through the rear-view mirror. He wasn't a dog person. It didn't matter most of the time as he'd simply ignore any dog he came into contact with, but unlike most dogs who also ignored him, Mitzy was a different species. He sensed Pops' anti-dog stance and mistook it for hostility. Rather than dealing with it by yapping or snarling, Mitzy would growl softly and wee all over Pops' trouser at the first chance he got. The last time it happened was at one of Aunty Maleeka's parties, while he was busy socializing. At any rate, there was no danger of that now with Pops in the front seat.

"I'm so glad you came, Aunty Maleeka," I said. "Mom and Pops were discussing the stress in my life."

"Oh, great, can I play?" Aunty Maleeka asked, elated.

"This is not a game of Monopoly or charades," Mom grumbled. "It's about Ila."

Aunty Maleeka raised her eyes questioningly. "Really? Pray do tell more."

"Ila is really stressed about gaining weight," Pops said.

"Weight gain has nothing to do with stress," Aunty Maleeka said before I had a chance to respond. "Stress is a by-product of insomnia. It happens when you wake up screaming, and you realize you haven't fallen asleep yet."

"Sounds more like depression to me," I said, intrigued by her description.

"No, depression is when you find that you can't wake up," she replied.

I couldn't tell what she was trying to convey, but then, donkey's years of knowing her had taught us all that one doesn't attempt to 'comprehend' Aunty Maleeka—one simply listens for entertainment. And so I did, and I added my two bits of inanity: "Or that when you do wake up, you are still tired."

The conversation was going way above Pops' head.

"Wait, you are not depressed are you, baby girl?" he asked with sudden concern.

"Ila depressed? Not a chance" Aunty Maleeka said with her characteristic cackle. "We've been hanging out quite a bit lately, so I know." She winked at me.

"Now *that* puts me in depression," Pops said under his breath, putting on his ugly face once again.

"JJ!" Mom barked. She was obviously sensitive about her friend's feelings.

"It's okay, Veena. JJ is just joking," Aunty Maleeka said. "Aren't you, JJ?" She looked at him a little threateningly.

"Yeah, joking; I'm joking," came the reply.

Now, Mom jumped in to defend Pops. Honestly, she gets very confused in situations where everyone is in the room, or in this case, the car. She can't decide whom to stand up for or whose side to take. The good thing was, the focus had shifted from berating me.

"Maleeka, if you are going to chide him like that, blowing things out of proportion, then of course, he will submit and say he's joking." Mom rolled her eyes even more.

Aunty Maleeka looked at Mom as though she had gone bonkers. "Did you say *chide*? Seriously, Veena, nobody talks like that. Save your literary fundas for your books. Besides, since when has JJ ever been submissive to anyone but you?"

"Hey, hey, ladies. I'm still here, remember?" Pops said.

I, too, was amazed by their flippant banter about him in his presence. Mitzy began growling at Pops.

"Cut it out, Mitzy," he yelled.

Mitzy jumped off Aunty Maleeka's lap and squished himself behind the front seat with this miserable look on his face.

"Oh, stop being such a drama queen," Mom said, looking disdainfully down at the self-pitying dog.

Drama queen. I remembered Dev's words yesterday. And the scene on the landing outside his apartment. And that swoony kiss! But right then, the awakened dream state I was about to enter into was disrupted by Aunty Maleeka's protest. "Hey, that's my Mitzy!"

"You stop being a drama queen, too." Mom was glaring at Aunty Maleeka, who decided to toe the line and change the subject.

"So, it's like this. We have a date."

Mom groaned. "*We*?"

"You, me, your date, and my date." She looked at me and winked.

There it was—my chance to jump in and build up the drama. "A double date?" I asked, feigning complete ignorance. "Wow, Aunty Maleeka, that's great."

"What's so great about that?" Pops asked wryly. He clearly wasn't amused.

Mom was clearly not happy with her best friend's announcement. She began to twist her left hand around her right wrist.

"Who are these so-called dates?" she asked suspiciously.

"Well, my date is blind," Aunty Maleeka replied. "As in a blind date. Nothing wrong with his eyesight. And your date is, well..."

"Yes?"

"The truth is," Aunty Maleeka admitted, "I have to figure out who your date is."

"Oh, good," Mom said, throwing her hands up in relief. "Why don't we simplify the situation by turning the double date into a single one? You go on your blind date without me."

"That's not going to work." Aunty Maleeka contorted her face. "You are my friend. You are supposed to support me."

Dad glanced at me from the corner of his eye with a mildly disgusted expression. I knew exactly what was going through his head—why was everyone yanking on Mom's chain for her support?

Mom was indignant. "I am supporting you, but I don't want to be a kebab mein haddi."

"In a double date situation, there's no question of haddi. It all just becomes one big kebab. And it's not an unreasonable request, you know, Veena. After all, I was there for you during your erotomaniacal stalking days," Aunty Maleeka insisted.

Mom rolled her eyes at the reference. "I see that Deepali has got under your skin."

Aunty Maleeka shrugged, "Maybe."

"By the way, you do realize that in all her psych research, she mischaracterized the syndrome? Erotomania is a delusion in which a woman believes that another person, typically of higher social status, is in love with *her,* and not a situation in which she is *stalking* him."

It was now Aunty Maleeka's turn to roll her eyes. "Details-shmee-tails. Why get so picky about these things, Veena? The point is that I was there for you when you wanted to stalk George Michael."

Dad and I shot a glance at each other, shaking our heads. The next several seconds of dead air made for an awkward gap in the conversation. Can't say anyone was to blame. I mean, how do you carry on a conversation that has got to this level of ludicrousness?

Aunty Maleeka tried again. "Come on, Veena, I need your help to break the ice!"

But Mom knew that breaking ice had never been her buddy's problem.

"Listen, Ice Queen, are you going to play ball or just leave me in the lurch?" Aunty Maleeka asked, feigning hurtful annoyance.

Aunty Maleeka knew that Mom is the very last person in the world who would leave her in the lurch. She was diving deep into the drama.

"Where am I supposed to even begin to find a date?" Mom asked, pouting.

Pops took it upon himself to get involved in the conversation. "I can help out. I can be Veena's date!"

Of all the directions in which I had envisioned the conversation could turn, this certainly wasn't one. Was he out of his mind? Mom clearly wasn't expecting this voluntary display of helpfulness either. She started with a look of surprise that quickly morphed to mild annoyance. Pops' face darkened as he caught her expression and immediately tried to make amends.

"Just to help Maleeka," he said, clearing his throat. "A sort of pretend date?"

I was quite distressed as my mind's eye caught a glimpse of a very real hell. Aunty Maleeka, on the other hand, perked up big time.

"JJ, that's an amazing idea." She turned to Mom all pumped. Mom responded by crossing her arms into an 'X'.

"Tell her, JJ," she said to Pops. "Tell her not to screw up my chance with this guy!"

Mitzy began to yap ferociously but shut up when Pops wagged his finger at him equally wildly.

"Come on," he said to Mom, smiling sneakily. "It might be fun."

Mom scrunched up her face. "If I wanted entertainment, I would go to the movies."

"But this *is* like going to the movies," Aunty Maleeka exclaimed. "Only *you* will be on set."

Mom was beginning to fume. I could practically see the smoke emerging from her nostrils.

"JJ, were you ever planning to take us home?" she snarled. "Or are we going to sit around in Worli Seaface for the rest of our lives?"

Pops made the kind of face he wears when he's been in the presence of and dealt with Aunty Maleeka and Mom's for too long. He's always said that Aunty Maleeka is zany and neurotic and that Mom feeds off of her energy. So as a result of hanging out with her, Mom has also become significantly more neurotic since her forties.

I had no idea that neurosis could be contagious. Pops insists that it's just an excuse cooked up by forty-something women to conduct an adult version of the girl in *The Exorcist*.

My phone lit up right that very moment—it was Dev and Deepali, both texting in a group chat.

Dev: How's it going?

Deepali: Any action?

I took it upon me to respond.

Me: It's the weirdest thing. To satisfy her infrastructure needs for a double-date, Aunty M has somehow convinced P to go on a so-called 'pretend' date with M.

Deepali: 'So-called'??!!!

Me: Shut up Deepali, they are separated.

Deepali: Yeah, like Siamese twins.

Dev: Wait, what? Why would she do that? And why would he agree?

Me: I don't get it either, but knowing Aunty M, she's got some trick up her sleeve.

Dev: Translation please?

Deepali: Impossible, Dev, I told you they were dysfunctional!

Alas, she was right. Truer words were never spoken!

Pops revved up the engine, checking the mirrors carefully this time as he backed up the car. The ride home had Mom and Aunty Maleeka arguing about the wisdom behind a single versus a double date, interspersed with odd monosyllabic comments from Pops. As we entered our building's parking lot, Mom finally put a brake on Aunty Maleeka's plan.

"Thanks, but no thanks," she said. "I really don't need the added drama in my life."

At some level, though, I thought she actually did. Need the drama, I mean.

Pops insisted on parking the car and coming upstairs. He wanted to talk with Mom in private, but she wasn't keen. She muttered in agitation for a good ten minutes in the building lobby, causing me to become even more anxious. Seriously, didn't she know better than to throw a fit in front of the watchmen? Before long, the gossip-mongering building staff would spread the news like wildfire. Finally, in the interest of keeping the peace, Mom relented. She knew she was in everyone's bad books—Pops', mine, and now Aunty Maleeka's.

Sakkubai opened the door and gave Pops a toothless grin. Even now, she thought he was the best thing since chaat masala. Much to Mom's dismay, of course. She couldn't stand it that Sakkubai continued to fuss over her estranged-husband, whom she had gone through a lot of pain to separate from.

Mom and Pops quickly disappeared into the kitchen. I finally had a chance to ask Aunty Maleeka what was going on.

"Either I am a complete idiot, or you are trying to set Mom up with Pops," I said indignantly.

"You are a complete idiot," came Aunty Maleeka's quick response.

"Excuse me?"

"Okay, fine, you are not. Here's the deal—Veena has been set up with Colonel Jhunjhunvala, who's showing up to meet her tomorrow from Pune, but if we tell her that, she's going to kick and scream and refuse to go."

"Seriously? His name is Jhunjhunvala? I thought you were talking gibberish because you couldn't remember his name."

"Yes, Jhunjhunvala. Maybe his ancestors used to make payals for a living. Anyway, this way, she thinks I am set up with a blind date—who is actually the colonel—but I need her to come with me as for support. Because she can't come alone, your Pops goes with her. All this time, she thinks she is going on a pretend date with him just to keep me company, but then when we reach the venue, we just flip it."

Wow! All this time I had been worried that Aunty Maleeka was going rogue, but now I realized that there was a method to her madness. I had to admit; it was a pretty brilliant plan and probably the only way she could have got Mom to concede. Yet, the finer details were nagging me.

"You mean she finds out that she's actually there to meet Colonel, and you are on a date with Pops?" I clarified.

"Exactly!" Aunty Maleeka proceeded to tickle Mitzy behind his ears.

At one level, the plan was genius. Mom flipping out when she realized that she'd been duped was the least of my worries. She was unlikely to throw a tantrum in public. But I couldn't reconcile the fact that Aunty Maleeka was effectively setting herself up on a date with Pops. It just didn't seem right for many reasons. Besides, even if she fancied Pops, she probably didn't realize how he always avoided her like the plague. Aunty Maleeka needed to take just one look at me to read my thoughts.

"Ila, you don't honestly think I am trying to set myself up with your father, do you? Don't be stupid. He would never stand for it, and neither would Veena. It's just that this way, she can't possibly say no."

"But she just did," I pointed out.

"That's going to change."

"What do you mean?"

"Why do you think they just left the room?" Aunty Maleeka took my chin in her hand and squeezed it affectionately. "So mature, yet so much to learn."

Mitzy yapped. He always did that when Aunty Maleeka gave attention to anyone else.

She continued, "Right now, JJ is giving her a lecture on what a lousy friend she is to me, given that I have known her all these years and blah, blah, blah. She'll never be able to say no to him. And my work—sorry, *our* work—will be done."

Aunty Maleeka was a true tormented genius! She knew exactly how to get under Mom's skin—and Pops' too. Within moments, Mom reemerged from the kitchen with an I-really-can't-stand-the-idea-but-I-am-doing-this-for-you expression. Mission accomplished! We were back on track!

chapter
twenty-four

OPERATION MOM, THE FINALE - HOPE IS A DESPERATE FEELING

There are moments in your life that you anticipate. You spend days, weeks, sometimes even years, preparing for them. There's a latent anticipation, and you are convinced that this is one of the most important events in your life. Then, you pray hard and harder that you don't do something to screw it up.

The moment of Mom's big date was finally upon us, and I was extremely nervous. I felt like the mother of a bride on her wedding day.

Deepali, Aunty Maleeka, and I had gone over the plan a hundred times. As far as Mom was concerned, Pops and Aunty Maleeka would both show up at home so that he could drive both ladies to Indigo, the designated dinner venue. Little did she know that, in actuality, Colonel Jhunjhunvala would show up at her front door. This little nuance was Deepali's idea, which I agreed because it would offer us a front-row view of Mom's reaction.

Aunty Maleeka had not been so enthusiastic, however. "I would rather get Veena out of her comfort zone," she said. "She's too control-oriented at home. If anything goes wrong, chances are, she'll send us all packing and won't leave the place herself."

It's true, Mom is the quintessential dog who loves barking in her own yard, but what could possibly go wrong? We'd all but had a dress rehearsal. Unless, of course, the colonel chickened out of the situation. But judging by his texts, this didn't seem likely. Aunty Maleeka could not be relied on for due diligence, so I'd texted the colonel back and forth for the last twenty-four hours. Reading between the lines, he appeared to be quite agog.

"I'll be there with a single rose," he'd said in one text. "Red, to indicate the passion in my heart." The last guy who made comments like this was Rahul G. I shuddered at the thought.

However, the Colonel seemed more cheesy than psychotic. Of all the guys we'd screened over the course of the last two weeks, he appeared to be the best bet. Besides, Aunty Maleeka was underwriting the whole deal since she'd found him in the first place.

Dev wasn't so sure about the red rose. "Sounds kind of cliché," he said when I called to give him the low-down. "The guy hasn't even met her, and he's already into red roses? He might not be crazy, but he could turn out to be colossally boring."

Deepali held me back from allowing Dev to check Colonel Jhunjhunvala's full profile. She insisted that, whether or not he was qualified to make a judgement call, he'd only distract me from following through with the project we had taken forever to get off the ground.

"It's a matter of just one more day," Deepali said. "After that, I'll be in Nainital, and the Ishams can both reinvigorate their sex... uh, *romance* potential—the older Isham with Jhunjhun and younger one with Dev."

Eww! That said, in some way, truer words were never spoken. I just couldn't believe I was hearing these words these words, in such a matter-of-fact way.

"Deepali, are you giving me your blessing?" I asked.

"Blessing for what?"

"Dev, of course!"

"Ilz," she said, staring at her nails in that Deepali-esque way. "Neither am I Dev's mother, nor am I your family pundit. Who am I to give blessings?"

"You're my best friend!" I shrieked. "Dev is...well, he and I...you know..."

"Spit it out, Ilz!"

"What I mean is, are you sure you've benched him? You're okay with he and I being together?" I asked her sincerely.

"Are you kidding, Ilz? Have you not realized by now that this has been a double whammy approach to ridding both you and your mom of your classic Isham obsessiveness? Why d'you think Dev has been bread crumbing you all this time? He was interested in you all along. And I was interested in him being interested in you, and having you be interested in him. Anything but that godawful Ali Zafar!"

So it was a ploy all along! "Deepali, you sneaky little... brilliant strategic planner! As always, her smarts had reigned. She had carefully craft the entire sequence of events, knowing what to do to make her plan reach fruition. And it *had* actually worked!

Right that moment, I loved her more than anything, and I threw my arms around her in a massive bear hug.

"Calm your heels, woman!" she laughed.

I whipped out my phone to text him instantly.

Me: I think you should be here tomorrow to witness the colonel for real.

My fingers fidgeted with the phone cover as I waited for the grey bubble, indicating a response in the making. Luckily it was just a matter of moments.

Dev: Hey you!

Hey you? A shiver of paradise radiated its way through my torso and down to my fingertips.

Dev: I should probably sit this one out. Not sure that I'd be entirely useful. I'd love to be a fly on the wall though. Or better still, see you the next day to get the blow by blow in person.

In person—we could arrange that, I thought giddily. Just thinking of Dev put me in my happy place. It was my turn to throw open my arms and sing on the mountain tops like Maria in the *Sound of Music*. Yes, I was dying to see him again!

———

The colonel had not posted a picture on his OkCupid profile, so all through the day, I had done little beyond visualizing the moment he would walk through the door. Like some kind of fairy tale, I envisioned him to be the perfect Prince Charming who, dressed in a khaki military uniform and armed with his long-stemmed red rose, would sweep Mom off her feet. Frankly, daydreaming about it was enough to sweep me off mine.

"Give me a break," Deepali said when I shared my thoughts with her. "Why would he be wearing godawful khaki? It's not like he's still in the Army."

"I know, but the thought of a man in uniform gives me goosebumps."

"You've been watching too many American Navy Seal shows," Deepali said, remaining unimpressed. "Don't confuse patriotism with romance."

She was right, but I couldn't readily admit to that. "No, those uniforms are something else," I insisted.

"The only kind of military guy who looks good in a uniform is a jawan off to fight the next war," she said. "Jhunjhunvala is a retired colonel, and that's an entirely different cup of tea."

I didn't think about that. What if he turned out to be a doddering old man with a walking stick? Like those bridge-playing military types at the CCI club on Friday evenings? My apprehension must have showed.

"That said, it's absolutely Aunty Veena's cup of tea," Deepali said, always quick to smooth things over.

I looked at her questioningly. How did she know about Mom's tea preferences?

"You know, yaar–kadak. Nothing needed to dilute the flavor."

I frowned, not sure if the metaphor was appropriate. It could be interpreted in many ways.

———

Mom emerged from her room at seven sharp. She wore a silken black sari with a jaamewaar border in red and burnt orange. Her hair was combed back in the modern Hema Malini style that the hairdresser at Silloo's had so painstaking taught me, and I had, in turn, taught Mom. Despite her face being bereft of make-up, save for a thin line of kajal on her eyelids and some translucent lip gloss, she looked absolutely ravishing. Even Deepali did a double take.

"Aunty Veena, you're smokin' hot!" Deeply exclaimed.

"Hot-schmot," Mom growled, her head held high and cheeks flushed. At first, I thought she was embarrassed by the compliment and was blushing out of modesty, but then I realized that she was actually red-faced. This meant she was either upset or angry—or both.

"Now, Deepali," she barked.

I knew it. Something was wrong.

"Aunty Veena?" Deepali asked, eyebrow raised at Mom's apparent agitation.

"Let's get this perfectly straight. I am thrilled that you and Ila are such close friends, but 100 percent full disclosure, this is *not* going to fly," she said, wrenching her pallav over her shoulder.

Deepali was dumbfounded, as was I. Mom directed her gaze towards me.

"Ila, don't play around with me. I haven't said anything yet, but I am no fool. Here we are at the crucial moment, and I will have you know that I am livid."

"Mom, what crucial moment are you talking about?" I asked.

"The moment *he* walks in!"

She was nervous about the double date. "Mom, it's just a date," I said gently.

"*Just* a date? All this drama for days on end, and my daughter tells me it's *just* a date?" Mom looked like she was going to explode into a thousand pieces.

Luckily, the doorbell rang right then. Before Sakkubai could shuffle up to it, Mom marched up to the door with an overly authoritative air.

I crossed my fingers that it wasn't the colonel already. Poor thing, she would crap all over him before he even had a chance to hand her the rose. Luckily, though, it was Aunty Maleeka showing off her curvature in a tight, white, embroidered maxi dress.

"Veena, check you out," she exclaimed, making her way into the living room. "Sati-savitri, sari clad and all. We are headed to Indigo, not a wedding at the Turf Club."

Mom ignored Aunty Maleeka's catty comment. Her anxiety was rising. "The girl has the audacity to say to me that it's *just a date*!"

"Who?" Aunty Maleeka asked.

"My brazen hussy of a daughter, who else?" Mom screamed.

I stared back, shocked. 'Brazen hussy' is a term Naani and Pops reserved for speaking about Aunty Maleeka. Now, I was being lumped into the same category.

"What's going on around here?" Aunty Maleeka looked at us quizzically.

I piped up. "It's time for the date, but now Mom is getting out of control."

Mom spun around to look at me viciously. "Don't even think about talking to me like that after what you've done!"

"Quite right." Aunty Maleeka was insincerely wagging her finger at me. "Don't talk to her like that."

I scowled. The double games weren't helping. What was pissing Mom off? Had she found out about Colonel Jhunjhun? I looked at Deepali for solace, but in true ostrich-with-head-in-the-sand style, she was focusing intently on her fingernails. "Seriously though, Veena," Aunty Maleeka said. "What's upsetting you?"

"You have *no* idea what is going on?" Mom yelled. "You have *no* idea what these girls have been up to? And, frankly, you have *no* business having *no* idea, given the amount of time they have been spending with you lately. *Completely* corrupting them with your useless ideas."

"Great, now I am in the doghouse with you girls," Aunty Maleeka said, trying to look dejected. "What have I done this time?"

Mom was so riled up by this point that the redness of her face was competing with the burnt orange of her sari border.

"You and your talk about dating? Have you any idea how you influence the girls?" she shrieked.

"Okay, you are still upset about the double date?" Aunty Maleeka said, trying to piece it together. "But what influence, why are you biting my head off?"

"It's not *your* date that's upsetting me, or the double date. That really doesn't thrill me either, quite frankly, but—"

The doorbell cut her off mid-sentence. Aunty Maleeka rushed to open the door. There stood a dashing-looking Pops, all suited and stylish in a pair of black jeans and a dark linen jacket. All the women in the room did a double take, Mom included. But then, she immediately turned back to settle her saree pallav in an effort to look like she had regained composure.

"Good evening, ladies," he said with a brilliant, Close-Up-ad smile. He had no idea about the frantic scene he had just walked on to.

Aunty Maleeka grimaced. "Aiiyaaa. Not a very good evening so far!"

He looked at Deepali and me cowering by the sofa and pursed his lips into a hard line. "Let me guess, did I miss some drama? What's the matter?"

Mom practically bit his head off. "*Your daughter* is the matter! I just don't know how to put it in words!"

It's classic—whenever she is annoyed with me, I am promptly labeled as Pops' daughter. There should be laws about how parents label their kids. And considering her focus in life was all about fine penmanship, since when did she ever have a problem putting things in words? But now, of course, I was worried about her eruption. Had she figured out something about Colonel Jhunjhunvala? My feet went cold at the thought.

"You will not believe what she has been up to. Lying, cheating, stealing!" she shrieked.

All this time, I had attributed Mom's mental state to the fact that she wasn't thrilled about humoring Aunty Maleeka with a 'pretend' double date, mostly because Pops was in the mix, but this was something else. Why was she accusing me of lying, cheating, and stealing? And how dare she admonish me for who-knows-what in front of all and sundry? I could kick some butt and show that I could be pretty fierce too—like mother, like daughter.

"What?" I protested. "When did I do any of those things?"

Mom pierced me with choleric eyes and proceeded to list out her grievances. "You have been *lying* to me about where you have been these last several days and weeks, *cheating* me into believing that you wanted to lose weight to support Deepali, and *stealing* internet correspondence with lecherous middle-aged freaks!"

Hai Allah! She *had* found out. What other incriminating evidence had she gathered?

Pops, who had been silently watching all this time, now realized that this flagrant display of wits was well beyond the regular dosage of mother–daughter dysfunction he was attuned to. "Whoa, whoa, what is going on here?" he asked, suddenly hot under the collar.

"Yes, seriously, what's going on?" Aunty Maleeka echoed, adding some extra masala to the mix.

Deepali and I stole a guilty look at each other. We knew exactly what Mom was referring to! Our cover was blown!

"I am two steps ahead of you, pipsqueak," Mom thundered. "I've hacked into your online dating profile."

My online dating profile?

"Wait, Ila has an online dating profile?" Pops' face was beginning to turn crimson too.

In a flash, it was clear why she had gone off the deep end. Mom thought it was *my* dating profile. Crikey, of all the miscommunication that could have possibly occurred, this?

Aunty Maleeka finally got the picture too. Her confused expression first morphed into an amused one. Then it morphed again, but this time into one of sheer disappointment. "Jesus Christ!" she whined, "Did this have to happen today of all days?"

Her words added fuel to the fire.

"My daughter is meeting strange men online, and all you care about is your stupid blind double date?" Mom now directed her glare towards her best buddy.

It was now Pops' turn to add fuel to the fire. "And *you* endorse the fact that Maleeka spends all this time with *your* daughter?" he said to Mom, his eyes blazing.

Glares all around. Gosh, one needed a pair of sunglasses just to stay in the room.

"Calm down, JJ" poor Aunty Maleeka said. "You don't understand!"

"Darned right about that," Pops yelled.

If Pops decided to attack Aunty Maleeka, she'd be sure to strike back, and then all hell would break loose. I had to defend her. And myself. I decided to add my two bits.

"No one's been supervising me," I said indignantly to Pops.

"Damned right about that, you are!" Mom shouted.

"Wasn't it your job to be supervising her, Veena?" Pops demanded. "I mean isn't that why she is living with you?"

"She's seventeen. I assumed that, like other seventeen-year-old girls, she'd be Instagramming and Tik-tokking. Not having online chats with some dinosaur called Colonel Jhunjhunvala."

"Jhunjhun-what? What kind of screwed-up name is that?" Pops demanded again, looking like he was about to have a coronary. For a man with a family history of heart disease, this could hardly be a good thing.

I avoided Mom's gaze. She thought *I* had been cavorting with the colonel. Of all the things that could have gone wrong! Aunty Maleeka, clearly annoyed, stormed over to where we were standing.

"Seriously? Colonel Jhunjhunvala?" she said, wrenching my hands away from my face to look me in the eye. "Could you girls not have been a little circumspect, today of all days?"

"Wait, you know about this?" Mom asked Aunty Maleeka who responded by closing her eyes and shaking her head.

I felt an ache in my side—whether it was real or psychosomatic, who knew. Deepali must have felt the same; she groaned loudly. Mom was about to unleash further vitriol when the doorbell rang again. Deepali and I froze to the bone, knowing full well who it was. Nobody moved. How could any of us be incentivized to let the poor man in?

"Who is that?" Mom barked.

"I don't give a damn who it is," Pops barked back. "I want some explanations. *Now!*"

Sakkubai came shuffling into the room but receded as Pops grimly waved her off. Aunty Maleeka sprang up from the sofa. "Let me see if I can—"

"*You* will do nothing," Pops said. "Forty-three years later...and you are still causing problems." Poor Aunty Maleeka always got the fuzzy end of the lollipop. I jumped to her rescue.

"Pops, wait," I begged. "Don't speak to her like that. I can explain, really."

"Start explaining right now, young lady," he demanded, looking as though he was about to lead the charge of the light brigade.

The doorbell rang again. This time, Deepali dived out from behind the couch and raced to the door.

"*Don't* open it," Aunty Maleeka screeched, trying to spare the poor Colonel the embarrassment he was about to endure.

How could you blame her? The Isham household had turned into a game of Russian roulette. The appearance of any new person was like the spinning of the cylinder—first Mom, then Aunty Maleeka, then Pops, and now the poor colonel!

"I *have to*, Aunty Maleeka!" Deepali said, shooting us a helpless glance. "It's the only way!"

"*Wait!*" Aunty Maleeka screeched even louder.

But by then, it was much too late. There, on the landing, stood Colonel Jhunjhunvala in a dark grey Nehru coat, his slicked back silver-grey hair combed neatly down to the side. He sported a massively long handlebar mustache, which gave him the appearance of the Air India Maharaja, but he was decidedly not fat. In fact, he was the opposite—tall, thin, lanky even.

"Look who's here, everyone," Deepali yelled. "The last member of the blind date foursome."

Mom and Pops' jaws dropped. Neither was expecting the date to show up at home.

"The last member of the blind date foursome?" Mom stuttered. "You mean..."

Deepali nodded. "The four of you should really leave for Indigo now."

Mom looked over at Aunty Maleeka—who nodded in response, her mouth creasing in a weak smile—for verification.

Pops scratched his chin, befuddled. "I thought we were supposed to meet your date at the restaurant," he said to Aunty Maleeka now in a loud whisper.

"We...were...*are*...kind of...not," Aunty Maleeka responded in an equally loud whisper, then cast her eyes downwards to look at her toes.

"I just thought it would be easier if we all drove together...you know, in the same car and all...rather than him going all by himself, you know, all lonesome on his own-some."

She shot him a feeble smile, but neither Pops nor Mom was in the mood for her lame excuses.

"Spare me the poetic crap," Dad glared at her. "You're lousy at poetry, anyway."

"Maleeka," Mom hissed. "Care to explain what's going on?" She looked at me, then at Deepali, and shook her head. "Right," she said, taking the matter into her own hands. She marched to the front door, pushing Pops and Deepali out of the way.

"A pleasure to meet with you," said the Colonel politely. "I am here for the...er...blind date."

Mom looked over to Aunty Maleeka with acid eyes and then turned back to the visitor. "Sorry, Maleeka didn't tell us you would be coming here. We were expecting to meet you at the restaurant. We are a little unprepared."

Mom thought he was Aunty Maleeka's so-called date, but she wasn't aware that he was also Colonel Jhunjhunvala, the so-called lecherous freak that she assumed I had been cavorting with online.

"Maleeka?" he asked, confused. "Isn't this the right address?"

Deepali piped up. "Yes, yes, you have the right place. Let me explain." She looked around the room with an expression that said, 'I think it's time to come clean.'

"He is not here to see Aunty Maleeka. He's here to meet Venus," she blurted out.

Jeez, Deepali! Thanks a lot. You really have a knack for clearing things up. I could sense Mom jumping in her skin as she thought that the handlebar-mustached guy had stepped out of my computer screen and into my life!

I had to interject. "No, no, you *don't* understand," I said to Mom. "You've totally got the wrong idea."

"Excuse me, what's your name?" Mom asked the visitor.

"I am Colonel R.S. Jhunjhunvala," he responded, plainly confused.

Mom looked like she had seen a ghost. I had never seen her react that way before, but before I could take in her expression properly, Pops muscled his way to her side. He was overloaded with testosterone. "You bastard! You have the audacity to show up here?"

The poor Colonel jumped back, startled. He gaped at Pops, grappling for clarity. "Sorry, sir. You are...?"

"I am her father, Jhunjhun! Who do you think I am?" Pops yelled.

Argh! Why, in my life, do situations just *have* to go from bad to worse?

"Pops, calm down," I said. "You don't get it."

"Damned right, I don't." He was livid for the second time in fifteen minutes.

Deepali tried to come to the Colonel's rescue. "He's not really her father, you know..."

Pops turned to Deepali with smoke coming out of his ears. He obviously did not know what to make of her statement, but he wasn't happy to hear it. We were all caught in the crossfire now. Despite this, Aunty Maleeka was still content with staring at her toes.

"Aunty Maleeka!" Deepali implored. "You need to help us before Aunty Veena and Uncle JJ kill us, along with this poor man."

Aunty Maleeka looked up from her toes, her expression going from sheepish to 'take-charge.'

"Right!" she said, slapping her hands together several times as though shaking dust off her palms.

Mom and Pops whirled around to look at her, quite baffled. "This man," she said, pointing to Pops, "is not her father. He's her jealous husband."

The poor Colonel didn't know what had hit him. "You didn't tell me that you were still married," he said disapprovingly to Mom.

Mom was clearly taken aback by his judgmental statement. "Me? I'm separated. But how is that any of your concern?"

I looked at Pops closely to ascertain his next move. All of a sudden, the blood drained from his face, and he went from monster to mouse. Or relatively, at any rate, as he quickly inferred the truth. "Wait a minute. I see what's going on here," he said to Aunty Maleeka. "This isn't your date at all, is he?"

Aunty Maleeka had gone rabbit-eyed again. She shook her head guiltily.

Then, a completely unexpected turn of events happened. Pops' anger melted like snow on a sunny day. He burst into a full-throated guffaw. "Oh Maleeka, you are priceless! I can't believe you set up my wife on a date."

"No, not me," Aunty Maleeka protested. Then she saw the humor in the situation and started giggling. So did Deepali. I wanted to laugh too, I but ran the risk of angering Mom, who didn't see any hilarity in it.

"Can someone *please* explain what's going on?" she yelled, her forehead saddled with lines of disconcertion.

My heart went out to poor Mom. As for the Colonel, I was surprised he hadn't he retreated by now.

I jumped to Mom's rescue. "Mom, this is Colonel Jhunjhunvala who is here to go on a date with *you*."

Mom's eyes opened so wide that they could extend beyond her forehead. "With me?"

"Aren't you, Venus?" the colonel asked her, his face turning even more disapproving now.

Mom's expression morphed from cluelessness to cognizance as she pieced together the possibilities. "Venus? Oh, Venus!"

She and Pops looked at each other and nodded, then both turned to me. "So, this is *your* doing?" Pops began, but Mom cut him off midsentence and turned back to the Colonel.

"Actually, my name is Veena. And yes, of course you are referring to our correspondence on Tinder. I mean Bumble. No, sorry, OkCupid, I believe."

Mom had hacked my phone and gone through all of my Venus profiles in full detail! Shit! Colonel Jhunjhunvala stood there, his gaze shifting to look at each of the characters in this ridiculous drama. It occurred to Mom that he was still standing at the door.

"Please, come in and sit down, so that I can explain this confusion," she said sweetly.

Unbelievable! She had just done a complete about-turn on all her fury.

Deepali and I looked at each other, feeling dismayed, guilty, and confused at the same time. Mom was about to spill the beans. What had we led this poor man into? Aunty Maleeka shot a questioning glance to Pops who simply shrugged in return.

Poor Colonel Jhunjhunvala, completely unaware as to what awaited him, followed Mom's orders and positioned himself at the far end of the couch, with the obedience of a domestic lamb. Why he still wanted to be a part of this, I had no idea. He began to twirl the end of his mooch nervously. Then, he cleared his throat.

"I...I am sorry if I interrupted your domesticity this evening," he said. "I...I can leave now if you'd prefer not to go ahead with this."

Domesticity? This guy spoke in real life in the same way he wrote on the internet. Did he have a stutter, or was he just weirded out by all the drama? I couldn't tell.

"No, no, you have not disturbed anything at all," Mom replied, smiling wryly. "It's just that...well, given the scenario of, you know, a blind date, Venus got a bout of cold feet. These things are perfectly natural, no? In an online dating situation, especially considering how taken she is with you!"

The Colonel's face lit up like a diya on amavas. "Taken with me?"

"Enchanted," Mom replied. "Bewitched, in fact. This evening is arguably Venus's most important in many years."

The Colonel was delighted by Mom's announcement. Much as she was enjoying this, Pops was clearly not happy with the situation and crossed his arms in disapproval. Aunty Maleeka, on the other hand, was perplexed. She looked on with both eyebrows raised. Deepali and I just stood there glued to each other like two halves of a cracked plate desperately trying to look pristine.

"Which really is the reason why she is so utterly nervous tonight," Mom continued. "In fact, when you said in one of your texts that you loved the idea of her pink toosh shawl against her soft, tanned arms, she was all set to wear it tonight."

Bewilderment overtook the Colonel again, and he wasn't the only one.

His light grey eyes bored into her. "Just to be sure...you are not Venus?"

"I am not," Mom replied calmly.

Where was she going with this?

"Yet, you are privy to all of our correspondence?" He twirled his mustache suspiciously.

"Come on, were you really expecting a single woman, aged forty-five, to hold back from sharing her most eagerly anticipated moment in dating history from her best friend?" Mom asked innocently.

Aunty Maleeka's expression softened at the words 'best friend.' Pops, Deepali, and I exchanged glances, intrigued. Mom was playing the poor colonel along as though she had rehearsed this scene for days. But why? Had she decided to go on this date after all?

"Colonel-ji, please wait for just one moment in the graceful company of my family. Give me a chance to summon your date for this evening." So saying, Mom disappeared hastily down the corridor.

The rest of us sat in our living room staring at each other in silence. What can one actually say in situations like this? The poor Colonel continued to twirl his mustache with one hand and stare awkwardly at the marble under the glass top of the coffee table. He fumbled with the long-stemmed rose still in his fingers. I felt the urge to jump in and help.

"Apologies for the situation, Colonel Saheb," I said awkwardly. "I know this evening has not turned out exactly as planned, but rest assured, my mom will have everything straightened for you soon."

The Colonel smiled weakly for a brief moment and went back to fidgeting with the rose.

Deepali motioned to me to ask what I meant by that. Pops and Aunty Maleeka also looked at me intently. I shrugged. I had no idea how Mom was going to fix the situation. It was like sixth standard drama class; I wished she would just explain in plain English rather than in cryptic riddles. Mom reemerged moments later with a wicked grin and her pink toosh shawl.

To all of our surprise, Mom marched over to where Aunty Maleeka and Pops were standing. With a jab of the elbow, she pushed Pops out of the way—it was the second time in the last fifteen minutes. He winced as his ribs received the blow. She arranged the shawl around Aunty Maleeka's bare shoulders, and then, grabbing her by her now toosh-covered arms, she ushered her forward.

"Colonel Jhunjhunvala, meet your date for the evening. This is your

Venus. But that, as you know, is her online pseudonym. Her real name is Maleeka."

None of us was expecting this outcome—least of all Aunty Maleeka, who wore a frazzled look. But, Mom seemed as if she had the whole thing under control. "Come, come, Maleeka. You've been prolific all this time and now you are seized by nerves? It's your big evening. Look at this dashing colonel here to enchant you even more than he has done online. Go on, enjoy yourself!"

An uneasy silence pervaded the room, which was finally broken by Pops who released his arms from their crossed position and began to clap. The Colonel looked pleased as punch. Aunty Maleeka, on the other hand, looked flabbergasted, albeit in a good way.

With her pure genius, Mom had got herself out of the situation and Aunty Maleeka into it. Most impressively, neither had she embarrassed us girls, nor had she let down the poor Colonel who, just moments before, had looked despondent at the thought of having his date dreams shattered. There was no recourse but to join in the applause. Mom deserved it. So, I began to clap—so hard that my hands stung. Deepali followed suit, bringing the applause to a crescendo.

Poor Aunty Maleeka just stood there blushing—her head cast down like that of a shy bride. It was as close to being a bride as she had ever come. The colonel on the other hand, continued to grin from ear to ear. It didn't occur to him that we were all clapping for Mom. He stepped forward and held out his arm to Aunty Maleeka, ready to lead her out.

"I...I..." she began, but Mom cut in before she could finish her sentence.

"Say no more. Hurry off now, or they'll give away your reservation," she said, ushering them towards the door. "And that's that," Mom said, closing the door behind them. "Let's hope it's not a flash in the pan."

Deepali and Pops stood there, looking somewhat uncertain. I sought comfort in the fact that I was not the only one with apprehensions. Deepali and I knew that keeping our mouths shut was the best plan of action.

"Veena," Pops began as soon as Aunty Maleeka and the colonel had left, but Mom wasn't in the mood.

"Save it, JJ," she said, holding her hand up to his face. "Time to cut short what could have been a long, long evening. I'm going to get out of this ridiculous chaiyya-chaiyya outfit, and you...I think you should make tracks." She glanced at Deepali before turning to glare at me. "As for you, Ila, I am too tired to deal with it right now, but rest assured that your mother does not lead such a lame existence that her daughter needs to pose as her and set her up with some moochad paanwalla lookalike from a dating app."

"Wow," Deepali said, new respect for Mom glistening in her eyes. "Aunty Veena, you kicked some serious butt!"

Pops nodded. He and I couldn't agree more.

He kissed me goodnight and left. Deepali left soon after. Her family was to depart for Nainital the next evening, so she decided to get home and help with the packing. Besides, even though she wanted to stick around to help me face Mom's wrath, I figured it was something I needed to do on my own.

I considered engaging with her to apologize for, or at least acknowledge my role in the fiasco, but she'd retreated to her room and closed the door—a clear sign that she didn't want to have anything to do with us—or me, rather—that evening.

I crawled into bed feeling quite foolish and could barely sleep all night. I tossed and turned, trying to console myself with the thought that my intentions were good, that I had done it for Mom and the greater good of the Ishams. That I had really tried to take care of everything down to the last detail, and this was just plain dumb luck. That it's near impossible to rationalize a situation or blame anyone, and that I should make peace with the fact that the disaster had happened—which was easier said than done.

chapter
twenty-five

THE NEXT MORNING, I was still wracked with anxiety. Mom had emerged early and left without a word to anyone about what she was doing or when she'd return. I couldn't help but take it personally.

The usual comfort of home seemed threatening that day. The silence of the May morning was deafening. Sakkubai moved quietly around the apartment like a seasoned sleuth contracted by Mom to watch my every move. She had prepared kanda poha, my favorite breakfast that never fails to light up a dull day, but even that wasn't particularly appealing. As I sat at the dining table, forcing it down my throat, I imagined the mechanical cuckoo in the clock flying out to attack me. This is what stress does to you...you begin feeding off of your own insecurities.

When I heard Sakkubai making her way into the room, I ducked out of the way. I didn't want to be interrogated by her about lack of appetite. At that opportune moment, Dev called to get the blow-by-blow account of the previous evening. "Hi, Ila. Deepali said yesterday was quite the saga."

At the sound of his cute voice, the usual flutter emerged from its resting place and began circling my insides.

"Are you sane?" he asked.

I couldn't tell whether he was enquiring after my well-being or trying to ask me in a roundabout manner whether I was completely cuckoo.

"Just dandy," I said.

No sound from the other end of the phone. He probably thought I losing my mind.

I continued, "Deepali and I got carried away by the whole dumb idea of Operation Mom, so it's probably worked out for the best."

I was met with silence.

"But you were great...er, great...to...help me that is, in creating the profile for Mom and all," I offered.

I heard him take a measured breath. What I'd give to see his face!

"So, does this mean no further dates?" Dev asked.

"Probably not. She's kind of repulsed by the whole dating thing right now," I replied.

"I wasn't referring to her, actually."

Did he mean what I thought he meant?

"Ila, you still there?" he asked.

Barely. I couldn't focus.

"She hasn't put *you* off the idea, has she?"

"The idea of what?" I asked warily.

"Dating?"

Now my heart skipped a beat. He *was* scoping me out.

"Since ice-cream doesn't seem to be your thing, would you be up for a juice this afternoon?"

"Juice?" I said weakly.

"How about we meet at Lal Nariyalwalla in a couple of hours from now? It's around the corner from Microwave Snacks and Juice Center. We could get a juice or nariyal and then take a stroll down Worli Seaface."

A date. It was a bona fide invitation for a date. Now, Worli Seaface was too public a place to engage in passionate, swoony kissing, but some inner voice told me that we probably needed to start with a more relaxed public acknowledgement of togetherness. A stroll by the seaside was perfect—who knew where it would lead to?

"Ila, are you still there?"

In my head, I was already at Worli Seaface.

——

Mumbai is filled with any number of coconutwallas whose stalls, set up courtesy the Bombay Municipal Corporation, are perhaps the city's signature attraction, along with vada pav, behl puri, akuri, and frankie stalls. Lal Nariayalwalla was no different. What I love most about his stall in Worli is the fact that he has his mobile phone number printed in bold letters up on the header, right beneath the Marathi invocation to Lord Ganesh. What does a nariyalwalla need to advertise his phone number for? I suppose if you are planning to show up in herds, calling ahead can ensure that he's prepared for the party. I know what you're thinking—the idea of a party at the nariyalwalla is a totally 'out-there' concept, but with so many foreigners flocking to Mumbai, even nariyal stalls have become tourist traps.

I was about to ask Lal Nariyalwalla why he had mausambis hanging from the sides of his stall when my cell phone started vibrating frantically to indicate an incoming text. It was Jaggi.

Jaggi: I'm worried about Deepali. She said she was leaving for the airport at six. She hasn't answered her phone since three.

Jaggi doesn't habitually contact me, but it wasn't too odd that he was seeking her out so actively. Deepali had blown him off the last few days. It was partly my fault—we'd been up to our neck with Operation Mom. But any free time beyond that, she'd spent with Vik. Deepali the three-timer was showing signs of becoming a one-dude gal. She was probably cozying up to him right now. Poor Jaggi was undoubtedly feeling neglected. Who could blame him? I wished she'd come clean with him, but then it wasn't my place to interfere.

Me: Sorry, don't know where she is.

"I hope you don't have a texting habit like your buddy, Deepali," said a distinctly recognizable, cute male voice. I looked up to see the tousled-haired angel in the guise of a teen boy. The familiar flutter set my insides into a state of disarray once again.

"That's just Jaggi, hyperventilating about Deepali not answering his texts," I said, trying to conceal a blush that was working its way all over my face down to my bare shoulders.

"You mean, he doesn't know she has the hots for Vik?" Dev grinned.

"Hey, I've heard that when Vik turns on the charm, he's an unstoppable juggernaut of passion."

"Eww," I said, gently slapping him on the shoulder. "Vik? Don't be gross!"

Dev whipped out an imaginary notepad from his backpack and made as if to jot something down. "Note to self: avoid all jokes about Vik with semi-sexual context. The mental damage they cause is not worth it."

"Where's your ethic, Dev?" I said indignantly. "Deepali is my best friend."

"And Vik is my bud," he grinned. "Besides, Deepali is a well-oiled machine, I mean nothing but praise and flattery."

She *was* a well-oiled machine. And unlike me, she'd never take offense at Dev's references. But how did he know that about Deepali? The comment nagged me, not for any other reason besides the fact it takes time, a long time at that, to understand how well-oiled a person is. Had he indulged in episodes on the landing with her too? How could I find out more without appearing to be nosy?

"You've obviously spent a lot of time with Deepali, haven't you?" I said as casually as I could manage.

"That would be your doing," he responded.

My doing? I was surprised. Did he really mean what I hoped he meant? But I was too nervous to prod further.

"Look, I figure it's time to come clean with you," he said.

"About what?"

"About the fact that all the time I've spent with Deepali, I've done with an ulterior motive."

"And that is?"

"To get to know *you* better."

My heart leapt up. This *was* happening. He was into me!

Lal Nariyalwalla handed us a couple of nariyals—ripe, with plenty of malai to feast on afterwards.

"In fact, I helped Vik smooth out his moves with her. Deepali figured you weren't ready for any guy besides Ali Zafar. Well, until recently," he said.

Deepali had played along without ever once spilling the beans! Still, I felt the need to confirm what Deepali had already told me.

"So, let me get this straight. You were *never* interested in Deepali?" I asked.

Dev laughed. "Deepali's cousin, Jay, is a good pal of mine. Let me explain the basics of bro code. If you've known a guy for more than twenty-four hours, his cousin is off limits forever."

"And so, the other day..." I started.

"...was perfect timing, all roads had been leading to the proverbial Rome."

Right then, I got another text from Jaggi.

Jaggi: You know, Deepali spends all that time with Dev too. It bothers me. I think I should speak up.

"Dev, take a look at this," I said. "Even Jaggi is upset about you and Deepali."

Dev grinned. "Jaggi doesn't realize that it's Vik who's stealing his thunder, not me. It's Deepali who's leading him on. Poor guy, he's on a 'through' route to the land of the unexplainable."

He took my left hand in his right and closed his fingers around mine. My heart began to pulsate like an erratic clock that needed winding.

"Shall we walk?" he asked.

Walk? I was barely able to stand.

My phone buzzed again. "It's probably Jaggi," I said. "What should I say to him?"

"Nothing. He needs to get on the road to discovery that exists beyond the limits of his current existence. But let's begin our walk down our road, shall we?"

Was he talking about Worli Seaface or was this was a metaphor for something else? I couldn't tell, but, either way, I didn't want to miss any of the excitement of the journey.

chapter
twenty-six

SOMETIMES, the desire for space outweighs the need to sort things out. This was the case with Mom, who hadn't spoken to me about 'the episode' even two days later. Perhaps it was her way of punishing me—laying on the guilt to ensure that I would regret my actions for the rest of my life. At least that's what Pops thought when I conferred with him. There had been no word from Aunty Maleeka, either. Whether her date with Colonel Jhun-jhunvala had turned out to be pure bliss or a complete disaster, I had no idea.

On the second morning after the blind date fiasco, I woke up to find Mom missing again. According to Sakkubai, she had left in the wee hours with no word about when she might return. But there was a note from her on my bedside table: *Meet me at the CCI sauna room at noon. Maleeka to reveal all at lunch.*

What could one possibly make of a note like that? Mom still hadn't as much as referred to the Operation Mom thing, yet she was all set to hang out in the sauna with me? And then we were to hash out Aunty Maleeka's rendition of her evening with the Colonel? No, I needed to get my apology out of the way before Aunty Maleeka came into the picture.

Having spent the entire morning rehearsing, I arrived at the CCI a few minutes before noon to see that Mom and I had been signed in as guests for the day. I wondered what else was on the agenda for the day.

Mom wasn't kidding about the sauna. I found her standing by the lockers in the ladies' changing room, a towel wrapped around her. It hardly seemed like the ideal moment to throw in the towel, so to speak, but then when are things ever ideal? I gulped and went for it.

"Mom, I've been trying to find a less cliché way to say sorry, but nothing comes to mind. Deepali and I got carried away. We obviously didn't really think through the issues," I said.

Contrary to my expectations, Mom beamed at me. "Actually, it's kind of flattering," she said.

"It is?"

"For sure. Nice to see that you care about your old mother." She actually seemed to be good humored about it.

"Puh-lease, you are far from old," I said, relaxing into the conversation.

"Well, that moochad paanwalla Colonel who walked through the door was not exactly the youngest chhokra on the planet, was he?" she said raising her left eyebrow.

Mom had clearly forgiven me, but I would never forget what a naive idiot I had been. I looked sheepishly at my hands.

"Hurry up," she said, stepping into the sauna. "Let's get the toxic stuff out before lunch."

All morning I had been on edge about how to apologize without somehow getting Mom upset again, and here she was, calm as a cow about the whole thing. I quickly changed and followed her into the sauna.

"I'm sorry, Mom. We tried to vet these guys, but somehow they all fake it on the internet," I said woozily. My senses had been assaulted by the overpowering heat of the sauna.

"Oh? Like Venus, the character you created, was all about telling the truth?" she replied with an amused smile.

"A thousand apologies," I said, squeezing her arm.

I was becoming adjusted to the sauna. It didn't seem that hot anymore, but Mom had a different opinion. I could tell from the fact that she had begun to huff and puff.

"I have to admit, the dialogue back and forth was kind of fun."

"Are you kidding? It was fantastic. Perfect story for a screenplay," Mom said, whooshing her breath like she does in yoga.

"Hey, that's an idea!" I grinned. "You should write it."

"Nah, I think that's one for you to write."

"I can't write like you."

She looked at me skeptically. "You can write way better than me," she said.

"You think so?"

"I know so."

"Then why do you always cut me down to size when it comes to grammar, and proofreading, and pretty much everything in life?" I joked.

By now, there were rivulets of sweat running down Mom's face and neck. She was redder in the face than she had been the other night. This time, however, it was thanks to hormones. I, on the other hand, was cool as a metaphorical cucumber.

"Ila, you are right," Mom replied, dabbing her brow with a wet face cloth. "I am obsessive—too much so—about you being the best. Obsession, as you know, can be a problem. In fact, it worries me that you might have inherited this particular trait from me."

I listened as she covered her eyes with the face cloth. "That thing with Ali Zafar— that was my life too. I went above and beyond to stalk George Michael when I was your age. My mother was livid about it— not because she had anything against him as a pop star, but because she was worried that my obsessive tendencies when I was just seventeen would lead to who-knows-what years later."

Seventeen. That was exactly my age now.

"I couldn't see it then, but today I understand exactly why she freaked out. I knew the Ali Zafar thing wouldn't last; see, you've already pivoted your interest to the idea of a real boy. But that's not what worries me. It's the O trait. You have no idea how much it cost me when I was your age."

"O as in...."

"Obsessive!" she finished my sentence with a raised brow. It spoke volumes.

How did she know I had pivoted my interest? Up until yesterday, she thought I was stalking middle-aged men online. Still, the part about the *O* trait intrigued me.

"Really, Mom? Tell me more," I said.

"After that picture came out in the *Mid-Day*, my life was terrible. Nobody let it pass as the cute story of a love-stricken seventeen-year-old groupie. I became known as Veena the Obsessive. It was impossible for me to have a boyfriend. Boys that age don't want to deal with women they perceive to be obsessive nags." Mom began to fidget like a child strapped into a harness. "And the stigma continued for years after, along with the trait. I can't bear to see that happen to you, Ila."

So, this was why she had been so against the Ali Zafar thing all that time, and why she had been so surreptitious about her George Michael history. It all made sense now. As I was musing, Mom dialed up her fidgeting. She began wringing her hands this way and that, scrunching up her face and sucking on her lower lip. "Oof, I can't deal with this heat anymore. Saunas and perimenopausal women aren't a good match for more than fifteen minutes."

I followed her out, wondering if I should ask about her previous comment referring to my interest pivoting towards a real boy. Or would that open up another can of worms? It wasn't even anything significant —not yet, anyway. Dev and I had only just started walking down that proverbial road.

Back in the changing room, Mom poured herself a large glass of water from the filter and gulped half of it down within seconds. She then held the glass away from her and stared into it.

"Half full or half empty?" Mom mused. "The truth is, Ila, I just don't know. And when I look at you, I see so much of myself that it makes me nervous." She pursed her lips in obvious dismay.

"Mom, did it ever occur to you that when you say that, you might be giving me the biggest compliment of my life?" I said.

She responded with a forlorn smile.

I smiled gently. "Why wouldn't I want to be like you?"

Mom sighed and held the cold glass of water against her cheek. "You know I get conflicted between trying to see you from the eyes of a mother versus being an objective person who sees you exactly as you are."

"Meaning?"

"Meaning, it's all very well and flattering for me to want you to be like me, but the truth is, I have made a lot of mistakes in my life, some of them too grave to go back and fix. I don't want the *O* trait to take over and turn you into some pathetic type who's stuck at the crossroads and has no choice but to take a hard left. Ila, I guess I'm just trying to prevent you from becoming me."

I could see that the *O* trait had profoundly impacted her. I gazed deep into her eyes, preparing to ask the question that I had never asked in all of these years. "Do you mean that the *O* trait has led you to make mistakes as in, like, splitting up with Pops?"

Mom sighed. She looked wistfully into the distance, a glazed look in her eyes. "That might have been one of the biggest mistakes, yes."

"Which part?" I asked. "Marrying him or splitting up?"

"If I hadn't married him, you would never have showed up now, would you?" Mom said. "So that could hardly be a mistake."

I couldn't tell what she meant. I said nothing.

Mom looked intensely into my eyes. "You know, what I admire about you is that you march to the beat of your own drum. Ilz, you are exactly who I want to be when I grow up." She stepped back and smiled. "Come on, hon, time to shower."

As the cool water sprinkled down on me, my head raced with thoughts about how the Ali Zafar chapter of my life was finally over. It was time to come clean with an update.

"About that pivoting interest thing," I said slowly, as we both emerged from the shower stalls. "The good news is that my own teen pop idol obsession is, well, no longer an obsession."

She smiled wickedly. "Let me guess. The tête-à-têtes with Dev are going well?"

I felt myself turn pink as I thought once again about the warmth of his hand against mine on World Seaface. "How'd *you* know?"

"I'm your mother," she said simply. "It's my job to know."

I blushed even deeper. "I was actually going to tell you about that."

"I know you were."

"You did?"

"Like I said, it's my job to know these things."

Neither of us said anything for the next few minutes as we dressed. It wasn't awkward, though—if anything, it was kind of comfortable. Mom finally broke the silence.

"You know, Ila, I am not necessarily...*not* in favor of Dev."

The butterflies in my stomach gave a little rumble. "What? So, you are saying that you *are* in favor of Dev?"

"That's what I am saying. But I am also hoping that it doesn't mean that Ali Zafar is completely out of favor," Mom replied in a strangely capricious tone.

"What do you mean by that?" I asked, raising an eyebrow.

"Well, since Deepali is off to Nainital, who are you planning to take to that Ali Zafar concert next week?"

I opened my eyes wide. She was referring to the tickets Deepali had bought me during math class. I had completely forgotten because I was so caught up in Operation Mom!

"What I am saying is, can I go with you?" she grinned. I opened my eyes even wider.

"You mean you'll go with me?" I said excitedly.

When a middle-aged mother deigns to go to a rock concert with her teenage daughter, it's impossible for the daughter to truly vocalize what she wants to say. Actions are so much easier. I flung my arms around Mom's neck, practically choking her.

Her towel dropped to reveal the most hideous pair of granny panties I had ever seen. Made of spandex and printed with a pastel floral design, they began directly under her boobs and covered her entire butt and thighs. I was overtaken by total and utter stupefaction. When it comes to glamour, her potential is undoubtedly Rodeo Drive, but the reality is that Mom's fashion sense never ventures beyond Lajpat Nagar. To think I wanted to set her up on a blind date. How embarrassing!

Mom caught me staring at her, aghast. "At forty-five, it doesn't get easier for your ass to defy gravity, you know," she said, fighting to get her jeans up her thighs.

I was certainly not in favor of Mom sporting anything that didn't suit her, so I didn't mind listening to her gyaan on underwear.

"Besides," she continued, "since I haven't had a date in years, I really don't know any better."

"Mom," I said, slowly calculating the meaning of her words, "I know that Operation Mom didn't quite work out the way we planned it, but did we turn you off the idea of dating for good?"

Mom shook her hair loose and laughed. "You know what, you and Deepali have no idea how far off the market you were regarding my taste in potential dates. A little more research into my past might have revealed that my George Michael obsession was followed by a quest to pursue a Latin lover!"

"Eww, Mom! Too much info!"

"Right you are, too much information indeed. But, I think you might have turned me *on* to the idea of dating. It's just that life is all about timing," she said. "You got me seriously thinking about something else."

I widened my eyes. Was she considering getting back together with Pops?

"Why should I resort to granny panties at forty-five? I'm thinking I'd rather lose some weight by having some fun. Maybe I'll enroll in that six-week flamenco class in Salamanca, the one that Reina talked about."

I couldn't believe she'd actually taken the time to think about this and come to terms with what was involved—taking the time out of her life to go to Spain! It wasn't at all a matter of having second thoughts about her separation. Why did that even cross my mind? If anything, she wanted to own her newfound freedom!

"Are you serious?" I asked, astounded. "You know you have to perform at the end of six weeks, right?"

"Fortune favors the brave!" she exclaimed. We both laughed. "However, I have on one condition," she said, smiling triumphantly.

"What's that?"

"You come with me." Mom finished with a smack of lip gloss. She was ready to go and looked fantastic—with or without her granny-panties.

I flash-forwarded into our Spanish sojourn—sombrero-clad hunks playing the flamenco guitar and beautiful women who defined the meaning of style. I immediately gave Mom a thumbs up.

"Let's get out of here," she said. "It's time to unravel the story of Aunty Maleeka and Colonel handlebar mooches!"

I pulled back and tried to look at my mother objectively. What pulsated through my emotional center was pure admiration. Or perhaps pure adulation. Veena Isham is one-in-a-million. To her ex-husband, she's a fearlessly opinionated partner-adversary; to her wanton buddy from childhood, she's a dating disgrace; to publishing mavens, she's a revolutionary writer; and to seventeen-year-old me, she is a role model, my emotional roadmap, and, simply, Mom. Chak de phatte, old girl!

But, above all, this is a lady who consistently epitomizes and over-comes the impossible dilemma of Indian womanhood. How does that even happen? The only way to understand was to dig into her own experience about the whole journey.

"Mom, there's one more thing I need to ask you," I said.

"Ask away."

"You know those mistakes you were talking about earlier, the ones that you said can't be fixed?"

Her face wrinkled up into a question mark.

"You and Pops still get along so well, even after the separation," I acknowledged. "It makes me wonder... how bad could marriage really be?"

Mom cocked her head to the side and placed her finger on her right cheek. "A loaded question for a seventeen-year-old, no?" she asked, though I knew she didn't expect an answer. She grabbed her handbag and headed for the door, then continued, "Life's about taking risks, Ila; not all of them work out. However you toss the coin; you've got to figure the value. Can you de-obsess enough to make a marriage last? Or can divorce give you the opportunity to really get to know your partner? Either way, you can hit the jackpot."

That's when I finally got it—getting Mom a life and a man was a gratuitous endeavor. She already had both. Perhaps it was time to pivot from Operation Mom to Operation Dev.

acknowledgments

If I were to stop to think about the random acts of wackiness that life hurled at me during my teenage years, it's a wonder that I actually made it to adulthood. Growing up in a dysfunctional Punjabi household in Bombay's late eighties was not the easiest task in the world, but it was certainly soul-strengthening. So, when I sat down to write a story about a teen in my native city, my first thought was: How difficult could it be?

Talk about being naïve! Firstly, Bombay had long since become Mumbai, a multi-layered transformation that transcended pure semantics. The landscape had changed, the slang was different, and understanding the context of Mumbai's young adults was like hiking an uphill course. The good news is that I like hiking and am always up for a challenge. So once I got going, the story began to flow.

But even the most entertaining of stories require a supportive cast of characters. So there's a bunch of people I'd like to thank for helping me bring this one to the page:

My daughter Ilya Hora and my mother Veena Malhotra—they continue to exemplify the insanity that comes from being the daughter of a mother and the mother of a daughter.

My husband Neeraj Hora, my son AryaVir Hora, and my dog Dumbledore—for skillfully stepping into the sidelines when the female energy in the household gets overpowering (which is all too often the case).

My sister-in-law Ashima Arora for her fine academic advice.

Thank gosh for physics teachers...and family!

My childhood buddy Maleeka Lala and my colleague Noreen Mir—for being fantastic friends and literary inspirations. That's two for the price of one as far as I'm concerned.

My agent Jennifer Wills of The Seymour Agency for subsequently bringing it to the attention of Gen Z Publishing.

The team at GenZ - Shannon Marks, Fiona Suherman, Lisa Wood, Courtney, Jessica, Madison — for all the time and effort they have put into this book.

All the readers of this book—thank you for the audience.

And last but not least, George Michael of Wham! —without you, my teen years would have had no definition!

9 781958 503089